# Planted by the Waters

## J. Carter-Ball

Ideas into Books: Westview®
Kingston Springs, Tennessee

Ideas into Books: Westview®
P.O. Box 605
Kingston Springs, TN 37082
www.publishedbywestview.com

ISBN 978-1-62880-139-2 Paperback
ISBN 978-1-62880-140-8 Ebook
ISBN 978-1-62880-141-5 Cloth with Dust Jacket

First edition, March 2018

Printed in the United States of America on acid free paper.

# ACKNOWLEDGMENTS

My sincere appreciation goes to **Gloria McKissack,** my friend and fellow church member. Gloria, a history professor, edited the novel and served as an advisor. Her contribution helped bring these characters to life.

I thank **Agatha R. Asemota,** my friend since we met in law school, who took the time to edit the novel.

I thank **David J. Johnson,** Museum Specialist at Fort Monroe, and other staff, who shared publications, reports and contraband images from the Casemate Museum, and other information about the history of Fort Monroe.

A special thank you to **James H. Ball, Jr.,** my husband and friend. James patiently drove me to Fort Monroe, Charleston, Savannah, Fort Pulaski, Tybee Island, Jacksonville, New Orleans and several locations to explore the sites discussed in the novel.

I thank **Joyce V. Coakley** for the information I found in her wonderful book about sweetgrass baskets.

Ultimately, I thank **my heavenly Father** who blessed me with the desire and ability to write.

## DEDICATED WITH LOVE

To the Unity, Strength and Perseverance of my

**FAMILY**

# Chapter 1

There is something special about being near a large body of water; it's peaceful; it's refreshing; it calms my soul. I feel close to God when I am near the water. *And he shall be like a tree planted by the rivers of water, that bringeth forth his fruit in his season; his leaf also shall not wither; and whatsoever he doeth shall prosper.* Mammy spoke this scripture often when my sister and I were children on the plantation in Mississippi. Perhaps this is why I feel healed and refreshed near the water.

I left my home this morning to walk near the Ashley River in Charleston, to reflect on my life; a life filled with much pain and suffering. Still, it is a life I am proud of, and proud to talk about; a life that may inspire others to push forward.

The year is 1875. It has been ten years since the Civil War ended. My children love to hear the story of how I reunited with my family after I was snatched away from them around the age of ten. My parents, Bertha and Joshua, have two offspring, my sister, Sarah, and me, Tom Johnson. We were all born into slavery. After being separated for more than twenty years, we finally reunited in Boston in 1863.

I am forty-three years old, and very fortunate to have had the opportunity to get an education at Hampton Normal and Agricultural Institute, founded by General Samuel Chapman Armstrong, a Union Commander of Colored Troops and an abolitionist. Two wonderful teachers worked with me and other newly emancipated pupils and taught us to speak grammatically correct English. I spent over thirty years of my life as a slave, and learned many valuable lessons from my parents. I want my children to know what it was like to be a slave.

Thank God, they do not have to live that life. I want them to know as much as possible about my flight to freedom. Most importantly, I want them to know what it was like the moment I saw, and embraced, my parents and sister again after all those difficult years.

Although it has been ten years since slaves were declared free, some of our scars will never completely heal. Telling my story has helped me move forward. My story begins with a confrontation with John Mundy, the slaveholder who owned me for more than seven years. After that confrontation, I decided I would live my life as a free man, or die. I will never forget the morning I approached John Mundy to ask him to allow me to buy my freedom. It was not a pleasant scene.

I was around twenty at that time, and was getting tools together to go to work on a house not too far from the plantation. John Mundy stood nearby and told me which tools to bring. He enjoyed watching over his slaves. I think it made him feel powerful. John Mundy was a big man and quite tall. His thick, grey hair was always neatly combed back from his face. He wore nice clothes, which appeared to be expensive. He did not talk a lot, but when he did speak, it was usually in a cold, demanding tone. He rarely had a pleasant look on his face.

At that time, I was very much in love with Hannah, an intelligent, attractive young lady John Mundy brought to the plantation to clean and cook for his family. I had saved enough money to buy our freedom so that we could be married, or "jump the broom" as we called it in the quarters, because slaves were not permitted to wed legally. I will never forget what happened when I approached him that morning in April 1861. I showed him my money and asked him to accept it as my offer for my freedom. Not all slaves were allowed to keep the money they earned, but some of us were allowed to keep a small portion of our money. Slaves were hired out to make a profit for the master, not to benefit the slave.

"Mastah John, some years back you told me dat if I eva had de money, I could buy my freedom. Well, Mastah, I dun save my money ova de years, an I got 'nuff to buy my freedom. I got it right heah. I didn't spend my money, 'cept for things dat wuz nessary." I decided to wait for his answer before I asked to buy Hannah's freedom as well.

"So, are you *telling* me that you want your freedom, and that you have the money to buy it, boy?" he asked. The color of his skin changed to a reddish tone. I had seen John Mundy angry many times. At that moment, he had that same angry look in his eyes.

"I ain't *tellin'* you nuttin, Mastah." I felt as if I had done something terrible, something I needed to apologize for. "I jes axin if I kin buy my freedom. You said I could some time back, if I had de money. I dun save my money, Mastah, an I kin pay you for my freedom." He still had that angry look in his eyes.

"There is nothing worse than an ungrateful nigger!" he shouted. "I bought you and gave you a place to lay your head and food to eat, and this is the thanks I get! It is because of me that you have had the opportunity to leave this plantation and work throughout Georgia and South Carolina. People from far and near ask for my skilled slaves to work for them. You would be nothing, a nobody, if it was not for me, boy. And, now, you want to leave this wonderful place and get your freedom. What in the hell do you know about freedom? You are a nigger, an uneducated nigger, who cannot make it on your own. Where in the hell would you go and what would you do?"

"Mastah John, you told me dat I could buy my freedom iffen I eva got de money, an Mastah, I'se got de money right heah. I ain't dun nuttin wrong."

"Why, you proud, smart talking nigger, I should whip you until you bleed. The nerve of you to stand here and tell me that this plantation isn't good enough for you!"

"Mastah, you been real good to me, an I 'preciate all dat you done for me. I got de money right heah to buy my freedom. I have wucked hard for you, Mastah." John Mundy was furious with me that morning. I was clever enough to be quiet and listen because I did not want him to think I was arguing with him. I was simply trying to get him to remember that he had told me I could buy my freedom one day, if I had the money. Either he did not remember saying that, or

3

he did not *choose* to remember his own words. I still believe he chose not to remember what he said to me.

"It's niggers like you that are causing problems for all of us southern planters. You get these crazy, big ideas about being free and leaving, and you don't know a damn thing about living on your own. Next thing I know, all of my slaves will be talking this foolishness about being free and leaving the plantation. Then, what's going to happen to our crops – our corn, cotton, sugar and rice?"

"Mastah, I ain't runnin' off. I jes axin if I kin buy my freedom from you. You been a good mastah to me, an I'se gratefal to you. I ain't neva cause no trouble for you ova de years. I respec you for all you dun for me." John Mundy was still angry.

"Benjamin Stark, a planter right across the county line, just lost three of his slaves in one week. Those ungrateful niggers ran off for no reason, and left Ben with no one to care for his horses or to cook his meals. Something has to be done to keep you niggers in line. We pay a lot of money for our slaves, and you *are* our *property*. Let me warn you, boy, we have the slave patrol, and their job is to watch, catch and beat slaves who get out of line."

"I guess I can't buy my freedom." I felt like someone had driven a nail through my heart. All those years I had served John Mundy and endured his brutal punishment, and came to him to buy my freedom, and he went into a rage. I believed him when he told me I could buy my freedom if I ever saved enough money.

"Hell, no, you cannot buy your freedom from me!" he yelled. "I never told you that you could buy your freedom. You niggers are getting out of control and something has to be done. You got a house to finish building, and you need to get to work. Boy, don't let me hear you talking any more foolishness about being a free man. I've been good to you, but believe me, I can make your life hell if you continue to be an ungrateful nigger. Now get your tools and get to work!"

As I walked away from John Mundy that morning to get onto the wagon to go to work, I hurt badly, but my spirit was not crushed. It would almost kill me to tell Hannah that I could not buy my freedom, or hers. I had waited so long to jump the broom with her. I loved her so much and wanted her to be my wife, but not as a slave. I wanted us to live our lives as free people.

I had seen other slave men jump the broom, still the masters had their way with slave women. Jake, a slave I worked with near Atlanta, had been beaten to death because he tried to protect his wife from her master. Jake was a decent man who loved and respected his wife, but her master made it very clear to Jake that his wife was the master's property, and that the master could have his way with her at any time. I was capable of killing John Mundy, or anyone who harmed Hannah.

To my knowledge, he had never touched Hannah. If he had, Hannah had not told me. There were several slave women on his plantation. I had no idea how he treated them because I was hired out to work a lot, and did not spend much time on the plantation. John Mundy hired his skilled slaves out to allow us to work for other people. Sometimes I stayed with the people and worked for weeks, and sometimes months. I was very valuable to him, and he worked me as if he did not think I was human. I made a lot of money for him over the years and was certain that was why he became furious when I asked to buy my freedom.

John Mundy did not know that Hannah and I loved each other. We were intelligent enough to keep our feelings for each other a secret, because we knew that some of the other slaves would talk, and before long John Mundy would know everything. Next to Mammy and my sister, Hannah was the most special lady I had ever known, and would ever know. Her large, brown eyes were captivating. Hannah spoke in a calm, caring tone. Her light brown skin was soft and clean. She was thin, and not very tall. She smiled a lot, and her big smile revealed white, straight teeth. Her hair was long and thick, and neatly styled in a single braid. I thought of her as an angel, living here on the earth.

As I traveled back to the plantation a few days later, I thought about the conversation Hannah and I had before I asked John Mundy if I could buy my freedom. We met secretly near some large oak trees behind the big house. Although Hannah was nervous about me asking John Mundy to allow me to buy our freedom, we were quite excited about the thought of being free; free to leave the plantation, and free to jump the broom. We were young and in love, and had wonderful thoughts about our lives together as man and wife.

"Hannah, I dun saved 'nuff money to buy our freedom from Mastah John. A few years ago, he told me dat I could buy my freedom. Well, I been wuckin hard for many years, an I dun saved a lot of money. I bleeve dis is more den 'nuff to buy our freedom. We will be free, Hannah, den we will jump de broom. Dis is a proud day for me."

"Tom, Mastah said you could buy yo freedom, but he ain't said nuttin about you buyin' my freedom. You gotta think about dis befo you go to Mastah John."

"Hannah, listen to me. I been thinkin' 'bout bein' free since dey took me from my famly. I ain't seen my famly but one time since I wuz a pickanniny. I seen Mammy an my sista, Sarah, in Atlanta many years ago. I seen dem 'cause I wuz wuckin at de house whur dey came wit Mastah Wilmington. I ain't seen dem since. Pappy could not come wit dem to Atlanta, so it been longa den dat since I seen him. I ain't gonna spen de res of my life as a slave."

"What do you think Mastah John will say to you, Tom? Lord, I been prayin' dat we can be free, but I know what dun happen to udder slaves who wonted thar freedom. When will you go to Mastah John to tell him dat you got 'nuff money to buy yo freedom?"

"Tomorrow is de day dat I been waitin' for for so long! I been a good wucker for Mastah John. He hire me out to do carpentry and bricklayin' wuck, an I been one of his bes wuckers. I done wucked hard for him, an I been honest 'bout de money. I ain't stole nuttin from him, an people hab told Mastah John dat I's a good carpenter and bricklayer. Mastah John dun made lots of money through my labor. I dun saved my money, an now I wont to buy my freedom, an yo freedom, so dat we kin jump de broom."

"Tom, I wanna be free, jes lak you, an I wont to be yo wife, but some of dese mastahs don't lak to lose thar strong slaves who got good skills. I pray dat he will take yo money an give us our freedom."

"I will talk wit Mastah early in de mornin', befo I go to wuck. We gonna be free, Hannah, free to jump de broom. Den, I's goin' back to Holly Springs to buy Mammy, Pappy an my sista. I saved my money. I's gonna get my famly back togetha, de way it should be."

"How do you know if yo famly still in Holly Springs, Tom? It's been a long time since you wuz sold an snatched from yo famly."

"My famly is lak me, Hannah. Dey is strong people, an dey got skills. I remamba dat Mammy could sew an mek dresses for Miz Wilmington an her chilluns. An Pappy wucked in our cabin to mek it comfertabal for his famly. An my little sista, I know she gonna be jes lak Mammy. I guess dat she kin sew an do all de things dat Mammy kin do. I guess she ain't so little no more, 'cause it's been a long time since I left dem. I know dat my famly is waitin' to be wit me, jes lak I been waitin' to be wit dem. We will all be togetha, soon.

"Our chilluns ain't gonna grow up bein' slaves. I wont betta for my chilluns. I wont dem to know how to read an rite, an to be free. Ain't no slaveholder gonna snatch my chilluns an hire dem out, de way I wuz snatched from my famly. Dey lied an said dat I would come back to my famly. I's a grown man, an I ain't seen my famly in years. Dis ain't gonna happen wit my chilluns! Hannah, you will be my wife, an you ain't gonna wuck in no big house de res of yo life. Our people is slaves, who wuck on plantations an in fields. Things gotta change, Hannah. I got de money to buy our freedom, an I will talk to Mastah John in de mornin'."

I hated to have to face Hannah, to tell her about my conversation with John Mundy, but I was certain she knew from the look in my eyes that I had not been able to buy our freedom. Painfully, I told her every word that John Mundy said to me that morning. Hannah cried on my shoulder.

"Tom, you tellin' me dat we can't jump de broom?" She continued to cry. That was one of the saddest moments of my life. I listened to the woman I had asked to be my wife, cry as if there would be no tomorrow.

"Hannah, listen to me. Yes, we will jump de broom, but not at dis time. Somehow, an someway, we will jump de broom an spen de res of our lives togetha, as free people, de way God wont us to. Mastah John done beat me down, agin, but my spirit ain't crushed. We will find a way, Hannah, bleeve me."

# CHAPTER 2

It took some time to get myself together after that confrontation with John Mundy. I should not have been surprised about what he said because I was quite valuable to him. I had been on his plantation for several years and worked hard as a carpenter and bricklayer, and at whatever he needed me to do.

I was whipped by Edward Carnes, the slaveholder who bought me when I was a child, and by John Mundy. Still, I believed there was some decency in them, because we are all created by the same God. Mammy said over and over that God did not create bad people. Perhaps God did not create bad people, but at times, His people did bad things. John Mundy was no exception.

Reflecting on my confrontation with John Mundy many years ago, I suspect the only reason he would consider my freedom was because he never believed I was intelligent enough to save money all those years. I earned a lot of money working for him. John Mundy and Edward Carnes allowed me to keep some of the money. Buying my freedom was a dream I held close to my heart for years. That dream inspired me to push forward.

John Mundy probably assumed that I had forgotten about what he said to me. Did he actually believe I was content to be his slave for the rest of my life! Yes, I was fed and lived in the slave quarters on his plantation, but that was by no means the life I wanted for my family. I was determined that our children would not grow up in bondage. We were created to be a free.

Hannah wanted us to jump the broom and make the most of living on the plantation, but I refused to accept that. A voice within continued to speak after John Mundy refused to let me buy my freedom. That voice was clear about the life I wanted for my family. I was determined that we would jump the broom, and would wait for Hannah, no matter how long it took to get my freedom. She was the woman I loved, and nothing would change that. I believed she felt the same.

The only choice was to accept the situation and show respect for John Mundy, although I was very angry with him. Over the years I learned that it accomplished nothing to let the master know you were angry with him, other than perhaps get a whipping for being disrespectful. John Mundy carried on as if nothing had happened. In fact, he seemed proud of himself that he had rejected the offer to buy my freedom.

I continued to work hard building cabins for slaves on farms and plantations, and building stately homes for white people. More than once I overheard white men tell John Mundy about the quality of my work. I also heard him tell them that he taught me most of what I know, and that it was because of him that I had developed into a skilled carpenter and bricklayer.

"I'm mighty proud of Tom," he used to say. "I been working with that boy for years, and he has caught on quickly to everything I taught him. Some of them don't learn as quickly as Tom…"

That was not the truth, and John Mundy knew it. Pappy taught me basic carpentry skills, and I learned to lay bricks by watching others, and by working hard on various jobs. The more I worked, the more I learned, and there was always plenty of work to do. John Mundy had little to do with me being a skilled carpenter and bricklayer.

Whenever I made mistakes, Edward Carnes deprived me of food. He often said he would not tolerate sloppy work from any of his slaves. It did not matter that I was little more than a child when he first hired me out to work. He had the same expectations of all slaves, regardless of age.

"Tom, you get this work right, or you don't eat tonight," he would say. "You may be young, but you've got to learn that if the work ain't done, you ain't gonna eat. It takes money to buy food, and you gotta earn your keep."

About a month later, in May 1861, John Mundy told me to prepare to go to Charleston, South Carolina. Someone he knew was building a house there, and the man wanted his slaves to help. I did not want to go, not because I did not want to work, but because I would be so far from Hannah for so long. Sometimes we would be away from the plantation for months. There was a time when I looked forward to being away from the master and the plantation, but after I met Hannah, everything changed.

Being close to Hannah made the long days on the plantation seem a little brighter and a little shorter. Although we could not spend time together, like white people who loved each other could, just the sight of Hannah during the day filled me with joy. Her smile was always warm and kind. Like Mammy, she never complained about her chores in the big house. There was "something special" about Hannah that captivated my attention the moment I saw her. She never lost that "something special."

First, I had to tell Hannah that I could not buy my freedom, and that we could not jump the broom as soon as we wanted to. Then, I had to tell her that I was leaving the plantation to work in Charleston, and had no idea how long I would be away. Hannah looked at me and did not say a word. I could see the pain in her eyes. Still, she smiled and said, "Tom, I luv you. Go, do what you gotta do. I will be heah when you git back."

Her words gave me the "push" I needed that morning to get into the wagon and head to Charleston. There were seven of us; John Mundy, two other slaveholders, two white carpenters and Joe, another slave on John Mundy's plantation. Joe and I sat in the back of the wagon. John Mundy always brought Joe along to keep the work place clean and safe. Joe was a hard worker and a good person. He was very loyal to his master. John Mundy often talked about how the rest of his slaves should try to be more like Joe. From time to time, he called all of his slaves together and boasted about Joe's good behavior.

"Joe was born on this plantation, and I have never had any trouble with him doing what he's told to do. Joe is a model for all you slaves to follow. I can leave Joe anywhere, and never have to worry about him running or loafing about. I don't like to punish my slaves, and if you behave like Joe, you don't have to worry about getting punished. Joe, keep up the good work."

11

John Mundy always came along to help his slaves get settled whenever he hired us out to work for someone else. We could be gone for days, weeks or months. We usually stayed in a cabin on the person's property we were hired to work for. After John Mundy gave strict orders about what his slaves were allowed to do or not to do, he left.

On that warm morning in May 1861, John Mundy and the other slaveholders talked on and on in the wagon about a war that had started between people in the North and those in the South. They spoke in a harsh tone, as if they were very angry. They talked about Abraham Lincoln.

"Abraham Lincoln got no interest in us planters down here in the South," John Mundy said that morning. "He's talking about saving the Union, but I don't believe a damn word of what he's saying. They ain't saying it, but none of those Northerners want us to keep our slaves. They're only thinking about what's good for their economy. They can't tell us what to do with our slaves because that's our property."

"This talk about slavery being a burden on the country is nothing but nonsense," Mr. Douglas, another slaveholder said. "Thank God for South Carolina and the other states that had the good sense to secede from that damn Union. Those Northerners only want what's best for them, with no regard for our livelihood. If they take away our slaves, who will work in our fields and grow our crops? They need to mind their own damn business and leave us planters alone. We ain't trying to tell them how to run the North."

"They're trying to get the new states joining the Union to come in and ban slavery," Mr. Robertson, the other slaveholder said. "They don't want us Southerners to have no power in the national government. They're trying to destroy us, our families, our crops, our way of life. Damn those Northerners, and all that they stand for!"

"Lincoln believes what they believe," John Mundy said. "Those Northerners want a Union where slavery doesn't exist, where they can tell us planters and farmers what to do, how to live, what to believe, how to raise our children. They want to destroy everything we value, everything we believe in. That's why South Carolina left the damn Union, right after Lincoln was elected."

"We got to protect our families, our properties, and everything else that belongs to us," Mr. Douglas continued. "Lincoln ain't ready to compromise, to work with us, to bring us back into the Union. South Carolina, Georgia, Mississippi, Florida, Alabama and Louisiana met in Montgomery, and now we got our own constitution. Thank God for the Confederate States of America! Thank God for Jefferson Davis! He's the president we need. He's the president I support!"

It seemed as if they became more angry as they talked on about Lincoln and people in the North, and their plan to destroy the South. I sensed that they were afraid of what lay ahead for them, their families and their crops. They saw Jefferson Davis as a leader who could save the South, and they were prepared to do whatever it took to defend their rights, and their property.

"He gave his word that the Union Army would protect the property rights of slaveholders, but there ain't no truth to that," John Mundy continued, after a short silence. "They got no right coming down here and interfering with what belongs to us. There ain't no cause for them to think they're superior to us. I'm prepared to do whatever Jefferson Davis needs me to do to protect what belongs to the South."

"Just last month, South Carolina attacked the Union's Fort Sumter," Mr. Douglas said. "They have every right to protect their property from the Union. I am prepared to fight, to kill, to wipe out every Northerner from our soil. I been talking to lots of farmers and they feel the same as I do. Ain't no cowards here in the South. We got every right to rebel, to fight for what's ours."

"Say what they may about this being a moral question, but it all comes down to slavery," John Mundy said. He scratched his head and looked back at Joe and me. "They want to abolish slavery, but we ain't gonna let 'em. I got fifteen slaves and I treat 'em good. I feed 'em and cloth 'em and give 'em a place to lay their heads. What more can any of 'em ask for?"

"The war done started, and I salute South Carolina for attacking Fort Sumter," Mr. Robertson said. "Somebody's got to stand up to those damn Northerners and show them that they can't have their way here in the South. We got our own president, and we don't need Lincoln telling us what to do or how to do it. God bless the Confederate States!"

I became more anxious as the three of them talked on about the war that had already started. Those Southern planters clearly hated President Lincoln. I suspected the slaves would pay a price for the growing conflict between the North and the South.

I had been hired out to work in Charleston more than once. While building homes in Charleston, I heard white people talk about the city, which is situated at the fork of the Ashley and Cooper Rivers. Most of the money in Charleston came from commerce, and many of the citizens were quite wealthy.

Charlestonians had a sense of pride about themselves and their city. You could see it in the way they walked and in the way they talked. They appeared to honor and respect their families.

Rice was harvested between October and March, which was a very busy time in Charleston. Some Charlestions believe it was introduced to Charleston back around 1690, when a ship that left Georgetown, South Carolina, bound for England, was forced into Charleston for repairs, after it was damaged during a storm. It is reported that the Captain gave the governor of the colony a handful of rice seeds. From that small amount of seed, Charleston was eventually able to supply all the colonies with rice. Rice mills were on the Ashley River. Ships carrying goods entered and left Charleston throughout the year.

Charleston has some of the most beautiful homes in the South. Many of the homes have a veranda on the first and second levels. The wood columns have intricate designs. The spacious verandas are graced with large pots of flowers and plants, and with wooden chairs that rock back and forth. A white bricklayer from Charleston explained that the grand architectural design of the homes in this city reflects this country's colonial period. Working in Charleston helped me to realize more than ever that life is a gift, and that all people should be free to enjoy it.

We finally made it to the location where we were hired to work. I was tired of riding, and of listening to John Mundy and the others speak about their dislike for the President and Northerners who wanted to destroy the South. After we got out of the wagon, John Mundy showed Joe and me the cabin we would stay in while working there. He then introduced us to the man we would be working for, James Forrester. He was a tall, well-dressed, big man, who walked with his head high and his shoulders back, as if he owned the city of Charleston. His thick, curly dark hair, with streaks of grey, gave him a distinguished look. Although a big man, he spoke in a moderate voice tone, had a pleasant smile, and did not appear to be a cruel person.

John Mundy made it very clear to his slaves that we were to address the men we worked for as "Master" and the ladies as "Mistress." James Forrester was told that Joe and I were good workers, and that he should not have any problems with us.

"Tom and Joe work hard and do a good job, but if they should get out of hand, don't hesitate to whip them. I don't tolerate any foolishness from my slaves. They are to behave here as they do on my plantation." The next day John Mundy left Charleston to return to Savannah. I was glad to be rid of him, and resented him more than ever. Although I missed Hannah dearly, I had no desire to be near John Mundy or his plantation.

We went to Charleston to build another house for James Forrester. He was already living in a smaller house on that same property. We began working on the house the day after we arrived in Charleston. That was one of the largest homes I had ever worked on. There were six columns in the front of the brick, three-story house, with a veranda on each level. The front of the house had six windows on each level. Several workers joined Joe and me that first day. Some were working class white people who lived in Charleston. Other Negras worked with us as well. Jessie, a skilled bricklayer, did not hesitate to let us know that he was a free Negra. He knew a lot about the South and the North. It was a pleasure to listen to him.

"I guess thar's around a thousand free Negras heah in Charleston," Jessie said. "Some is free 'cause thar mastahs no longer got any use for dem, either 'cause of thar age or 'cause of thar health. Many of dem is in need of food, clothin' and a place to live, but some got skills and work hard, and is able to provide a good life for thar famlies."

Jessie knew of a few free Negras in Charleston who owned slaves. I could not understand why our own people would choose to support a system that had been so destructive, so cruel, so inhumane to us. He made it very clear that he did not own any slaves, and that he never would.

Jessie was probably the shortest man I had ever met. I clearly remember his big ears and pale green inquisitive eyes. I had never seen a Negra with eyes that color. Although his skin was brown, I wondered if he had some white blood running through his veins. Jessie talked about what it was like to be a free Negra in Charleston. He explained that there were things white Charlestonians could do that free Negras were not allowed to do.

"We ain't allowed to gatha in large groups, 'less a white person is present. An, thar is restrictions on educatin' free Negras. An, like slaves, free Negras gotta have papers at all times to show dat we's actually free."

Jessie said things began to change in Charleston shortly before Abraham Lincoln was elected president. I asked why, and he explained.

"White people, 'pecially politicians, feared dat his election meant dat Charleston an udder cities in de South was doomed. Many white Charlestonians bleeve dat President Lincoln an his supportas hate dem, an is workin' to destroy what dey bleeve in, an thar way of life. Dey bleeve people in de North is thar enemy.

"Before de election in Novemba, thar was talk dat South Carolina would likely leave de Union. Afta de election, South Carolinians was afraid, an dey took action to protect demselves from Northerners. Dat's when South Carolina attacked Fort Sumter, a sea fort heah in Charleston. I bleeve dis war is all about slavery. People in de North is 'gainst slavery, an people in de South is fightin' to keep it."

Jessie then spoke some words I could not get out of my mind. "I heard dat free Negras an slaves is offrin thar service to de Union, at

Fortress Monroe in Vaginia, followin' de attack on Fort Sumter. I also heard dat dey been 'cepted thar."

If free Negroes and slaves were willing to fight for the Union, I wanted to join them. We had a duty to help ourselves. "You think de President will let us fight?" I asked. Jessie was a free Negra who knew about what was going on outside of Charleston and the South. Still, I had to be careful not to ask too many questions, because I did not know Jessie, and did not want to get in trouble with John Mundy or James Forrester.

"You talkin' 'bout dose of us who's free?" he answered. "I don't see why not, 'cause de North go need all de help dey kin get to win de war. 'Course, I got a famly heah in Charleston, an I got to support dem. I ain't got no plans to fight 'cause my famly need me."

"I would fight if I wuz a free man, an if dey would have me," I said. "Do you think de war is really 'bout settin' us free?" I believed that the war started because people in the North were against slavery. That was all John Mundy and his friends talked about as we traveled to Charleston. They hated the President and his supporters.

"I bleeve it got a lot to do wit de slaves, whetha dey should be free or not," Jessie answered. "Course, ain't no need in you thinkin' 'bout fightin', 'cause you ain't free. Yo mastah sho ain't gonna let you leave de plantation an join no war. You a good bricklayer an carpenter, an ain't too many slaves got yo skills. Betta git dat thought out yo head."

"I wuz jes axin, dat's all." I continued to work and did not discuss the war any more. Jessie was right; I was a slave and very valuable to John Mundy. He was probably still angry with me because I asked to buy my freedom. Also, he believed that the President and others in the North wanted slaves to be free. I felt that he and his friends would watch their slaves more closely than ever.

I had never been to Virginia, but had enough faith to believe that I could make it to Fortress Monroe. I learned new things quickly, and had always been a good listener. Jessie had been to Virginia more than once, and I asked him about his trips. He loved to talk, and talked endlessly as we worked on James Forrester's house each day. I listened carefully.

"We got famly in Philedelphia, an we gits to go up thar at leas once a year," he said. "Let me tell y'all, Philedelphia is a fine place. I think we might jes move on back up thar one of dese days. Some of our famly doin' real good up thar."

"Whur is Vaginia, an how do you git thar?" I wanted to learn as much as possible. Jessie was an intelligent man who had lived in the North. He had never been a slave. He originally came to Charleston from Philadelphia with his wife to help build a house. He was a skilled bricklayer. After working on that house for several months, a wealthy Charlestonian asked him to stay in Charleston to help build his house.

The wealthy Charlestonian was very pleased with Jessie's work, and told several of his friends about him. Before long, Jessie had more than enough work to keep him busy. He loved to talk about where he had been and the people he had met, and I enjoyed his stories. I was eager to learn more, but was clever enough to keep the desire to learn and explore to myself. Edward Carnes and John Mundy made it very clear that they would not tolerate any such nonsense from their slaves.

"Vaginia is dat way." Jessie pointed in the direction as he tried to explain where Virginia was located. "You leave heah, den you go down to Hopper's Store on de corner, you turn, an den you stay on dat road. Afta a real long ride on dat road, wont be too long befo you git to Norf Carolina. Den you headed for Vaginia. Sho take a long time to git thar."

I never forgot Jessie's words. "Maybe I will git thar one day," I said. Jessie continued to talk about other places he had been, and the people he had met. He was a very interesting person. I am thankful to have met him.

That night at the cabin, Joe and I talked about the war. He had also heard some of the white workers talk about the war as he cleaned up around the construction site.

"Dese folks in Souf Carolina sho is mad wit de President," Joe said. "Dey all talkin' 'bout how dey so glad dat Souf Carolina done lef de Union. Dey say dey ready an willin' to fight to run dem Union men back whur dey come from. Dey say dat de war start 'cause people in de North wont to free us slaves, an dat it ain't none of thar damn businuss."

"Joe, whut if a slave wont to fight wit de Union? If dey fightin' for us to be free, den why should slaves not help dem? Seems like we should wanna help de Union win."

"Tom, you dun loss yo mind? Do you really think dem Union men gonna let a nigger fight wit dem? Dey white, Tom; dey ain't lak us. We don't even know if dey really fightin' for us to be free. Dat's jes whut I heah dese white wuckers sayin'. Tom, I know you wont to be a free man, but you need to git dat thaut of fightin' wit de Union out yo head!"

Suddenly, I realized I could not discuss the thought of fighting with the Union Army with Joe. He was a good friend, and I had known him a long time, but I also knew that he was very loyal to John Mundy. John Mundy had often described him as his "model" slave. Unfortunately, I did not know if I could trust Joe not to tell John Mundy or James Forrester that I had thoughts about fighting with the Union Army.

"I wont to be free, too, but mastah John ain't all bad, Tom," Joe continued. "We gits food an close to wure, an we got a place to sleep at night. We don't know nuttin 'bout livin' no whur else. We know dat a lot of our people dun run off, but neva made it to de Norf, 'cause dey was killed tryin' to git thar. Mastah John an a lot of white people is angry 'bout all dat's goin' on dese days.

"You betta keep yo thinkin' to yosef, Tom, 'cause mastah John ain't gonna have no slave of his talkin' 'bout fightin' wit no Union Army. He done said many times dat ain't no slave gonna disrespec him. I cure 'bout you Tom, an don't wont you to git whipped or worse. We been togetha for a long time, an you my friend."

"I guess you right, Joe. We got a house to build, an I need to think 'bout doin' de bes job I kin for mastah Forrester. I don't wont mastah John to be disippointed in my wuck." I said those words to Joe, but could not, and did not stop thinking about the possibility of getting to Fortress Monroe and fighting with the Union Army.

Joe was a good person. I had known him since John Mundy brought me to his plantation. He was a thin man, with a small body frame. Perhaps that was why he was afraid to run from the plantation. Joe had a pleasant smile, but also had a frightened look on his face. He tried so hard to please everyone, except himself. John Mundy said many times that all of his slaves should try to be more like Joe. He often reminded the rest of us that Joe had never caused him any trouble, and that he was very obedient. Well, I was not like Joe, and never wanted to be like him.

Joe was born on John Mundy's plantation. He was probably a few years younger than me. I thought of him as a younger brother. He often worried that my ideas and the way I thought would get me killed. I listened to him, but nothing and no one could keep me from dreaming; from believing that Negras were not created to spend their lives as slaves. If I got killed because I believed that, then at least I would die for what I believed in.

Over the days that followed, I did not say anything else to Joe or Jessie about the war. As we worked on the house, I listened to other workers talk about the war, and learned more about it. While working there, I had the wonderful opportunity to meet Miz Emma, a slave who cooked and cleaned for James Forrester's family. She had been on that plantation for several years. Miz Emma was a big woman, and very warm and kind. She appeared to be around my mother's age, perhaps about sixty years old. She always wore a black rag tied around her head.

At the end of the work day, Joe and I, Ed and Ethel, two of James Forrester's slaves, gathered at Miz Emma's cabin to listen to her stories about West Africa, and to watch her make baskets. Miz Emma weaved the most beautiful baskets. She explained that the baskets are called "sweetgrass" because of the smell of the grass when it's freshly harvested. She was teaching this skill to Ethel, a young slave girl, about seventeen years old. Ethel worked with Miz Emma in the big house. Ed was around forty years old, and he cared for James Forrester's horses.

Miz Emma loved to talk about what she remembered about her life in West Africa; about making baskets and cooking for her family before they were separated and departed to the many ports in the West. Her husband had been on James Forrester's plantation with her, but he died long before I came to work on the house. Miz Emma did not have children of her own. Perhaps that was why she was so warm and caring toward Joe, Ethel, Ed and me. As her hands worked the grass to make baskets, she told stories about her family; about how her mother, sisters and relatives made quilts and baskets in West Africa.

She explained that slaves knew that palmetto leaves and other grasses in South Carolina were ideal for making baskets. Her ancestors used palmetto leaves and similar grasses to weave baskets in West Africa. Miz Emma made lots of baskets, and explained that they were used to store rice, beans, nuts, sewing items and other things.

The five of us spoke Gullah when we gathered in Miz Emma's cabin in the evenings. I was familiar with Gullah words because I lived in Savannah for several years. We did not speak Gullah during the day, but when we gathered after work, we bonded with each other through telling stories and singing spirituals. I remember the words to a spiritual Miz Emma taught us:

> *I'ein comin back no mo,*
> *I'ein comin back no mo.*
> *Bid dis world a long fa'well*
> *an I'ein comin back no mo.*
> *Soon'z muh foot strike Zion,*
> *and da lampos' light up on dah sho'*
> *Bid dis world a long fa'well*
> *An' I'ein comin' back no mo.*

To this day, I miss Miz Emma. I enjoyed every moment spent with her. In some ways she was like a mother. She had a kind, loving spirit. Unfortunately, I would never see Miz Emma again, because I decided to run away from Charleston. I decided to offer my skills, services, and whatever they needed, to the Union Army at Fortress

Monroe. I would help the Union win the war against slavery, because I believed that was really what they were fighting about.

One night, after a long day at work, after leaving Miz Emma's cabin, I was tired, but ready to act. My mind was made up. After working in Charleston for about a month, the time had come for me to run; run to fight for what I believed in – freedom. I did not know if the men fighting for the Union would have me, but I would never know if I did not leave Charleston to try to find out.

Joe thought it was dangerous for any slave to attempt to escape slavery. He believed that, because of the war, any runaway slave who got caught would be killed. He was probably right. Joe also believed that we should accept our lives as slaves, and make the most of being enslaved, living on farms and plantations. He was definitely wrong about that.

Jessie was a free man and proud of it. Each day after work, he was free to go home to his family. Although Negras in Charleston did not enjoy the same rights and privileges that white Charlestonians enjoyed, Jessie was not a slave, or his wife and children. He did not think the Union soldiers would have anything to do with slaves.

Well, it did not matter what Joe and Jessie thought. God gave me a healthy brain, and I used it to do what could help me and all slaves. The only difficult part of my decision to run away to fight for the Union was my love and respect for Hannah. I desperately wanted to talk to her. There was so much I needed to say to her. In desperation, I wrote my feelings on some paper. Mammy taught her children to read and write simple words when we were very young. Mammy learned to read and write some words by being around the white children in the big house, who had a tutor to teach them. Hannah could read and write a few words as well. I knew enough words to write to her:

*My deer Hannah:*

*I miss you mor than eva I been wuckin hard heah in Charlston an dont no whin we wil finish up heah on dis house I hav luv you sinse de day dat we met an you de only lady I wont to be my wif but we cannot jump de broom til we is free peple I wont betta for you an for our chillen an I wil neva stop tryin to be free it is hard for me to tell you dat I hav ran away from Charlston to fight wit de Union dey dont bleev slavery is right an I wont to hep dem win de war Hannah plees bleev dat I wil cum bak for you one day but I gotta do dis for me an for udder slaves take cure of yoself an we mus pray for each udder evry day one day you wil be my wif an things wil be much betta for us an for our peple I luv you so much an I wil cum bak for you*

*Tom*

By the time I finished writing that letter, I was in tears. I believed Hannah would understand, because she knew and understood me. She was as intelligent and passionate as she was beautiful.

I wanted to give that letter to Joe to give to Hannah whenever he returned to John Mundy's plantation. Joe would never run from that plantation, and would probably be there forever, or until slavery no longer existed. Joe was loyal to John Mundy, and would more than likely give that letter to him, so I kept the letter with me. I felt better after I wrote to Hannah. Somehow, after writing those words, a heavy burden was lifted.

Before I left the cabin that morning, Joe pleaded with me not to run. I could see the pain in his eyes and hear it in his voice as he described the horrible things that could happen if I was caught.

"Tom, is you crazy? If dey ketch you, dey will kill you dis time! Dey is already angry wit us 'cause of de war. Tom, dey will whip you 'til you bleed! Dey might even let de hounds eat you! Dose white men fightin' for de Union ain't gonna 'cep no slave to hep dem win de war. Tom, whut 'bout Hannah? Dis is too dangrous for you…"

I heard Joe's desperate words, but my mind was made up. That morning in June 1861, I ran as fast as I could from that small cabin on James Forrester's plantation, into a bunch of huge, tall trees not so far behind the plantation.

# CHAPTER 3

As I sprinted from the plantation that morning, I could still hear Joe's desperate words, pleading with me not to leave. He said over and over that I would be killed if John Mundy caught me. He even described some of the horrible things that had been done to runaway slaves. "Some been hung, whipped 'til dey bled, or beat to death. Udders been deprive of food or force to wuck 'til dey dropped'". He was absolutely right. I tried to get away from Edward Carnes once and was severely whipped.

I thought about Hannah, and how much I loved her and wanted her with me. Still, I could not jump the broom with her and live on a plantation. I was capable of killing anyone who harmed Hannah in any way, including the master. It was definitely time to run and try to have the life I believed I was created to live. It did not matter if I got killed. I would fight to the end.

Before I left the cabin that morning, I grabbed the bread and fat back that was sent over for our supper, and put it in a sack. I wanted to give the letter I wrote to Joe to give to Hannah, but did not. I had to believe that Hannah would understand, and that she would wait for me to come back for her. Like Mammy, she was strong, loyal and patient. She believed things would get better for us.

I had to get out of South Carolina as quickly as possible because James Forrester and John Mundy would certainly have had the patrollers and hound dogs hunting me as soon as they got word that I was missing. Joe had no choice but to tell them that I ran off. I prayed that he would not be accused of knowing about my plan to run, because he knew nothing until the morning I left. John Mundy would blame someone for my escape, and unfortunately, that person would be Joe.

One of the saddest things about running away was that those you left behind were likely to suffer in some way. The first time I ran away from Edward Carnes, he whipped several slaves for not telling him about my plan to run. The truth is that none of them knew. I learned that the less you said to others, the better. That was a lesson Pappy taught me years ago.

It was a warm, peaceful morning. I ran as fast as possible into the wooded area to get away without being seen. To this day, I believe Joe allowed time for me to escape before he told James Forrester that I was gone. Joe was a good friend. I wish he would have come with me.

The patrollers were good at tracking down runaway slaves. They had caught hundreds of slaves and brought them back to their masters to pay the price for running off. That morning I believed I had spent my last day as a slave and was prepared to accept the consequences for running away, again, even if it meant death. The thought of dying was no longer frightening. I did not want to be severely punished again, but I had to run.

I ran and walked at a fast pace until it was too dark to see clearly. I had to find a place to rest for the night, but was reluctant to close my eyes. There was no telling who was out there. I tried to follow the path Jessie talked about, and prayed I was headed to Fortress Monroe, because there was no way to know. Faith in God would lead me where He wanted me to go.

Before I left the cabin, I grabbed my worn quilt. It was very old and very special. The clothes on my back were all I had. Slaves had very few clothes. Some were nearly naked and barefooted until the teen years. Unless you were a house servant, the mastah cared little about slave appearance. It was our labor that "represented" the mastah, not our looks.

Shoes were called "brogans". I remember Papa saying, "Most of us neva wore no brogans in de summa an mos times not in de winta, but some did. De shoemaka would come 'round once a year, den in 'bout six months, he would come back and haf sole an mek udder repars to de brogans. The mastah gave us one garment at a time, and that had to be slap wore out 'fore we got anotha one. Most of us was barefooted."

That first night in the woods, I spread the quilt over a bed of leaves, sticks and dry bush, put the sack under my head, and looked up at the moon, wondering what would become of me. I speculated about what was beyond the sky. Was God up there, or was He somewhere else? I sure needed Him that night.

I was tired, but did not want to fall asleep because I needed to stay alert. There were lots of sounds, some familiar and some not. Most of it probably came from bugs and other insects. I listened as something slowly moved across the crisp, dry leaves. Whatever loomed about in that wooded area, in the midst of the night, could not have been more harmful than those patrollers, who were probably hunting me.

Laying there, looking up at the sky and listening, afraid to fall asleep, was most uncomfortable, knowing that I may have to run at any moment. My feet were swollen and blistered because the shoes did not fit well. Running through the woods had not helped.

John Mundy had his slaves' feet measured like "shoeing a horse". Shoes never seemed to fit comfortably. Slaves who were fortunate to get shoes reduced discomfort by rubbing grease into stiff shoes. Unfortunately, I did not have any grease in my sack.

I thought about taking the shoes off for a few minutes, to get some relief, but did not. The flight to Fortress Monroe was not about being comfortable or pleasurable; it was about getting to the other side, to be a free man. So I lay there, looking up and listening, body still, determined not to fall asleep.

Suddenly, I heard a different noise that got louder, and closer. As planned, I jumped up, grabbed my things and ran. It was dark, but thank God the moon provided enough light to avoid running into trees. With aching feet, I ran as fast as possible, with limited vision.

Before long, I recognized the noise that startled and forced me to jump up and run. It was the sound of hound dogs. The dogs, as expected, had picked up my scent! Those dogs were trained to catch and kill their prey, if necessary. I was familiar with hound dogs because John Mundy had some, and he used them to catch slaves, his as well as runaways of other planters. Edward Carnes used hound dogs to track me down several years ago.

Dogs were trained to strike terror in the slaves. They bit, mutilated, and if not pulled off in time, killed! Slaves used their wits against the dogs with conjurer's potions and or grave dirt rubbed on their feet. I was not able to get any of that before leaving the plantation.

I was not afraid of dying, but did not want to be eaten by hound dogs. I ran as fast as possible, stumbled over a tree stump and fell. My head hit a large tree. That was painful, but I had to get up and keep running. Even the pain could not stop me from running. I was no stranger to pain. I had been whipped many times before and survived.

I stumbled again, over what must have been an opening in the ground. I fell hard, with my right arm under my body. It took a few minutes to get my breath. As I got up from the ground, one of the dogs grabbed my shirt and pulled me back. "Let me go, let me go!" I tried to pull away from his large, sharp teeth, but could not. Finally, I looked into his fierce eyes.

The hounds' eyes were ferocious, vicious, and as bright as the sun. The brightness of their eyes was almost blinding. I covered my genitals with my hands to protect them. I had been caught, but I was still a man.

I opened my eyes, prepared to look into the eyes of hound dogs, but did not see any dogs. Where had they gone? Surely they had not been called away. Perhaps the patrollers had decided to spare my life, but none of that made any sense.

Although I did not see any dogs, or white men, my eyes hurt. I rubbed them and slowly realized that it was the brightness of the sun that had blinded me. I pulled my body up from the ground and realized that nothing and no one had been chasing me. I had done exactly what I had been so determined not to do – fallen asleep and awakened from a bad dream! That blinding brightness was the beautiful sun, shining in my face, trying to tell me to get up and get going, quickly.

I rubbed my arms to make sure I was completely awake. What a horrible dream. I had tried so hard not to fall asleep, but my body had done what it needed to do – rest. My body knew it had to rest in order to keep moving. I thanked God for getting me through that first night, grabbed my things and started running.

I had no idea if I was still in Charleston or not, or where I was headed. Regardless, I had to get away from the patrollers and those hound dogs. James Forrester must have known about the escape, and was probably furious with everybody, especially Joe. I prayed that Joe would not be hurt or punished for something he knew nothing about. Joe was truly a decent person.

I was hungry, but would not take the time to stop to take a few bites of the fat back in my sack. I would eat when it was too dark to find my way. That was not the first time I had been hungry, and it would not be the last. I had to keep running, and think about getting away, not about what my body needed.

It was extremely hot at that time. Still, I was thankful for the sun, because its brightness had awakened and reminded me to get up and keep going. Mammy always said that in everything we endure in this life, there is something to be thankful for; something we can learn from having gone through it.

I stopped running for a few minutes to drink some water. Oh, how I wished I had brought more than that small animal skin pouch filled with water. I walked at a quick pace and could feel my heart pounding. The sun got hotter as the day dragged on.

I saw a huge tree, with lots of roots, some larger than the branches. The lower branches had been cut off, perhaps to be used for firewood. Squirrels ran and jumped around in the top branches, safe from harm, because no one could get to them. There was a small space between the roots, and I decided to sit for a few minutes. That tree provided lots of shade. I took my shoes off, rubbed my sore feet, tore an old rag in my sack and wrapped them before putting my shoes on. I did not think to ask the plantation conjurer to give me some of the potion made from grease that slaves used. That potion would have been so useful.

I slowly got up to continue running. Thank God, my feet felt a little better. The days seemed longer in the heat than in the colder months. That was a good thing because I needed to get as far away as possible before dark. I wondered how many other slaves had taken that path. Jessie said James Forrester lost two of his slaves earlier in the year. Things would probably be much harder for his slaves who stayed on the plantation out of fear that they, too, would escape.

There was an opening through the trees, and I saw what appeared to be a house. I stopped running and hid behind a large tree to see if anyone was around. I did not see anyone, but heard voices. I desperately wanted to ask someone if I was still in Charleston. I patiently waited to see who was speaking. Finally, I saw a young white boy come from around the front of the house. Apparently he was talking to someone inside the house. The boy walked toward the wooded area where I was hiding. I was close enough to get his attention, but I could not trust a white child any more than an adult. No white person was to be trusted by a runaway.

I watched the boy get some water from a large bucket, then waited until he went into the house. I decided to try to get some water because my throat was dry, but my body was wet from the heat. I slowly approached the bucket of water, filled my pouch, and stuck my head in the bucket to cool off. It felt wonderful. There were apples on a nearby tree and I grabbed some and put them in my sack.

I had never stolen anything from anyone, but had to survive. Water and food were necessary to continue on my flight. As I ran from the apple tree, I heard a door shut. The boy came out of the house and stared at me. He yelled, "Moma, Moma, there's a nigger out yonda!"

# CHAPTER 4

The day Mammy, Pappy, and I—Sarah—reunited with my brother, Tom, was the happiest day of my life. That was more than a decade ago. Over the years, I have learned that nothing is more important than family. I want my three children to understand how fortunate they are to have the opportunity to grow up together. They don't have to worry about being sold or separated from family, as we were, because our people are no longer enslaved.

It has been twelve years since my family reunited in Boston. My children need to know and appreciate their family history, and the history of their ancestors. They need to hear and learn about our flight to freedom, and the pain and struggles we endured as slaves. They need to know this so they can tell their children, and their children's children.

I am blessed to have a loving, close family, and to own a propersous business as a dressmaker and designer. As I reflect on my flight from a Holly Springs plantation, to New York City, and then on to Boston, as a fugitive slave, there is still some pain. Talking about what happened to us helps to ease the pain. My story is one of love and devotion to family; of faith and persistence to fight for what you believe in; and of courage to stand for what is right. These are the principles that helped my family survive, and reunite after being separated for years.

Fifteen years ago, in 1860, my parents, Bertha and Joshua Johnson, came to Boston to live with me, after I devised a plan to get them away from the plantation where they spent most of their lives. Shortly after they arrived in Boston, William and I were married. A year later, our first child, William Thomas Harper, was born. I wanted to call him "Tom", but there were too many painful memories of my brother. Instead, we decided to call him "Will". At that time, I did not know if I would ever see my brother again. We had not seen each other in years.

Frank Wilmington, our former master, allowed my parents to come to Boston to care for the mother of Daniel Broughton, his friend. This was planned to get my parents away from that plantation. After Mrs. Broughton died, Mammy and Pappy discreetly moved in with William and me. They cared for Will while I worked at the dress shoppe I opened soon after arriving in Boston. William was quite busy as well. He was a writer for the *The Liberator*, an abolitionist newspaper. *The Liberator* was founded by William Lloyd Garrison and Isaac Knapp. Garrison co-published weekly issues of *The Liberator* from Boston from January 1, 1831 through December 29, 1865. It was one of the most famous antislavery newspapers in the country.

I started my business in 1845, working alone from sun up to sun down. Two dear friends, Aunt Clara and Mrs. Baker, rescued me as a young runaway slave in New York City, and helped me get an education and learn to speak grammatically correct English. They also sent customers to my shoppe. I was determined to please each customer and asked them to tell a friend or relative about *The Dress Shoppe*. Thank God, they did, and my business grew.

As the business grew, I needed help with cutting and sewing dresses and hired three women, who, like me, escaped slavery in search of a better life. I met Callie, Cora and Naomi at the African Methodist Episcopal Church my family attended. Our church was small and the members cared about each other. One Sunday I welcomed these ladies who were new to our church. While talking to them, I learned that they had sewing skills and were looking for work. They appeared to be around the same age, perhaps in their late twenties.

They escaped from farms near Raleigh, North Carolina. On Sundays, slaves were usually allowed to visit and socialize with other slaves. Callie, Cora and Naomi lived on different farms, but one Sunday they met when a group of slaves got together on a farm to celebrate the birth of a baby. They talked about how they enjoyed sewing, and, about how they wanted to be free. They began meeting secretly on Sundays after church and soon came up with a plan to escape. After running for weeks, they made it safely to Baltimore, with the help of the Underground Railroad. In Baltimore, they met other fugitive slaves headed to Boston, so

Callie, Cora and Naomi joined them. They decided to settle in Boston.

Callie was tall and thin. She had a scar on her left cheek, which she got when her mistress hit her with a stick because the master brought Callie out of the fields to work in the house. The mistress resented her husband's interest in Callie, and Callie paid a price for that. Even with the scar, she was quite attractive. Her big, brown eyes gave her an innocent, childlike appearance. Her pleasant smile revealed two deep dimples. Callie was kind and soft-spoken.

Naomi was somewhat of a mother figure. She wasn't very tall, and not as thin as Callie or Cora. She was firm, and always thinking ahead about how they would stay safe and not get caught. I can still hear her saying, "Don't forgit, we still slaves, eventhough we in de Norf. Lord knows, we can't go back to dose farms. We gotta be careful, an look 'round us at all times." Callie and Cora often turned to Naomi for advice.

Cora was comical and cheerful. She kept us laughing as we worked tirelessly at the shoppe. She knew very little about her parents and family, because she was sold and separated from them at an early age. Perhaps her comical nature helped her cope with the pain of losing her family. Cora was of average height. Her high cheek bones gave her a distinguished look. Her dark skin was smooth and flawless.

I was very fortunate to have met those women. They were brave and courageous, and always eager to work. They worked hard to help build my business, and I paid them well. Our church helped them find a home. They lived in a house owned by a prominent Negro family in our church. The family rented the upstairs rooms to them. They were so grateful to be able to earn enough money to buy food and to have a comfortable home to live in.

My dress shoppe was within walking distance of my home, in a two-story building that one of Aunt Clara's friends owned. He was a pleasant white man. He ran a bakery on the first floor, and I rented the second floor for the shoppe. It was a wonderful place to work because the smell of hot cinnamon rolls and other delightful pastries lingered throughout the building. Some days it was simply too difficult to resist running downstairs to buy pastries. We often reminded each other that we would not be able to wear our clothes if we were not disciplined. We strived to take care of our bodies, and to look fashionable and stylish. After all, we were in the fashion business.

Many years ago, in October 1861, Mrs. Baker and Aunt Clara came to The Dress Shoppe with Jane Merritt, Helena Austin and Eve Grant. They were prominent white women in Boston society. I had seen them at a social event I attended with Mrs. Baker and Aunt Clara. They were active in organizations that opposed slavery, such as the American Colonization Society.

"Sarah, do you remember meeting Jane, Helena and Eve?" Aunt Clara asked.

"Yes, I remember meeting each of you. How are you?"

"We are just fine, thank you," Jane Merritt answered. "Sarah, we have heard wonderful things about your dresses. I know several ladies who bought your dresses, and they are quite pleased with your work. Helena, Eve and I are here to ask if you can design and make dresses for us for the Christmas Ball. That's our biggest fundraiser of the year, and it's well attended. Our charities depend upon us raising lots of money each year. We know exactly what we want, and we want you to make our dresses."

Jane Merritt was quite gregarious. She was tall, somewhat thin, with large, expressive blue eyes. Her blonde hair was neatly pinned back in a bun. The blue dress she was wearing, with three-flounce skirts and full sleeves, complimented the color of her eyes. As she spoke, she waved her arms and hands about as if she was directing a choir or an orchestra. She appeared to be around forty years old. I found her quite amusing.

"This is the social event of the year," Helena Austin added. "Why, the three of us have never missed it. It's a lovely event and lots of people attend. Of course, most of the money goes to charity. This year the three of us are on the planning committee."

Helena Austin was of average height, and not so thin, with probing brown eyes. The skirt of her pale green dress was plain. Her short, brown hair was covered with a bonnet decorated with ruffles. She looked around the shoppe as she spoke, perhaps wondering if I had enough of what was needed to get the job done.

"I want all eyes on *me* when I enter the ballroom," Eve Grant interjected. "I love getting compliments on my dresses. Why, Jane and Helena will attest that I will travel quite a distance to buy a beautiful dress. My husband has tried for years to cure me of my infatuation with fancy dresses, and the accessories, but it's no use. It's a hopeless cause, and he finally realizes it." Eve Grant broke into laughter, along with Helena and Jane.

Eve Grant was very attractive. She appeared to be in her late twenties. Her smile was warm and somewhat mischievous. Her long, curly red hair bounced as she turned her head. She spoke with much enthusiasm about her love for fashion and social events. Her violet eyes sparkled with excitement as she described the dress she wanted me to design and make for her. She was very clear, even down to the minute details, like the color of the thread.

"I'm always on top of what's in style," she continued. "My gown will have an enormous skirt, with a vast quantity of material. It will be decorated with lace and embroidery. The neckline will be low, wide and off-the-shoulders, with lots of ruffles. I want short, puffed sleeves. Oh, by the way, my skirt will have several rows of flounce, the more the better. All eyes will definitely be on *me* when I enter the ballroom."

I sensed that Eve Grant was a kind person who loved fashion, and lots of attention. Jane Merritt and Helena Austin appeared to be amused with her youth and sense of humor. I, too, was somewhat captivated as she talked on and on about the Christmas Ball, the shoes she planned to wear, and how her hair would be styled.

"I'll stick with a gown that has a fitted, less decorated bodice," Helena Austin added. "I don't quite have Eve's figure." They all laughed. "We're going shopping for the fabric today. I hope we have given you enough notice, Sarah. Once we get the fabric, we'll be back with more details about our gowns."

"Sarah will do a fabulous job for you all," Aunt Clara said. "She works hard and takes so much pride in her work. I can assure you that you will be pleased. She is skilled in sewing custom-fit fashions."

"I'm sure we will be perfectly happy with our gowns," Jane Merritt added. "Well, I must leave because I have a hundred things to do today."

"And so do I," Eve said. "Sarah, we'll be back as soon as we get the fabric to discuss the details about our dresses. Thank you so much, dear. Oh, if only I could sew; but, if I could, I probably wouldn't. That would take up much too much of my precious time that I could use shopping and spending money." Eve Grant burst into laughter and they left the shoppe. Mrs. Baker and Aunt Clara said goodbye and left as well.

I was thrilled about designing and making gowns for those ladies. Callie, Naomi, Cora and I would have plenty of work to do with Christmas coming. The white women in Boston did not mind spending money to look glamorous. Most of them were quite specific about what they wanted, which made my job easier.

I immediately looked around the shoppe to see what supplies we needed to purchase. There were three sewing machines, and I had saved enough money to purchase one more. Thank God for sewing machines, which helped me and countless others make crinoline skirts. These were especially popular with prominent women in Boston and other places. As the number of clothing factories and textile mills increased throughout New England, so did the demand for sewing machines.

We worked together day after day, and I learned more about Callie, Naomi and Cora. Naomi was very good at decorating dresses with flowers, ribbons, lace and ruching. Our customers began to spread the word about her special finishing touch to their dresses. Callie's gift was hand-sewing. She had repaired garments, as well as made new garments for the house slaves on the farm she grew up on. The field slaves got hand-me-down dresses from the mistresses. Cora designed and cut pattern pieces for sleeves, collars, sashes and skirts. Her mistress was a seamstress, and she taught Cora how to make pattern pieces for clothes for her family and friends.

Callie, Naomi and Cora were prepared to begin working in a clothing factory before they met me. I heard that women worked long hours in those factories under bad conditions, and earned a meager salary. Some of the factories lacked proper heating, and there was a low level of illumination. I assured them that I would never force them to work under unpleasant conditions in my shoppe.

By the time we began taking orders for Christmas gowns, in October 1861, Callie, Naomi and Cora had been working for me for about a year. One day we took a break from sewing and decided to celebrate our lives, our ability to sew and our friendship. We enjoyed a delicious chocolate cake that Callie made, and chatted about how much we love to sew.

"We can do it, ladies," Naomi said. "Dese dresses can't be more difficult den some of dose I had to make for my mistress. Lord, dat lady was hard to please. She would make me wuk 'til her dresses was perfect."

"That is a good thing," I said. "Now you know how to sew, and how to do it well. Our trials can help us become stronger, better people. We have good skills, and no one can take that from us, ever."

"Sho can't, praise de Lord," Cora added. "I'm startin' to bleeve in myself, dat maybe I can have a good life afta all I been through. Lord knows, it ain't been easy, but it's got betta. Thank you for hirin' me, Sarah."

"Thank you, ladies, for your hard work, for your ideas, and for all you have done to help this dress shoppe grow. I appreciate you. And, thank you, Callie, for the best chocolate cake I have ever tasted."

We were laughing when someone knocked at the door. I went to the door and there was a colored woman with two young girls. I opened the door and asked them to come in. The woman looked tired. I invited them to sit down and gave them some water.

"Hello, how can we help you?" The woman looked at me and then at the young girls. She appeared to be frightened, but answered the question.

"Hello, my name's Liza, an dese is my childrun, Rosa an Ella. We come heah 'cause we heah dat you mek purty dresses. I wont to buy two for my two girls. Dey ain't neva had a purty dress. I wont dem to know whut it's lak to wear a purty dress."

"Hello Liza, Rosa and Ella. My name is Sarah, and these ladies are Callie, Naomi and Cora. We work together here. Who told you about this shoppe?"

"Some ladies from my church said some real nice thangs 'bout yo dresses," Liza continued. "I wont two for my girls. I got some money, an I kin pay for de dresses. We come heah from Kentucky not long ago. I pray evry day dat my husban will mek it heah wit us. I bleeve he will. I clean an cook, an have saved some money. I wont my two girls to have a purty dress."

"When do you need the dresses?"

"As soon as you kin mek dem. My girls will only wear dese dresses to church. I got 'nuff money to pay you."

When I lived on the plantation, we dressed up for church and special occasions. During the week we belonged to the mastah, but on Saturdays and Sundays slaves were proud men and women who enjoyed our time with each other. Dressing up helped us feel special.

"Liza, thank you for coming by. We appreciate your business. We will have your dresses ready on Friday. Your daughters are lovely. Cora, please get their measurements."

"Thank you so much. We's gratefal." After Cora got their measurements, Liza took her daughters by the hand and they left the shoppe. They had obviously found a decent place to live because they were neat and their clothes were clean. I did not want to ask too many questions. We talked about what to make for the girls.

"We got some calico fabric dat we haven't used," Naomi said. "We can add a white collar an cuffs, wit a little black ribbin bow at de neck. Dat will be simple to make."

"We can also add some bodice buttins down de front, wit shoulda wings at de armhole," Cora said.

"Don't forget de white apron," Callie added. "We can make dat de same length as de dress. Dat's what we wore on de plantation evry day. What do you think, Sarah?"

"I want Rosa and Ella to have fancy dresses, unlike anything we wore on the plantation. I will never forget what it was like to watch the Wilmington girls prance around in pretty dresses, while I wore simple, plain dresses every day. No, we are not making plain dresses for Rosa and Ella. We are going to make beautiful, fancy dresses for them to wear and prance around in.

"I want Rosa and Ella to have dresses they will remember wearing for the rest of their lives. I want the dresses to be made with the finest cotton. Their dresses will have wide, slightly dropped-shoulder lines. The dress bodice will point in front, and the skirt will have side and back fullness. The neckline and sleeves will be trimmed with white lace. I also want wide grosgrain ribbon sashes to complete the look, perhaps cut from very nice, patterned silk. Rosa and Ella will wear long, lace-trimmed pantalets under the skirt."

We had two days to purchase the fabric and make the dresses. On Friday afternoon, Liza and her daughters came to the shoppe to get the dresses. Cora presented the dresses to them. They looked as if they could not believe what they saw.

"Lawd, we wont spectin nuttin lak dis," Liza said. "Dese is fancy dresses, de kind dat specia people wear. Ain't nuttin specia 'bout me an my girls."

"You and your daughters are very special, Liza," I responded. "I want Rosa and Ella to put their dresses on so we can see how well they fit. We have enjoyed making these dresses for your lovely daughters."

Callie took the girls to the back room to help them get dressed. When Rosa and Ella walked out wearing their dresses, Liza cried. She sat in a chair and wiped her eyes. "My babies look lak my mastah's childrun used to look in thar dresses. I ain't neva seen my babies look dis purty."

Rosa and Ella pranced around in their new dresses, as if they were royalty. They certainly looked like royalty. Rosa's large brown eyes sparkled with excitement. She was eight years old. Her red dress looked beautiful against her dark skin. Ella was six years old, and appeared to be somewhat shy. Her big smile, which exposed two missing front teeth, indicated that she was very happy with her red dress as well. We chose red because red was a royal color in African society. The color also has a connection to life and fertility.

"You look beautiful, girls. Tek off yo dresses, 'cause we gotta go," Liza said. She stood and began digging in the bag she was carrying. She pulled out some money and began counting it.

"I don't know how much you wont, but I hope I got 'nuff heah to pay you." She extended her hand with the money.

"Liza, I want you to keep your money. Save it for Rosa and Ella. Your daughters are special and they have every right to wear beautiful, fancy dresses. Take care of yourself and your daughters." Liza, Rosa and Ella hugged Cora, Naomi, Callie and me.

"Thank y'all," Rosa said. "I likes my dress a lot." Rosa jumped around the floor, holding her dress close.

"I thank y'all, too," Ella said. She jumped around with Rosa. Liza was crying, but Rosa and Ella left the shoppe skipping, with big smiles.

# CHAPTER 5

Shortly after the boy yelled, "Moma, there's a nigger out yonda," a man and a woman, who I assumed were his parents, ran to him and began screaming harsh words at me. I had not realized how fast I could run until that moment. I knew it would not be long before others joined them, chasing after me through the woods. After drinking the water, I was refreshed and ready for whatever lay ahead.

My shirt was wet from the sweltering heat, but as I ran through the woods, the breeze actually cooled my body. The heat was a blessing. Complaining accomplished nothing, and I managed to keep going over the years by thinking positive about the future. I had been sick numerous times, but my body and mind were strong and healthy.

I forced myself to believe that I was headed in the right direction, and not back to Charleston. Positive thoughts helped me make it through the woods in that sweltering heat in June 1861. After running for a long time, I stopped to catch my breath, and looked around, but did not see or hear anyone. That did not mean that they were not chasing me. I sat behind a thick bush to rest for a few minutes. As I lay against that bush, something hard hit my head. I thought someone had thrown something at me. I rubbed my head and was ready to start running, but looked up and saw some squirrels looking down from the branch of a large tree.

The squirrels were eating nuts, and one of the nuts hit my head. They stared at me for some time. Perhaps they wanted me to move on because I was an intruder. Or, perhaps they were trying to welcome me to their home in the woods. Another nut fell, but it hit the ground. I walked away and smiled at the thought that the little critters may have been trying to share their food with me, as opposed to trying to harm me.

My feet did not hurt as much as before they were wrapped with rags. Although they were swollen, I had to keep moving. I walked that day until just before dark. What bothered me most about that flight was being lost. Unknowingly, I could have been headed straight back to the plantations, to the life I so desperately wanted to escape.

It was almost dark and I could no longer see clearly, so I spread the quilt over some sticks and leaves and tried to rest. I ate one of the apples I took from those white people. Maybe those people had not been chasing me after all. Perhaps they were simply angry because I took their apples and water. I was desperate and hungry and could not ask them for water and food. I did not know what they would do to me, a runaway, except return me to mastah.

That night I stared at the stars and thought about Hannah. That was only the second day in the woods, and she probably did not know that I had run away. I missed her so much. Her touch, her girlish smile, her large brown eyes, her warmth and compassion were very special. I loved the way she giggled when I embraced her tiny body. Hannah's smooth, brown skin was soft, and she always smelled like hickory soap. Slave women often made their own soap with lye, hickory ashes, water, fat and grease. I missed the sound of her soft, but firm voice. Her words were comforting and pleasant. Like Mammy, she never complained about anything. She was always more concerned about comforting others than herself.

After I met Hannah, I wanted my freedom more than ever, because I had found someone to share my life with. Still, I was intelligent enough to know that neither of us could do, or become, all that we wanted to do and become if we were confined to plantations for the rest of our lives. Hannah wanted to be free as much as I did, but she sometimes had problems breathing, and did not think she could make it on the run. Running from plantations was very difficult.

As I lay there, thinking about my family and Hannah, I thought I heard someone approaching. Soon, I realized there was someone or something in the woods with me, other than insects and squirrels. As I grabbed my things and jumped up to run, a voice screamed, "Come back!"

It was almost dark, but there was enough light to get away from that stranger, or strangers. As I ran, it was clear that someone was chasing me. It appeared that the patrollers, or maybe the people from whom I stole the apples and water, had caught up with me. I ran for my life. The warm, pleasant thoughts of Hannah vanished, quickly.

Someone continued to scream, "Come back, come back!" That person was getting closer, eventhough I ran as fast as possible. Finally, he said, "Stop runnin', 'cause I ain't gonna hurt you!" Suddenly I realized that was not the voice of a white man. I stopped running, turned around, and looked into the face of a man whose skin was as dark as mine.

"Whut you doin' out heah in dese woods?" He stared at me from head to toe, and appeared to be around my age. He was obviously strong because he could run as fast as I could. "Is you a woodcutta?"

"No, I ain't no woodcutta, but I kin cut wood. Why you runnin' afta me?"

"Cause we been out heah cuttin' wood, an some of it's gone. Look lak somebody dun took some of our wood."

"You kin see I ain't got yo wood. Dis is all I got wit me." I held up my sack. I did not say too much because I did not know that man. "Whur is yo mastah?" I wanted to know if he was a free Negra or a slave.

"He back yonda at his house. Mastah don't come out in de dark. He sen us out to cut wood all day, an den we go back to de farm. Two of his woodcuttas ain't well. You sho you kin cut wood? We sho need some hep. You out heah by yosef wit no whur to go. Ain't good to be livin' dis way."

It sounded as if that man wanted me to join him and the others to cut wood for their master. I did not let on that I was a runaway. He continued to talk about the wood they cut, and returned to find that it was gone. His master sent him to find out who took the wood. He had strict orders to catch the thief and bring him in. I apparently convinced him that I had not stolen his wood.

"Well, it's too dark to fine de one dat took our wood. I will come back tomarrow. You need to git on while you kin still see out heah."

He turned and walked away. I assumed he was one of those slaves who was loyal to the master and wouldn't run off, like Joe. Thank God he was not chasing me. I turned and called out to him.

"Kin you tell me whur I am?" Surely he had some idea where we were.

"Whut you mean?"

"Is we in Charleston?"

"I don't know much 'bout dis place, but I dun some wood cuttin' near heah, in Wilminton. Dat's 'bout all I kin tell you."

"Thank you. Hope you find yo wood." I walked away quickly from that stranger. He told me what I wanted to hear. Jessie mentioned going through Wilmington on his way to Virginia. Thank God, I was headed in the right direction and did not have to turn around.

It was getting dark, and I could not see anything in those thick woods, so I cleared a space to rest until the sun came up the next morning. I still had a long way to go to get to Virginia. I took my shoes off, rubbed my sore feet, and actually felt a sense of peace that night.

I woke up early the next morning and continued the flight. Mammy believed that singing sometimes helped us get through the really hard times in our lives, so I sang with joy:

> Could I but climb on Pisgah's top
> And view the promised land,
> My flesh itself would long to drop,
> At my dear Lord's command.
> "This living grace on earth we owe,
> To Jesus' dying love;
> we would be only his below,
> And reign with him above.

That was one of the hottest days ever. The water was gone and my body was wet, but there was no cooling breeze that day. I was used to working in sweltering heat, but on the plantation we always had water to drink. Unfortunately, there was no water.

I thought about stopping to rest, not because I was tired, but to avoid collapsing from thirst. If I stopped walking, the patrollers and hounds could possibly have caught me. I did not have the luxury of lying around in the woods, so I kept moving.

After walking for several hours in that heat, I felt faint and had a difficult time breathing. I fell to the ground. Sharp pains ran through my body. I asked God for help. Any hound or patroller could have done whatever they chose to do with me at that moment.

I thought about Hannah, my parents and Sarah, and said over and over that I did not want to die. I was not afraid of dying, but to die deep in the South Carolina woods, where my body may never have been found, was not desirable. Hannah and my family would need to know what happened to me. I opened my eyes to look up, but the trees were all a big blur. I tried to take the shirt off, to stay cool, but was too weak. I managed to roll over with my face down, away from the scorching sun.

I could still hear Joe's words, "Tom, don't run, don't run. Dey will kill you if dey ketch you dis time." I guess Joe did not think to warn me that the sweltering heat, without water, could also kill. As I planned my escape to Fortress Monroe, I only thought about being free; not about the sweltering heat.

I certainly did not want to die in the deep woods, alone. There was one comforting thought – if I died in the woods, trying to get to Fortress Monroe, at least I would have died trying to do something I truly believed in – that all people have a right to be free.

I was probably out for several hours. The sharp pains were gone. My face was buried in leaves and dirt, but the leaves were no longer dry and crisp. I wiped leaves and dirt out of my mouth and attempted to turn over.

Suddenly I heard loud noises. It sounded like trees falling on top of each other. My body and clothes were drenched. As I lay on my back, still in a daze, I opened my eyes, but could not see anything. I rubbed my eyes, desperately trying to see, and screamed out for help.

Lots of water hit my face and body. I could not see because the heavy rain blinded me. Slowly, I stood up, raised my hands and thanked God for water – wonderful, wet, water. I cupped my hands and gulped as much rain as I could get in my mouth, as it poured over my body. That moment was blissful.

I took my shoes off, hoping that the rain could somehow soothe my aching feet. It was a miracle God sent that day. I filled my pouch with water and drank as much as possible. I was given a second chance to continue the flight. First, the bright sun awakened me, then the rain revived me.

The rain and storm continued throughout the day. I was soaked from head to feet, and it felt wonderful. The rain cooled the earth and invigorated me. Even the birds and squirrels seemed to rejoice over my victory. The birds sang louder and clearer than ever and the squirrels ran freely, jumping from branch to branch. They appeared to want to join me on my flight, and they were welcome to come along. Sarah and I were taught not to take any blessing for granted. My parents believed that the more we counted our blessings, the less time we had to complain. I counted the rain, birds and squirrels as blessings, and continued on to Fortress Monroe.

It stopped raining by dusk. As expected, I was unable to sleep peacefully because surely those patrollers had not given up on catching me. Perhaps the heat had been as hard on them as it had been on me. Just as the rain revived me, it may have revived them as well, so I pushed on.

The next morning the bright sun woke me up. I grabbed my things and tried to run, but my feet were swollen and I could not. Instead, I walked as quickly as possible. My mind was focused on getting to Fortress Monroe. Jessie and Joe warned me that the Union soldiers would have nothing to do with niggers, but that did not stop me.

It was not long before the heat dried my clothes and body. I had no idea how many days and nights I'd spent on the run. Thoughts of my family lingered in my head. I often dreamed about seeing and actually touching them. As the years passed, the pain of not having them close eased, some, but it never completely went away. Although we were separated, physically, we were very close in spirit.

I could visualize the look on Hannah's face when she learned that I had, once again, run off. Hannah would understand. She knew me, and she understood what I wanted for her and my family. Like Pappy, I fell in love with a strong, courageous, lovely woman. Pappy said more than once that Mammy was a good woman, and that she helped him stay strong over the years. Likewise, Hannah's presence eased some of my pain. My parents and sister would love her. I believed that she, like Mammy, would be a wonderful companion. I also believed that she would wait for me.

I walked as far as I could that day and saw some water at a distance. It appeared that I would have to get across the water because I did not see a way around it. Thank God, I had no fear of water, and knew how to swim. Mastah Carnes forced me and another young slave boy to jump into some water years ago with him, because he said we needed to know how to swim. I remember going down and screaming for help. Suddenly, I was overcome with a determination to fight for my life.

In the midst of the struggle, I came up to get my breath, and heard mastah Carnes yelling, "Move your arms and kick your legs!" He said that over and over. I began moving my arms and kicking my legs, and praying. Then, I remember moving across the water and breathing again. The other slave also moved across the water. I will never forget that day. We survived, and I was never afraid of water again.

I had to cross the water in order to continue on my flight, so I took my shoes off and put them in my sack. I tied the cloth sack around my neck and threw it over my back. I jumped into the water and swam as fast as possible. The water was warm and refreshing.

Finally, I reached the other side. I climbed out of the water and looked around to see if anyone was watching. I did not see anyone, and sat behind a large tree to rest. I studied the huge trees near the water. I had always been fascinated with large trees. Mammy used to say that one day I would grow to be like a *Tree planted by the waters, and that spreadeth out her roots by the river, and shall not see when heat cometh, but*

47

*her leaf shall be green; and shall not be careful in the year of drought, neither shall cease from yielding fruit.* I wanted to be like those trees in the Bible.

I drank some water, ate the last apple tucked in my pants, then got up to move on. After walking a short distance, I thought I heard voices, but did not know if they were real or not. I soon realized that they were very real.

I quietly walked in the direction of the voices, praying that no one would see or hear me. The trees were large and the bushes thick in that wooded area, so it was easy to hide. As I walked on, the voices became clearer. It did not sound like the voices of patrollers. I stopped walking and tried to listen, but could not understand what they were saying. I sat for several minutes, trying to decide what to do.

I decided to keep going in the same direction to see who was speaking. Before long, I saw cabins that looked like the ones on my masters' plantations. There were four small, wooden cabins, painted white, in a single row. Each cabin had a door and a window. Those cabins made me think that perhaps the voices I heard were the voices of slaves. I moved closer and hid behind a large tree to watch from a distance. I then saw three colored men standing between the cabins, talking. It was their voices I'd heard.

It was almost dark and they could not see me standing behind the tree. I watched for a while. Apparently they had finished working for the day and had come back to the cabins for supper because I smelled food. Watching them made me think about Hannah. She cooked for John Mundy's family, and at the end of the day she came back to her cabin and cooked for other slaves on the plantation. She always had something good for me to eat whenever I was able to come by to visit with her.

Finally, I decided to take a chance and approach those men. They would either talk to me, and try to help me; or, they would run and tell their master about me. It was risky, but it was a chance I decided to take.

# CHAPTER 6

As I approached the three men, they continued to talk. Apparently they had not noticed me. Then one of them heard the dry leaves crumble under my feet and they all looked at me without saying a word. I was too tired to be afraid of what they might do or say to me. Two of the men appeared to be somewhere around my age, and one appeared to be much older. I extended my hand to the older man to let them know that I had not approached them to cause trouble.

"I heard y'all talkin', an I come to say hello." I carefully watched the expressions on their faces. The older man shook my hand and said, "My name's Buddy." I did not sense that any of them would harm me.

"Ya mus be one of dem new slaves from ova yonda at de udder farm," Buddy said. "I heah dat he got some mo slaves jes de udder day."

"Yeah, I's one of his new slaves." They thought I was one of the new slaves from a nearby farm. I was clever enough not to tell them that I was on the run.

"Glad to meet ya," Buddy said. "You hungry? We got some fat back an beans cookin'. Hep yoself."

"Thank you." I was more thirsty than hungry, so I asked Buddy for some water.

"Go git him some water," Buddy said to one of the younger men. The two younger men seemed to respect Buddy. I did not know if they were related and did not ask.

"Y'all been 'round here long?"

"I been 'round heah mos of my life. Mastah been good to me, cuz he ain't neva sold me. Dese two come heah 'bout a year ago," Buddy said, referring to the two younger men. "I's real good at plantin' an growin' beans, cabbage, greens an corn. Mastah said he don't know whut he would do wit out me."

"Do you sell dese vegetebles?"

"Do we sell vegetebles?" Buddy asked. He laughed aloud. "Lawd, yes; why, we jes got back from sellin' some in Vaginia."

I almost choked on the water when Buddy said, "Vaginia." Had I gotten to Virginia and did not know it? My heart pumped faster, but I stayed calm. Those men were strangers, and I did not forget that.

"I don't know too much 'bout dese parts," I said. "Is dis Vaginia?"

"No, it ain't Vaginia, but you ain't far from it. Keep goin' dat way, not far, an you cross ova from Norf Carolina to Vaginia. Whur you from?" Buddy asked.

"I come from Lousiana. My mastah got me from a sugar plantation down thar." That was a lie, but I had to protect myself. I did not tell them where I came from or where I was headed.

"You ain't gonna lak it 'round heah," the younger man said. "We wuk from sun up to sun down, plantin' an pickin' vegetebles. It kin git real hot in dem fields."

"Oh, hush up, Jack," Buddy interrupted. "Don't be puttin' no bad ideas in dis man head. Wukin ain't neva hurt nobody."

"Whut's yo name?" Jack asked.

"My name's Joe." Jack starred at me from head to toe. I started to eat the beans and fat back, and knew it was time to get away from them before they asked more questions. Still, I had to find out how far away Virginia was before leaving those men.

"You say you jes come from Vaginia? I ain't neva been thar. Is it far from heah."

"No, it ain't far," Buddy answered. "We go down to Lawrenceburg wit Mastah to sell vegetebles. Yo new mastah gonna have you goin' to."

"Ain't neva been thar," I said. "How you git thar?" After I found out how to get to Virginia, I intended to leave that farm as quickly as possible.

"Go down yonda road, an keep goin'. Ain't too far, an befo you know, you will be in Vaginia. Lak I said, yo new mastah gonna have you goin' a lot. He sell vegetebles down thar, too."

"Whut happin to yo feet," Jack asked. My feet were severely swollen and scratched because I had not been able to wear my shoes after they got wet crossing the river.

"Look lak you been runnin' through de woods," Jack continued. He made me uncomfortable because of his stare and questions. Unlike Buddy and the other man, Jack was much too inquisitive for me to stay around any longer.

"On de way from Lousiana, we stop to git some water, and my shoes fell in de water. I put dem on an wor dem while dey was wet. Mastah told me not to do dat."

"Heah, I got somethin' for you to rub on yo feet," Buddy said. He handed me some potion wrapped in paper. "I dun had dat same trouba wit my feet an, let me tell ya, dis stuff do wuk. Yo feet gonna feel betta real soon. Go head an keep it, cuz ain't nuttin worse dan sore, swollen feet, wit blistars."

I don't know why Buddy wanted to help me. Perhaps he was simply a kind person. I was thrilled to get that potion because it appeared to be what slaves on the plantation used on their feet. I thanked Buddy and told them I had to leave to get back to the farm. As I turned to walk away, Buddy warned me to be careful.

"Make sho you git on back to de farm befo somebody think you dat slave dat run off." Buddy's words startled me.

"Whut you talkin' 'bout?"

"I talkin' 'bout some white men dat come by heah lookin' for a slave dat run off some time ago," he answered.

"When did dey come by?" I tried hard to look calm, but my heart started to beat faster. Could those men have been looking for me? I wondered if they had followed me to that point.

"Dey come by heah some days ago, say dey was huntin' a slave who run off from a plantation in Chawston. Dey say dat slave got good skills, an dey aim to fine him an take him back. You be carful, an git on back to de farm, now. Yo mastah gonna be lookin' for you."

I turned and walked away slowly. It certainly sounded as if the patrollers were after me. Buddy said they had been there *some* days ago. There was no telling what *some* meant. I wanted to ask more questions, but Jack's stare reminded me that it was time to move on. I wondered if the patrollers described the slave they were hunting. Perhaps they had, and that was why Jack stared at me so intently. Maybe he did not believe I was one of the new slaves on the nearby farm, or that I came from Louisiana.

It was almost dark, but I decided to walk on. I needed to get as far away from Jack as possible because I sensed that he would tell his master about me. Then they would all know that I was not one of the new slaves on the nearby farm, and they might come after me. John Mundy had lots of money, and he would surely have paid anyone to catch me.

When I could no longer see clearly, I lay against a tree and rested for the night. I could not sleep because of what Buddy told me. I wanted to ask him if the men had hounds, but did not want them to get suspicious and think I was a runaway. It was frightening to think that I could very well have been the slave they were hunting, and that they were so close to finding me. Perhaps the hounds lost my scent after I crossed the water.

I lay against the tree and rubbed my feet with the potion Buddy gave me. They were sore and hurt, but the potion helped to ease the pain. I was no longer hungry or thirsty, thanks to Buddy's kindness.

Thinking Virginia was close, I was anxious for the sun to rise and to start running again. Once I got to Virginia, I would find my way to Fortress Monroe. If the soldiers turned me away, I would keep going to get as far away from Charleston as possible.

The next morning I got up very early, tore a piece of my shirt off to wrap my feet, then forced them into my shoes. They still hurt, but there was more potion if necessary. I walked as fast as possible through the woods. That morning I believed I could do anything. My mind was focused on the positive, not the pain and suffering.

I thought about my wonderful parents who loved and taught their children so much. Although I was snatched away from them at a young age, I still remembered most of the lessons they taught us. I had not seen Sarah and Mammy since I ran into them in Atlanta, when I was working on a house there. I tried to be brave for Mammy, because I did not want her to worry about me, but when they left to go back to the plantation in Holly Springs, I cried. My heart was broken for a long time.

The worst thing that ever happened to me was being snatched away from my family. Family was very important to us and to other slaves. I had been whipped and punished many times, but nothing hurt as much as being separated from my family.

I thought about Hannah, and how much I missed her. She probably knew that I was not coming back to Savannah, unless I was caught and brought back. We had prayed together many times, and promised that we would always pray for each other. I believed my parents and sister prayed for me as well. Their prayers were probably the reason I was still alive.

I could not run that day because my feet were very sore and swollen. The potion helped, but it would take time for them to completely heal. I walked with a limp that day. The thought of getting to Virginia was exciting, and I was filled with joy inspite of the pain. Buddy said that Virginia was not far away. I did not know where in Virginia Fortress Monroe was located, but I would certainly find it.

While walking in the sweltering heat, my left foot stumbled over some debris. I fell and saw blood on my leg. Apparently something cut it when I stumbled. I tore another piece of the shirt to wrap my leg to stop the bleeding. The pain was sharp. I needed help, but there was no one to ask. I prayed that my leg would heal so that I could keep moving.

Throughout that day, I tried to walk, but was only able to limp. While putting more potion on my feet and leg, I heard someone behind me. Unfortunately, the voice did not sound like Buddy's or Jack's. It was the voice of a white man.

"You nigger, what ya doing out here, by yaself? Ain't no free niggers in these parts, so where is ya master?"

I looked up into the face of a white man. He was not very tall, nor was he a large man. If my feet had not been swollen and sore, I would have knocked him down and kept running. Unfortunately, I could barely move and could not get away from him. I was so close to Virginia; but, it appeared that I had been caught, only because I could not walk.

"Answer me, nigger!" he continued. "Where is ya master, and where ya think ya going? I ain't heard nothing about no runaway slaves in these parts. Is ya running from ya master? Why ya by yaself? What happened to ya feet? Can ya even stand? Answer me!"

"I got loss out heah in de woods, an can't fine my way back," I mumbled. "The othas lef me afta I fell an cut my leg, 'cause my feet is swollen an sore."

"I don't know what ya talking about, nigger, but I can sure use ya to help around my place. There's much work to do in my fields, and things need to be fixed around the house. Ya coming with me, and you're *my property* now. Take those shoes off." He then called out to someone, and before long another white man came to help him drag me to the wagon they were traveling in.

That was extremely difficult to endure, because I could easily have beaten both of those white men and run off, *with* their wagon. Unfortunately, my feet could not support me at that time. They helped me climb into the wagon. I was angry with myself for stumbling and cutting my leg. Although my feet were sore and swollen, and my leg was bleeding, before I stumbled on the debris, I could walk. Suddenly, I was forced to sit in a wagon, with no idea where I was, or where they were taking me.

We traveled almost two days in that wagon. Finally, the wagon stopped in front of a white wooden house. The men jumped out of the wagon and told me it was time to get out. They helped me get down, and I limped along behind them toward the house. The man who found me talked about all the work that needed to be done around the house, which I assumed was his home.

"He's a strong one, don't ya think," he said to the other man. "Ain't but one problem I see, and that's his feet. He can't do nothing with those swollen, cut up feet. I will get someone to take care of his feet, and as soon as they heal, I will have him in the fields. I'm mighty proud of my catch."

"You done found yourself a good one," the other man said. "Where did he come from?"

"I saspect he's on the run from his owner. Ain't no free niggers around here."

"Somebody might come to claim him, 'cause he looks mighty strong. He probly can do just about anything you need him to do."

"I found him, and he's *my property*, now. I been needing some help around this place. A strong one like this could cost a lot. He'll be just fine, soon as he gets something to eat, and those feet heal. They are scratched up and swollen real bad. Look like he been on the run for days."

They took me to a small cabin in the back of the white house, where I spent the night. I was certain that someone watched me throughout the night because I heard voices. I would rather have been in the woods, hungry and bleeding, with sore feet, than have been in that cabin, confined like an animal. But, I had no choice but to make the most of it. That night I did not complain to God that I had been caught. Instead, I asked Him to help me to somehow continue on my flight to Fortress Monroe.

The next day a man who said he helped sick people get well, came to look at my feet and leg. He told Jim, the man who found me, that I was probably a runaway slave who had been in the woods for weeks. He said my feet were swollen and blistered because my shoes had gotten wet and were too small. He said it would not be long before I was as good as new. That night he put my feet in very hot water, and told me to keep them in the water until it cooled. He wrapped my leg with a white cloth.

Although the water was scorching hot, my feet immediately felt better. After the water cooled, he rubbed some type of potion over them. He told Jim to keep me off my feet for about a week, and that he would come back to do the same thing until they healed. I wanted to thank him for his help, but he was not my friend. He was only trying to get me strong enough to start working for Jim.

Within about a week, my feet and leg healed and I felt like a new person. I was confined, but had no pain. I could walk again. Jim immediately put me to work in the corn fields and around his house. I had no intention of telling him that I was a skilled carpenter and bricklayer, because he would not use me and make any money from my labor, as the others had.

I worked hard for Jim in his fields, planting and growing vegetables. He kept a close watch over me. Jim and I, along with some of his friends, worked tirelessly cutting down trees and traveling to sell the wood throughout parts of Virginia. Although I desperately wanted to run, there was no opportunity to escape. Jim's friends stayed in cabins close to my cabin, and, Jim had three mean dogs who watched me as closely as he and his friends.

Jim appeared to be around forty years old. He was not a big man. His face was full and round, and his thick eye brows gave him a sinister look. I could have beaten him and taken everything he had with no problem, but Jim was clever; he kept his friends and dogs close by.

I did not know a lot about Jim Greene, other than he had a wife, Mary. They did not have children. I did not see a lot of Mary, who appeared to be much younger than Jim. She had long, brown hair, and was about as short as Jim. Mary was not friendly, and definitely not attractive. She rarely smiled, and when she did, her crooked, stained teeth were quite visible. Based on some of their conversations, I sensed that Mary and Jim did not get along well. She was rarely at the house.

I was stuck with Jim for probably a year. John Mundy and James Forrrester had perhaps given up on finding me, because a lot of time had passed since I left Charleston. If anyone had caught me, I thought it would have been the patrollers. Never in my wildest dreams did I expect a short, stubby, poor white man, like Jim, to catch and keep me in bondage. Still, I never gave up on finding Fortress Monroe.

One day, while helping Jim cut down trees, I heard him tell one of his friends that they had to take the cut trees to a house in Williamsburg. I knew nothing about Williamsburg, but assumed it was not so far from Jim's house. Of course I had to go with them to Williamsburg to lift the cut trees from the wagon. Jim was proud of the fact that he found a "strong nigger" to do the heavy work for him. Unlike John Mundy and Edward Carnes, he did not have a large house with lots of land, crops and horses. He only needed one slave, and he found me in the woods, at no cost.

Jim did not know it, but I did not mind hard work because that was what I was used to. Whenever he asked me about my past, I pretended I had been in the woods so long, lost and weak from lack of food and water, and did not remember where I came from, or who owned me. It did not matter much to Jim, because he found a slave he did not have to pay for.

A few days later, I loaded the cut trees onto the wagon, and Jim, one of his friends and I headed to Williamsburg. As we traveled, I thought about ways I could get away from Jim, because on that trip, he only had one of his friends with him. Jim did not bring his dogs along that time because he needed the space to haul the cut trees. It appeared that he had grown comfortable with the idea that I would not run away from him.

I never had any more problems with my feet after they healed, because Jim gave me shoes that fit well. I came to believe that stumbling in the woods that day, cutting my leg and being caught by Jim, was a blessing. Mammy often said that sometimes things that looked bad for us could actually be good for us. She said we had to always walk by faith.

Williamsburg was a beautiful place. I had traveled throughout Georgia, Mississippi and South Carolina, working for my masters, but Williamsburg was somehow different. The unique design of the buildings caught my attention. The bricks were different from the bricks I used to build houses. I was curious and wanted to learn more about that place, but there was no one to ask.

As we rode through Williamsburg, I saw people walking in and out of shoppes, their faces covered with smiles. They all looked happy, as if that was the best place in the world to live. I did not see any people who looked like me. Perhaps there were no free Negras in Williamsburg. I did not see any colored people until Jim told me to follow him into some of the shoppes.

Jim went into a blacksmith shoppe where colored men, who I assumed were slaves, worked with iron that would be used for horse shoes. As he talked to the shoppe owner, I watched the men skillfully work with iron. I wanted to ask questions, but Jim made it very clear that I was to stay close to him and not speak to anyone.

We then went into a shoppe where men made jewelry and other items with silver. That was fascinating to watch. Jim knew the owners of several shoppes in Williamsburg. Based on their conversations, I assumed he had sold vegetables and wood to them. There were colored people working in some of the shoppes. We are creative people. Unfortunately, many of us had not had the opportunity to show or express our creativity.

When Jim finished visiting the owners of different shoppes, he told me to follow him back to the blacksmith shoppe. He and the owner talked about the vegetables Jim was to deliver to him, and other business matters. Then, the owner said something, and my heart felt as if it skipped a beat! He told Jim that he might not be in the shoppe the following week because he had to deliver some iron to Fortress Monroe.

"If I am not here, my brother will take care of you next week," the owner said. "They are expecting me at Fortress Monroe, and I will probably leave here on Tuesday. As you know, that is not far from here, and I will not be gone for long…"

His words rang in my ears: *that is not far from here…* Apparently I was closer to my destination than I realized. I had to somehow figure out which way to run from Williamsburg to get there. While Jim and the owner continued to talk, ideas of how to escape ran through my mind. Jim told his friend that we would return to Jim's house later that night.

We left the blacksmith shoppe and walked toward the wagon. There were far too many people around to run off at that moment. I jumped onto the wagon as the horses pulled it away from the shoppes and all the people. Because there were not many people in Williamsburg who looked like me, I would've been easy to spot. Also, there were no thick woods nearby to disappear into, unlike in Charleston.

We had not been traveling long when the wagon stopped at a house, and Jim told me to get out and start unloading the trees. That would take some time to finish because the wagon was stacked with as many cut trees as it could carry. Jim and his friend started out helping me, but soon another man came out of the house and they all began talking. They apparently got caught up in their conversation and moved toward the back of the house. The other man was showing Jim and his friend something that had probably fallen from the roof of his house. They picked it up and examined it. The cut trees were quite heavy, and I was attentive to lifting them off the wagon, to avoid dropping them on my feet. Jim and his friend forgot about helping me, or perhaps they changed their minds. Jim probably decided that his "strong nigger" should unload the wagon without any help.

I continued to unload the wood, and the three men continued to talk and examine the object. I watched them gradually walk behind the house, out of sight. The moment I could no longer see them, I dropped the wood, grabbed my sack from the wagon, and ran! My speed was proof that I was strong and healthy. I could not remember running faster. I was trying to get to Fortress Monroe as quickly as possible, and running for my life.

At a distance, I heard one of the men yelling, "He's gone! He's gone!" I did not look back to see who was yelling, or if they were coming after me. Thank God, Jim did not have his dogs with him that day, which was a blessing, because he usually traveled with his dogs. I made the most of Jim's decision not to bring his dogs along, and to travel with only one friend.

Jim found me in the woods, and I had been his slave for many months. During those months, he provided me with food and water. I was not thankful that Jim had caught me, but was thankful for the food and water. Jim found a strong slave to work for him, and I was certain that he, like the others, would do everything in his power to catch me because I was quite valuable to all of them.

I ran for maybe two or three days, and only stopped at night when I could not see clearly. I felt great, and was so thankful to be on the run again. With no dogs around, I knew I could run faster than Jim and his friend. There was something special about being *free* –*free* to run through the woods.

I ran until I saw a large body of water. Then, I wandered into a place that looked like nothing I had seen before. I watched from a distance, and saw white men moving around large buildings made of stone. I couldn't figure out what they were doing. Gradually, I realized that, by the grace of God, many months after running from Charleston, I had finally reached Fortress Monroe!

# CHAPTER 7

Several women came into the shoppe after Jane Merritt, Helena Austin and Eve Grant's visit to place orders for gowns to wear during the Christmas holiday. Callie, Naomi, Cora and I worked hard, and left the shoppe after dark each day. Mammy and Pappy loved caring for my son, but I felt guilty about spending such long hours at the shoppe. Although *The Dress Shoppe* was growing, I was a mother, and wanted to spend as much time with my son as possible. I wanted to be the mother to my son that Mammy had been to us. Mammy had no choice but to work long hours at the big house. Thank God, I had a choice. Still, I worked hard, trying to be the best dressmaker and designer in Boston.

William likewise worked long hours writing for *The Liberator.* Some of his articles were controversial, but were written to motivate people to reach out to our enslaved brothers and sisters. I saved many of his articles, including this one:

> *"We have brothers and sisters who have successfully escaped the cruelty and brutality of slavery, and are here in Boston and other cities in the North. As free Negroes, we have an obligation to reach out to them. They need food, shelter, clothing, skills, jobs, and most importantly, to know that someone cares. We must help them establish and live their lives as free people.*
>
> *"Throughout Boston and other cities around the country, there are advertisements for runaway slaves. Southern planters have no interest in the quality of life for our people. Their interest is in making a quick profit at the expense of Negroes. Their crops, tobacco, rice, indigo, sugar and cotton, thrive because of free labor provided by our people.*

*"Slavery is wrong. Our people are punished mercilessly when slaveowners aren't pleased with them for some reason, any reason. The punishment is intended to humiliate and demoralize the human spirit. Exhaustion, isolation and cruelty from Southerners have led Negroes to self-destruction and profound depression, and caused numerous illnesses.*

*"By the grace of God, many of our people are finding ways to escape to the great ports of Baltimore, Boston, New York and Philadelphia, looking for economic advancement, peace of mind, and the life they were created to have and enjoy. Many are skilled craftsmen and need jobs. We must help them find work at their old trades. Some do not have skills and are grateful to do menial tasks. Our people aren't afraid of work. They work untiringly for southern planters. It is now time for them to work to support themselves and their families. We must reach out to them and help them make the transition. We become stronger when we help each other."*

Each week the newspaper posted jobs that were available for our people. Wealthy Bostonians were looking for women to do domestic labor. Some newly freed Negroes found prosperity in the middle ranks of American society by establishing catering services, barbershoppes and opening stables. Some worked as bricklayers, carpenters, blacksmiths, plasterers and furniture makers. William's family helped Alfred, a slave who escaped from his master in New Orleans, open and establish his very own barbershoppe. Before long, men were standing in line, daily, at the door of the small shoppe. Within a few months, Alfred was able to provide for his wife and children.

Mrs. Baker, Aunt Clara, William's family and other prominent Negroes continued to work to establish institutions such as churches, schools and friendship societies to help support and encourage our newly freed brothers and sisters. Our people had informal, clandestine associations with each other as slaves on plantations and farms. They drew upon those experiences as they began living their lives as free citizens of this country. We understood that we had to come together if we wanted to be strong and prosper.

Fugitive slaves were eager to learn to read and write. Many worked and could feed their families, but their success was limited without knowing how to read and write. I taught several children in Boston to read and write. More than ever, I felt the need to teach those skills to adult Negro men and women.

I talked to my priest about teaching our people to read and write. He gave me permission to teach at the church on Saturday afternoons. I decided to teach two hours each Saturday because my shoppe was closed on weekends.

Six men and nine women came to the church that first Saturday afternoon in November 1861. I was excited because I love to teach, and was thrilled by the look on the students' faces, and the sparkle in their eyes, when they learned something new. I made an effort to bond with them by telling them a little about me; that I was a mother, and enjoyed sewing, but was careful not to disclose too much because I was a fugitive slave.

I then asked them to stand and share something about themselves. They looked frightened, almost like children who did not know what to say. Finally, a lady stood and introduced herself.

"My name's Vaginia." She lowered her head, as if she did not know how to continue.

"Hello, Virginia. I am glad you are here today. Is there anything you would like to tell us about yourself or your family?"

"I come heah from a farm in Vaginia. I come heah alone, 'cause my husban got caut. One night we run off wit some mo slaves. We wuz runnin' fas, but de patrollas caut up wit us, an got some of us. My husban told me dat if he dont mek it, dat I wuz to keep runnin', an I dun whut he told me to do. My two chillens died from de feva sometime ago."

Virginia wiped her eyes with the sleeve of the blue and white cotton dress she was wearing. Her brown eyes were sad. Her short, thick hair was braided. The black shawl around her shoulders was torn. Her brown shoes were worn. Virginia looked at me and continued to speak.

"Mammy wuz sold three times, an when she come to Vaginia, dat's when I wuz born. Dat's why she name me 'Vaginia'." She smiled, and looked down at her dark, scratched hands. She rubbed her hands together, then took a deep breath.

"I bleeve dat thangs gonna git betta fer all of us. My husban say he will be a free man one day, an I bleeve him. I wonts to learn to read, an dat's why I come heah today. I used to wuk in de mastah house, an I kin cook an clean. I kin mek purty shawls, lak dis one." Virginia held up the shawl she was wearing so that everyone could see it. She appeared to be proud of her work.

"Miz Sarah, I will wuk real hard to learn to read. Thank you fer heppin me." She sat down and wiped her eyes. I had to be strong because, like Virginia, each of them had a painful story to tell. I was not there to pity them, but to help them learn to read and write.

"Please call me 'Sarah'. Thank you, Virginia. Before long, you will be reading and writing well. You are going to be just fine here in Boston."

Virginia appeared to be around thirty years old. She had a big smile and clean, straight teeth. Although she appeared to be frightened, I felt that Virginia would do well as a free woman. She had been through some tough times, but if being enslaved had not crushed her spirit, nothing could.

The next person to stand was Marcellus. Marcellus was quite tall and somewhat heavy. His brown overalls and plaid shirt were soiled and worn. He had a deep voice. He looked directly at me as he spoke. Unlike the others, he did not appear to be frightened. He appeared to be around forty years old. The skin on his big hands was thick and rough.

"My name's Marcellus. I run off from a plantation in Nashval, whur I wuk as a blacksmith. I know a lot 'bout horses, 'cause dat wuz my job to take cure of de horses. I ain't got no famly. Far as I know, dey all done passed on. We wuz all seprated years back, an I wuz sold to my mastah in Nashval, to wuk wit his horses at de stable.

"I done run off befo an got caut, but dis time I made it! I ain't goin' back Souf neva agin. I wont to learn to read an write, 'cause I wont my own stable one day. I been wontin to be a free man for a long time. I knew dat one day I would mek it heah to de Norf."

Marcellus sat down and looked around as if to see who would stand next. The others slowly stood to introduce themselves. Some talked about the pain and suffering they endured as slaves, and about their flight to Boston. Some gave their names, but chose not to discuss their past. I did not force anyone to talk because I wanted them to grow to be comfortable with me. I was very proud of them. They each had the courage to escape slavery and start a new life.

"I thank each of you for coming today. You want to learn, and I want to teach you as much as possible. Please do not be afraid. Learning to read and write is not difficult. You are all very strong, courageous and intelligent human beings. I only ask that you come every Saturday, and that you get here by one o'clock. When you leave here each week, you will have to find the time to study and do the work that will be assigned to you. Soon, each of you will be reading and writing. We will work together to help strengthen and encourage each other. It is very important that we help each other."

As I spoke, they looked as if they trusted me. One man asked, "Is I too old to learn to read an write?" I answered, "Absolutely not." Another lady asked, "How long will it tek me to learn to read?" I told her that depended on how eager she was to learn. Some voiced their concerns about being captured by the patrollers.

"Please understand that there are posted advertisements around the country offering rewards for the capture of slaves," I explained. "There are also well-trained patrollers searching for slaves throughout the country, eager to claim those rewards. Still, you cannot live in fear. You must move forward and keep learning. Stay together, and help each other. That is the most we can do for each other."

Before we departed that day, I said I expected to see each of them the following Saturday. Some said they would be back, but some did not respond. Unfortunately, within a few weeks, I lost five students. Two of the men said they were simply too tired to come to class on Saturdays after working hard during the week. One of the ladies stopped coming because she was pregnant and quite sickly most of the time. Jacob, one of my best students, was captured by patrollers, and returned to the plantation from which he escaped in New Orleans. Jacob's master had advertisements posted throughout Boston, offering a large reward for his capture because he was a skilled blacksmith.

Marcellus told me the painful news that Jacob had been captured, and that he would be returned to his owner. Marcellus and Jacob worked together as blacksmiths, and he witnessed that most painful scene.

"Miz Sarah, dose patrollas come to whur me an Jacob wuz wukin on Monday. We kep wukin, 'cause we thought dey come to see de white man who own de horses. Den dey come an grab Jacob by his arms. Dey shouted, 'You ran off from yo owna, Robert Smith, an we come to bring you back to de farm whur you belong.'

"Jacob told dem dat dey wuz wrong, dat dey had de wrong man, but dat didn't stop 'em from takin' Jacob. Miz Sarah, Jacob fought lak a man. He hit 'em an kick 'em, an tore thar clothes, but Jacob could not fight off three large, cruel patrollas. I tried to hep him. I push dem off Jacob an threw one of de men on de ground. Dat's when one of dem hit me ova my head wit de stick he wuz holdin'. I couldn't get off de ground for a few minutes, 'cause my head hurt so bad. By de time I could stand up, dey had took Jacob." Marcellus looked away and wiped his eyes. He was clearly distraught about what happened to Jacob.

"That is terrible. I am so sorry for Jacob. Lord, bless him. He was doing so well learning to read." I hugged Marcellus.

"Marcellus, this is very difficult for you, but you must believe that Jacob will get away from that farm, again. Jacob is strong and intelligent. He will find a way to get back to Boston, or to wherever he can be free."

"Miz Sarah, I bleeve de white man we wuk for turn Jacob in to git dat reward money. If thar is any reward out for me, I bleeve he will do de same cruel thing to me. I gotta git outta thar an find me anotha job. I ain't jes a blacksmith, I's a carpenter, too."

"I will help you find another job. We've got to believe that Jacob will escape again."

"You ain't got no idea, Miz Sarah, whut dem patrollas do to us when we gits caut an brought back to our mastahs. I seen dem whip our people 'til dey bleed. I know some slaves who got thar arm, leg, hand or foot cut off afta dey wuz caut an brought back to farms an plantations. It ain't right, Miz Sarah, it jes ain't right." Marcellus wiped his teary eyes.

"Jacob is a good man, an he will do anything to hep you. I jes hope dey don't kill him dis time."

"They won't kill Jacob because he is valuable to them. They can make money by hiring him out." Marcellus was hurt, and I wanted him to feel better, but there was no way to know what would become of Jacob once he was returned to his master.

The Fugitive Slave Law of 1850 required citizens of free states to assist in capturing escapees. I was especially mindful that we could be captured at any moment and returned to our owners. I was almost captured by Frank Wilmington, the owner of the plantation from which I escaped. I will never forget what happened that dreadful day in the fall of 1860.

Frank Wilmington allowed my parents to come to Boston to care for the mother of his friend, Daniel Broughton, who had been quite ill. On that particular day, my parents were no longer caring for his mother because her condition had gotten worse. Her doctor advised Daniel to have a nurse care for Mrs. Broughton. After the nurse came, my parents moved in with William and me.

I was aware that Frank Wilmington had written to Daniel, to inform him that he was coming to Boston to get my parents to take them back to his plantation. He had written that he would arrive in Boston as soon as possible. Daniel did not know exactly when Frank Wilmington would arrive. Daniel had been very kind to me and my parents, and I had heard that his mother was not doing well. One afternoon I left the shoppe early to visit Mrs. Broughton. Shortly after I entered her bedroom, Daniel and his mother began a heated discussion about Frank Wilmington taking my parents, his slaves, back to the plantation. Daniel had received another letter from Frank Wilmington about coming to get my parents. I clearly recall that conversation.

"Something has to be done about those planters and farmers who think only of their own wealth and prosperity," Mrs. Broughton said. "It's time somebody took action to put an end to their cruelty, selfishness and greed. I am almost eighty, but I'm not afraid of Frank Wilmington, or any of those planters. I hope something destroys their way of life!"

"Mother, a man's property is his property, whether you agree with it or not," Daniel responded. "There are laws in this country, and the Broughtons are law-abiding people. We don't take what belongs to other people, no matter how we feel about it. I believe you taught me that lesson."

"I taught you a lot of things," Mrs. Broughton continued, "and I'm thankful that you are a decent man. But, Frank Wilmington and other slaveholders aren't decent, and it's about time somebody told them the truth. Yes, I protected Bertha and Joshua, and I will protect any other slave who comes to me and needs help. I'm proud to be an abolitionist, and I don't give a damn who knows it. *Broughton* is an honorable name, and we stand up for what we believe in. We are not afraid to say what is right and what is wrong. Slavery is wrong. If enough slaves escape, like Sarah, Bertha and Joshua, then there will be no one to work in those cotton, corn, rice and sugar fields. Perhaps that will bring the system down!"

Daniel left the room to get his mother a glass of water. Mrs. Broughton calmed down after her son left. She and I talked for a few minutes.

"Sarah, I want to see this injustice to your people come to an end before I leave this world. I don't know how much longer I have down here, but, by God, I will always stand for what I believe in. If I was able, I would go down to his plantation and tell Frank Wilmington just what I think about him and his fellow slaveholders. What they are doing is wrong, and if those of us who disagree with them don't take a stand against slavery, it will never end."

"Please calm down, Mrs. Broughton." I did not want her to be upset. She was not well, and I did not want her to get worse. I changed the conversation to talk about my dress shoppe and how busy we were. I was about to leave Mrs. Broughton and head home, when I heard someone knocking at the front door. I assumed it was one of Mrs. Broughton's friends stopping by to visit with her. Although she was candid and strong-willed, Mrs. Broughton was well-respected in the Boston community. People often stopped by to talk to her.

"That's probably Betsy coming to bring my bread," Mrs. Broughton said. She sat up in her chair. "That woman makes the best bread. Some days all I want for breakfast is a piece of Betsy's bread, with a little butter.

"Does she sell her bread? If she does, I would like to buy some."

"No, she doesn't sell her bread. She loves baking it and giving it away. Betsy is one of the kindest women I ever met. She bakes different kinds of breads and pastries. And, you know, she doesn't eat all those good things that she bakes. Baking is just something she loves to do. She and your mother cook the best food. I sure miss Bertha, and her cooking.

"I can send you some customers," she continued. "The women here in Boston love to look dainty and feminine. I did not have dainty dresses when I was younger. I was so busy with other things. My husband was always finding new ways to make more money. I should have spent more time finding ways to spend it." Mrs. Broughton laughed as she talked about some of the things she and her husband enjoyed. It was clear that she still loved him very much, although he had been dead for years.

"You know, Daniel is just like his father. I so wanted him to get married, but he always seemed to enjoy making money more than he enjoyed the company of women. He brought some lovely women here to meet me over the years, but one by one, they disappeared, after he refused to marry them. I cannot say I blame them. Every woman wants to get married. It has been said that I ran those women off, but that is not true, not a word of it. I made it very clear to each of them that Daniel is my son, and I expected him to treat them with respect, and I expected them to treat my son with respect." Mrs. Broughton continued to reminisce about her family. Although I needed to leave, I listened because I sensed that she wanted me to.

Then I heard someone climbing the steps. It was Daniel. He came into Mrs. Broughton's bedroom with a look on his face I had not seen before. He appeared to be troubled. I told him I had to leave in order to get home before dark. But, as I walked pass him to leave, Daniel gently grabbed my arm and told me I could not go downstairs.

"Sarah, you can't leave now. I need you to stay here, at least for now." He had a strange look on his face.

"What on earth is going on?" Mrs. Broughton snapped. "Sarah can certainly leave if she wants to."

"No, she cannot, Mother," he said, adamantly. "Sarah, get in that closet and be quiet. I will tell you when you can leave this house!"

"Now, wait just a minute," Mrs. Broughton said. She attempted to get out of her chair. "What in the hell is going on around here."

"Mother, Frank Wilmington is downstairs! He has come for Bertha and Joshua."

When Daniel said, "Frank Wilmington is downstairs; he has come for Bertha and Joshua," I froze. Although Daniel told me Frank Willmington was coming to Boston to get my parents, I could not believe he had actually arrived; and I was in the same house with him! I looked at Daniel, speechless. I could feel my heart pounding. I felt weak, as if I was going to pass out.

William was probably still at work, and I had no way to get word to him that I needed help. Suddenly, the days I spent as a slave on the Wilmington plantation flashed before me. I wanted to cry out for help. At that moment, I felt so helpless, so afraid, so vulnerable. After many years, Frank Wilmington had finally come to claim his *property*. In the past, I had had time to think, to come up with a plan; but, at that moment, there was nothing I could do.

I thought I would never see Frank Wilmington again, and that I was clever enough to avoid ever getting caught by him or his patrollers. I certainly had not forgotten about my life as a slave on his plantation, but chose not to dwell on the past. Instead, I made the decision to look forward. The Bakers, Aunt Clara and William helped me start and enjoy a new life in Boston. Although I was a fugitive slave, I believed I was a "free" woman.

Frank Wilmington had come to get my parents. I could only imagine how thrilled he would be to return to Holly Springs with Mammy, Pappy and me. My parents would not be punished, because they had not run away from him, but I would certainly have been severely punished. At that moment, I did not have the strength to pray. I just stood there, staring at Daniel in disbelief.

I was angry at myself for having come to visit Mrs. Broughton that afternoon, knowing that Frank Wilmington had written to

Daniel about coming to get my parents. Instead of checking in on her and leaving, I stayed around and listened to her talk about her family. Unfortunately, Frank Wilmington had arrived at her home, and I could not get downstairs to run for my life!

"He wants to come up to see you, Mother," Daniel said, breaking the silence. Mrs. Broughton was sitting in her chair. She sat up straight and looked directly at her son.

"I don't want that man in my house!" she snapped. "There is nothing about him that I respect!"

"Don't forget, Mother, it was Frank Wilmington who gave permission for Bertha and Joshua to come here to care for you. He did not have to allow them to leave his plantation to come here. I think you owe Frank that much."

"I don't owe Frank Wilmington a damn thing, and I will tell him so! He is not taking Bertha and Joshua back with him to that plantation, and he certainly isn't going to take Sarah. Sarah, get in my closet, and stay there until I can get this man out of my house!"

"Come on Sarah, get in here until he leaves," Daniel said. I walked into the closet, and he closed the door. I heard Daniel ask his mother if she could at least be polite, and respect the fact that Bertha and Joshua were Frank Wilmington's property, whether she approved or not. Mrs. Broughton did not respond. Daniel then went downstairs to get that horrible man.

I will never forget standing in that dark closet, listening to Frank Wilmington's steps as he climbed the stairs to speak to Mrs. Broughton. It frightened me then, and it frightens me to this day. I was also afraid of what Mrs. Broughton would say to him. Would she lose her temper and tell him that I was in her house, but that he was not taking me back with him? I asked God to protect me from that man. I did not want to go back to that plantation. I was a fugitive slave, and desperately needed God's mercy. Legally, I was Frank Wilmington's *property*; but, more importantly, I was a human being who wanted to be free.

Frank Wilmington came into Mrs. Broughton's bedroom and spoke to her. His voice had not changed. My body trembled as I listened to the voice of the man who had caused so much pain for my family. I put my hands to my ears to block the sound of his voice. Then, slowly, I calmed down, because I needed to hear what he had to say to the Broughtons.

"Mrs. Broughton, how are you? Daniel told me you have not been feeling well, but you look quite well. It is good to see you."

"I am well, thank you," Mrs. Broughton said, in a sharp tone. I thought she would continue talking about her health, but she did not.

"It appears that Bertha and Joshua have been taking good care of you," he continued. "They are just wonderful. They have always taken very good care of my family. When Charlotte was ill, Bertha never left her side." There was a brief silence.

"How is your family?" Daniel asked.

"Well, Kate and Melissa are married, and have families of their own now. They came to visit me several weeks ago. They are well."

Mammy told me that Kate and Melissa distanced themselves from their parents after they married, because of a dispute about money. Still, Frank Wilmington did not speak ill of his daughters.

"We are expecting a good cotton crop this fall." He changed the subject to what he loved most – cotton and making money. "Last year was a great year, and the demand for cotton continues to increase, here and in Europe." He and Daniel talked briefly about the increase in the demand for cotton. Then, Frank Wilmington asked about my parents.

"Where are Bertha and Joshua? I have not seen or heard them. I trust that they are doing well."

There was an awkward silence, then Daniel spoke. "Actually, Frank, Bertha and Joshua are not here."

"Not here. Where are they?"

"Toronto," Mrs. Broughton interjected, "Bertha and Joshua are in Toronto."

"Toronto! Who gave them permission to go to Toronto?" Frank Wilmington snapped. "If you recall, Daniel, I allowed Bertha and Joshua to come here to care for your mother."

"Now, just a minute, Frank," Mrs. Broughton interrupted. "*I* gave Bertha and Joshua permission to go with my brother to Toronto, not Daniel."

"Why would you do that? The only reason I allowed them to come here was to care for you."

"I gave them permission to go with my brother because I wanted to!" She did not sound as if she was intimidated by Frank Wilmington. She stood up to him, as she did with everybody.

"Daniel, you brought Bertha and Joshua here with you, and I hold you responsible for getting them back, as soon as possible. I expected more from you. Bertha and Joshua are *my property*, not *your property*. I only allowed them to come here because you needed someone to care for your mother. I never said they could leave the country, and run off to visit your relatives. Tell your uncle I am here to get Bertha and Joshua, and to bring them back, immediately."

"You don't order my son around," Mrs. Broughton shouted. "We are not *your property*, and don't act as if we are!"

"Calm down, Mother," Daniel said. "Remember what your doctor said about getting upset."

"I am not here to upset anyone. I am only here to get Bertha and Joshua, to take them back to Holly Springs. I promised Charlotte they would never leave the plantation, and I should have honored my word. Daniel, I wrote to you and told you that I was coming to get them. You had no right to let them go with your uncle. How long have they been in Toronto?"

"Not long," Daniel said. "I am so sorry about all of this. Bertha and Joshua have taken very good care of my mother, and I am grateful to you for allowing them to come here."

"How are they? Are they well?"

"Bertha and Joshua are just fine," Mrs. Broughton said. "We treat them like human beings *should* be treated."

"They were treated well on my plantation. When does your brother plan to bring them back?"

"I have no idea when they'll be back," Mrs. Broughton said. I became more anxious as I listened to the conversation between Frank Wilmington and Mrs. Broughton. I did not want her to make that man angry. He sounded as if he was quite irritated.

"I'll bring them back as soon as possible," Daniel said. "I am sorry, Frank."

"If I had enough time, I would wait here in Boston for their return. However, I have obligations at home, therefore I must leave tomorrow. Daniel, I want you to bring Bertha and Joshua back to Holly Springs. I think that is the appropriate thing to do."

"I think that is a reasonable request," Daniel responded. There was another brief silence. I expected Daniel to say more, but he did not.

"Mrs. Broughton, you look well. I hope you continue to improve. Good day to you." Mrs. Broughton did not respond. There was no way to tell what she was thinking, or planning, as Frank Wilmington prepared to leave her home. I heard him walk toward the door to go downstairs. Daniel said he would walk down with him.

I then heard Frank Wilmington speak again as they descended the steps. "By the way, Daniel, I have not given up on finding Sarah. She has been gone for years, but I *will* find her. I'm not sure if she's still in New York, or somewhere in New England, but I *will* find her. And, when I find her, she *will* pay the price for running away from me."

"You cruel, foolish man," Mrs. Broughton shouted. I do not think Frank Wilmington heard her because he was talking to Daniel about something else. I then heard the front door close. Daniel came back to Mrs. Broughton's bedroom and opened the door to the closet for me to come out.

"Sarah, you can come out. He is gone." I wanted to curl up in that closet and hide for days, but had to come out and find the strength to keep going.

I slowly walked out of the closet and looked around the room, to be sure he was really gone. I wanted to run out of that house and never return, but Mrs. Broughton asked me to stay for a few minutes. She knew I was upset and frightened, and wanted me to calm down before I left.

"Mother, you were wrong to lie to Frank about Bertha and Joshua being in Toronto."

"Yes, I lied, and I'll do whatever I need to do to protect Bertha, Joshua and Sarah. Frank Wilmington is a cruel man, and I have no respect for him."

"That was *not* the way to handle this, Mother. I have some matters to take care of, and we will talk later." Daniel left the room and went downstairs.

"Sarah, you are a brave young woman, and you have come a long way. Don't let that cruel man frighten you. He hasn't caught you, and he is not going to catch you. You must believe that."

"Right now, I don't know what to believe. You heard him say that he will find me. After all these years, he still has not given up. Perhaps I need to leave Boston and go somewhere, anywhere."

"Sarah, he does not know that you are here in Boston. Boston is a large city. He believes you might be somewhere in New England. I don't think you should leave Boston. Perhaps you just need to be less visible."

"Thank you, Mrs. Broughton, for all you have done for me and my parents. You and Daniel are good people. I must go home now." I hugged her and left her bedroom. That was the last time I saw Mrs. Broughton. She passed away a few weeks after that dreadful day. Shortly after she passed, Daniel left Boston and moved back to Canada. That was where he grew up, and where he chose to spend the rest of his life. I kept in touch with him over the years, through Mrs. Baker and Aunt Clara.

Before he left Boston, Daniel visited Mammy and Pappy at our home one evening. He wanted to speak with them before he left.

"Thank you for caring for Mother. Mother could be difficult at times. Over the years, I hired several people to care for her, and none of them stayed very long. However, she never wanted you and Joshua to leave or stop caring for her. She was very fond of both of you."

Daniel said he would never tell Frank Wilmington he was returning to Canada, or that my parents were living in Boston with me. He said he would break all ties with Frank Wilmington, and with the cotton industry. To my knowledge, that is exactly what he did.

# CHAPTER 8

I watched from a distance as a group of white men, dressed alike in blue pants and shirts, walked across a moat to enter the six-sided fort, substantially constructed of stone. I had finally made it to Fortress Monroe, and had to figure out what to do.

I decided to follow those men. Fortress Monroe was designed to protect the Chesapeake Bay's inland waters from attack by sea. Within the moated stone walls were several brick buildings surrounded by mature oak trees. Some of the buildings had fragments of stone between the windows. A group of men stood in front of a long, brick building, talking and laughing. Another group stood at the top of the stone wall, watching over the Bay. I stopped walking as some men approached me.

One of them shouted, "It's another one of those slaves, seeking refuge. This is a Union fort, not a shelter for slaves."

They stared at me from head to toe. I was tired, but not afraid, and calm, with a sense of peace that is difficult to explain. Perhaps it was because I had reached my destination.

"Why are you here, boy, and what do you want? Where did you come from?" One of the men asked.

Before speaking, I looked around and took a deep breath, but did not look at the men. It was disrespectful for a slave to look directly at a white person.

"I's heah 'cause I wont to wuk to hep de Union. I got good skills, an don't eat much, an don't mind wukin hard. I won't mek no trouble for nobody."

"What kind of *good skills* you got?" They all laughed. "We got enough niggers hanging around here looking for food and shelter."

"I kin lay bricks, an do carpentry wuk. I been doin' dis for years, an I wont to hep out 'round heah. I don't eat much, an don't mek no trouble."

"So, you're a bricklayer and a carpenter?" the man asked. He appeared to be in charge of the others because he asked all the questions. "Who taught you these skills, and where are you from?"

"I learned dese skills wukin for my mastahs. I come from Georgia."

"So, you ran off from your owner, and now you want the Union Army to take care of you? Did you know that we ain't enlisting no niggers? We can fight this war and win it without any help from your people. It costs money to feed and provide shelter for y'all."

"Tell us why you're here?" Another man asked.

"I come heah 'cause I wont to hep de Union. I kin do whateva you wont me to do. Please don't sen me away. I got good skills, an I will wuk from sun up 'til sun down. I wont to stay heah."

"There's plenty of work to be done around here. Tell me, what can you do?"

"I kin lay bricks an do carpentry wuk. I kin jes 'bout fix anything." Either they were not listening or they wanted to hear it again. Although they didn't admit it, they probably needed my help.

"This one is able-bodied, and we can put him to work over in the hospital," another man said. "There's plenty of work to be done around here, and several men are sick. We need to put these slaves to work to help prepare meals and clean up. This one needs to go on over to the hospital, so he can get busy repairing the roof and plastering walls and ceilings. He says he got good skills, so let him prove it."

One of them grabbed me by the arm and said, "Follow me." As we walked away, he turned around and said to the others, "This place has become a refuge for fugitive slaves. They may cost us more than they're worth. I hope General Butler hasn't made a mistake by letting them stay here."

I followed that man to a large building made of stone, which I assumed was the hospital. I was tired and hungry, but grateful that those white soldiers did not run me off. Thank God, I was allowed to stay at Fortress Monroe, and was assigned to work in the hospital. I was not a free man, but sure felt like one that day in June 1862, because my flight to Fortress Monroe was a success.

I thought about the hounds and patrollers who could still have been hunting me. Patrollers were known to be persistent, and they often tracked slaves into other states. I wondered if they would come as far as Fortress Monroe, and if I would be turned over to them. That was not a pleasant thought.

Inside the hospital, men were plastering walls. "I've got somebody to help you," the man I followed to the hospital said. "He says he's a carpenter, so he should be able to help you. Put him to work. Andrew, I want you to keep an eye on him." The man then left the building.

The man named "Andrew" asked, "What is your name?" I said, "Tom." He proceeded to explain that Fortress Monroe, or "Fort Monroe," as he called it, had been damaged by a hurricane, and that some of the buildings had internal damage. He gave specific details as to what he and his men were assigned to do, and then asked if I had any questions. I said "No," and started plastering.

"When did you get here?" Andrew asked. "I don't think I've seen you around."

"I got heah today."

"How did you get here?" I assumed he would have known that I was a runaway slave because of my appearance, with worn and soiled clothing. I was not a pleasant sight.

"I wuz wukin on a plantation in Charleston when I heard 'bout Fort Monroe. I cum heah 'cause I wanna hep de Union." That was all I said because I did not know anything about Andrew. He was a white man, and every white man I had ever known had been cruel to me. There was no reason to think Andrew was any different.

After a while, we moved to work on the roof. I noticed that Andrew had trouble putting nails in the roof. I asked if he needed help. He gave me the hammer and watched as I nailed pieces of roofing in place. I had been doing that type of work for years and enjoyed it. Then, to my surprise, Andrew asked a very interesting question.

"Where and how did you learn to do this so well?" The tone of his voice was different from that of other white men I had known. His was not a harsh, derogatory tone. Instead, he sounded as if he was impressed with my work and watched closely as I meticulously placed each piece of roofing. I finished that task and asked what else needed to be done.

"There are doors that need to be hung. Let's get this area cleaned up, and then we can get to work on those doors."

I picked up debris until the area was clean, then grabbed several bags of waste to make the area safe for the workers. Some of the soldiers complained about the heat, but the hot weather did not bother me. I had worked under much worse conditions. I looked around but did not see any fugitive slaves, and wondered if Fort Monroe was truly a shelter for runaways, and if I would be thrown out.

"There was quite a bit of damage done to the roof and to the interior of some of these buildings during the last hurricane," Andrew said. "We have been working for several weeks, but there is still much to be done. Follow me, and I will show you the damage."

I followed Andrew throughout the hospital and listened as he explained what had to be done. Parts of walls had been torn down in some of the rooms. By the time he finished showing me around, it was almost dark. He said we would continue the work the next day. I followed Andrew to a large white house made of wood near the center of the Fort. The design of that house caught my attention. It reminded me of the houses I worked on in Charleston. The house had three stories, with a veranda on the second and third levels. Six white columns supported the front of the house, which was graced with four windows on each story.

"This is Quarters 1, the commanding headquarters for Major General Benjamin Butler," he said. "General Butler is in charge here at Fort Monroe. We will start working early in the morning." Andrew then left for the night.

At that moment, a man came out of the white house and told me I would have to join the other fugitive slaves for the night. He pointed to some buildings and then left. I walked into the first building, filled with several male slaves. It had a kitchen, common mess-room and a commodious wash room. There were several small beds on the first and second floors. One of the men said three buildings were used to house fugitive slaves. He said women and children were in another building. I was thrilled because apparently fugitive slaves were not turned away, and were allowed to stay at Fort Monroe.

That night I slept well, with no worry about patrollers and hounds sneaking through the woods. I longed to be with Hannah, and envisioned her large, brown eyes and warm smile. I promised her I would come back for her, and was determined to do it. We would jump the broom one day and have a family of our own.

The next morning one of the Union soldiers came by early to get us up to work. I soon learned that Union soldiers were assigned to guard and police the fugivtive slaves, or "refugees," as we were called by some of the soldiers. Most of the refugees were assigned to do laundry, cook, clean and work as servants, stevedores, carpenters and laborers, for which they were given rations and a small monthly wage. Some made an independent living by fishing and peddling. A few who escaped from nearby farms and plantations attained the distinction of serving as guides and scouts for the union expeditions operating out of Fort Monroe, because they were familiar with the area.

I returned to my work at the hospital with Andrew and other Union soldiers and worked diligently tearing down damaged walls. Andrew stopped working and watched me work, just as he had done the day before. I was used to white men watching over me to make sure I did the job right, and did not run off. I soon learned that Andrew watched me for a different reason.

"I've never seen anyone work as fast as you do," he said. "We've been working on these walls for weeks, and have not made a lot of progress. I'm watching so I can learn to do this quicker. We still have lots to do around this place, and need to finish so we can move on to another building." He then called some of the other soldiers over to watch.

"Mastah Andrew, thank you for tellin' me dat. I will wuk hard, an you an Genral Butler won't be sorry dat you let me stay."

"I'm nobody's master," he replied. "I'm just a man from Philadelphia, who wants to fight for the Union. I think this is the best thing to do with my life. It's an honor to be here at Fort Monroe."

After working for several hours, Andrew said he was hungry and asked me if I wanted something to eat. I said "Yes." I thought he was going to send me away to eat with the other refugees, but he did not. Instead, he distributed food to the soldiers and to me. He gave us bread and beef with vegetables, and cold water to drink.

The other soldiers went off somewhere to eat, and I expected Andrew to join them. I sat down where we had been working to eat. I heard someone behind me, and looked around to find Andrew standing nearby. He sat near me and began talking about his family. I soon learned that, not only was he very close to his family, but Andrew was a decent person. That was the first time I had ever had a conversation with a white man who did not remind me that I was a slave, and that he owned me. I will never forget my first conversation with Andrew. He spoke to me like I was a human being, who had feelings, hopes and dreams, as he did.

"Last night I wrote to my parents," he said. "They like to know how I'm doing, and if I'm making progress with all of my assignments. Sometimes I have to force myself to write because I'm so tired at night. Still, I write because the last thing I want to do is to hurt Mother. She's a wonderful lady. I have two older brothers, but Mother still thinks of me as her 'baby'. I've asked her many times not to say that, but she doesn't listen to me. You know how mothers are.

"Tell me about your Mother, Tom." He took a bite of the beef, and appeared to be as hungry as I was. Andrew was about my height, around five feet, eleven inches, and rather thin. I was amazed to see him eat as much as he did. His pale blue eyes looked somewhat sad. If he missed his family, he probably would not have told anyone, for fear they would think of him as a "baby." He stopped eating, and looked as if he was waiting for me to respond to his question.

It took everything within me to fight back the tears that welled in my eyes. I had often cried about my family over the years. I had not seen Mammy and Sarah since that day we ironically ran into each other in Atlanta, when I was younger. I was building a veranda when Mammy screamed, "Dat's my boy, dat's my boy!" I will never forget that moment.

I hugged and kissed Mammy and Sarah, and did not want to let go. At that time, it had been about five years since I had seen them. I looked around for Pappy, but he was not there. Mammy said he had to stay behind to watch over Frank Wilmington's cotton crop. Mammy asked how I was doing. Although my heart was broken, I said all was well. I told her that Edward Carnes had not whipped or mistreated me. That was a lie, but I did not want her to worry any more than she already had about me.

"Tell me about your mother," Andrew said again. I was caught up in thoughts about my family, and did not want to share anything about them with Andrew or any white person. I had only talked about my family to Hannah because she was the only person who understood the pain and suffering I had endured. I did not even get to stay in Mississippi, close to my family, but was "hired out" to a slaveholder in Georgia. Inspite of the pain, I kept going, but did not think I would ever completely heal.

"I don't know much to tell you." I stopped eating and looked away at the Chesapeake Bay. Staring at that large body of water calmed by soul. "I ain't seen Mammy in years and don't know whur she is no mo." Andrew looked at me as if he did not understand my words.

"Didn't you grow up with your mother and your family?" I knew from that question that he did not understand the barbarity of slavery. I soon realized that he, like most Northern soldiers, came into direct contact with slaves for the first time during their service in the Union Army. They knew it existed, but clearly did not understand the institution of slavery, and what it had done to our people.

"I lived wit my famly 'til I wuz 'bout ten, den mastah sold me to anotha slaveholder. I ain't seen Pappy since de day I wuz sold, an I ain't seen Mammy an my sister since dat day in Atlanta. Dat's all I know to tell you." It hurt to talk about my family. Every time I discussed them with Hannah, it brought me to tears. Hannah understood my pain, and encouraged me to talk about them. She thought that would ease the pain.

Although Hannah was a slave, she had grown up with her mother. They were owned by a planter in Savannah. Shortly after her mother died from pneumonia, Hannah's master sold her to John Mundy, and we met on his plantation. Her father was sold when she was very young and she did not remember anything about him. Still, she was blessed to have had her mother with her until she became a young adult.

"I'm sorry, Tom," Andrew said. He stopped eating and starred at me with those sad, blue eyes. He looked at me as if he was shocked to hear my story. There was more I could have told him about my family, but Andrew was not Hannah. In fact, I was ready to talk about something else because I had nothing in common with a white, Union soldier from Philadelphia, who had grown up with his family.

"Do you think you will ever see them again?" Andrew clearly had no idea how much talking about my family hurt. Although I hid my feelings, he should have sensed my pain. However, that day I realized it was possible to ingratiate with Andrew. He asked questions which made me think he was actually a decent human being.

"I bleeve one day I will see my famly agin. I will neva stop bleeving dat."

"If they can make it to the Union line, as you did, they will not be returned to their owners. One of the commanders said that, as of March (1862), Congress adopted an article of war forbidding Union soldiers to return fugitive slaves to their owners. I don't know if that makes y'all free or not, but you can't be returned to your owners."

"Dat's good to know." I did not tell Andrew, but I never stopped thinking of ways to get Hannah away from that plantation. I did not know how, but it would happen. As for my family, I did not know if they were still in Holly Springs, or if they had been sold to other slaveholders. Although I was thankful to be at Fort Monroe, and thankful to know that fugitive slaves within Union lines would not be returned to their owners, I would never rest or have peace until Hannah and my family were free, and we were all together again.

# CHAPTER 9

It did not take long to realize that Union soldiers did not enlist in the army to fight to free the slaves. The soldiers at Fort Monroe could have cared less about our freedom. But, Andrew was different. He and I worked together every day, and he never disrespected me in any way. He was proof that all white men are not cruel.

Andrew talked a lot and I listened. The quality of my work had always been important to me, and I did not allow a kind, talkative, white soldier change that. So, as Andrew talked on about his family and his dreams, I worked.

Andrew's parents were Quakers who settled in Philadelphia when he was a young boy. I did not know anything about Quakers, but assumed they were decent people because of the manner in which Andrew treated people, including Negras. He was twenty-five years old. One day he talked on and on about Susan, a young lady he thought he was in love with. He met her in Philadelphia, shortly before he was sent to Fort Monroe. He liked her because she knew how to make him laugh. He said Susan was not the prettiest girl he had met, but she was the one he enjoyed being with the most. He then asked me if I had ever been in love. I said, "Yes."

"Tell me about her." I did not want to discuss Hannah with him. She was very special to me, and I had never discussed her with anyone. We kept our feelings for each other a secret. Hannah was a ray of light in my life, and thinking about her always lifted my spirit. Talking about her made me sad, because she was so far away.

"What is your girl like?" I wanted to ignore his question, but had not forgotten that I was a fugitive slave, and he was a young, white Union soldier, who had been assigned to watch over me. I had no choice but to answer him.

"She's very pleasant, an she's warm. She's a patient person, an she's kind to evrybody." I wanted him to change the conversation, but he did not.

"What is her name?"

"Her name's Hannah." I answered his question and proceeded to show another refugee how to lay the bricks to repair the wall. Several of the young Negra men asked if they could work with me, and I enjoyed teaching them about masonry.

"Hannah is a nice name," Andrew continued. "Where is she, and why didn't you bring her with you." His questions were irksome, but I knew how to hide my annoyance. He clearly had no idea how difficult it was for slaves to get away from their masters and from patrollers.

"It ain't easy for slaves to git away from thar mastahs. When I ran from Charleston, Hannah was not wit me."

"Tell me what you love about her." Andrew was smiling like an innocent child who wanted to know something that did not concern him. Although I thought he was a decent white man, I did not intend to share my feelings about Hannah with him.

"I like evrything 'bout her." Someone asked a question about the bricks, and that was my opportunity to change the conversation.

"Well, you ought to try everything in your power to get her here with you. If you think she's pretty, then so will other men." His comment made me angry. The thought of Hannah with another man was painful. Although she loved me, I could not expect her to wait forever.

"I will try to git her heah." I wanted to say to Andrew, "*I can't send for Hannah to come and visit me, as you can send for Susan, and have her come to visit you.*" However, getting angry with Andrew for asking questions about Hannah would not have accomplished anything, except to get me in trouble with the Union soldiers. I got over my anger and continued to work.

Samuel was one of the refugees who asked to work with me, and one with whom I enjoyed having close. He was quite tall, well over six feet. His hands were huge, and his shoe size was almost twice the size of mine. Samuel did not mind hard work, and he whistled as he worked. His wife, Lydia, was also tall and quite attractive. Her dark skin was smooth and clear. Her light brown eyes were bright and inquisitive. Her smile was big and warm. She was pleasant and kind, like Hannah. Samuel and Lydia came to the camp from Ashland, Virginia. They were good, decent peopIe. I spent a lot of time with Samuel working at the hospital.

The buildings within the Fort used to house fugitive slaves were overcrowded. Therefore, it became necessary to divert the flow into what the Union soldiers referred to as the "contraband camps," because the fugitive slaves at Fort Monroe were considered "contraband of war." The shanties in some of those camps were made of slabs, the rough side of logs which had been sawed into planks. Samuel, Lydia and I lived in the largest camp, the grand contraband camp, which was established in the ruins of Hampton. Hampton was burned by the Confederates in August 1861, reportedly to prevent Union troops from using the town for winter quarters.

The contraband camps were crowded as well, and not pleasant to live in. They were squalid shanty and tent communities, where the Union Army housed runaways. Still, the refugees thought that living in those camps was better than living on plantations.

As time passed, I grew close to Samuel and Lydia. They reminded me of my family because they got along well and loved each other. They were intelligent and worked hard. Watching Samuel and Lydia together caused me to miss Hannah more than ever. One night they asked me about Hannah. I felt comfortable enough to share my feelings about her.

They suggested I write a letter to Hannah, to let her know where I was so that she would not worry. Even if John Mundy got the letter, he could not come to Fort Monroe to claim me because of what General Butler had done to protect fugitive slaves. I told them I needed some time to think about writing a letter.

Although the Union soldiers were reluctant to admit it, the refugees' contribution to federal military success was quite valuable.

Some provided useful information to the Union Army, because they were acquainted with the roads, paths and other natural features of the area. They made excellent guides. In addition to doing most of the menial labor, such as preparing meals and cleaning camp, refugees scouted the countryside and built fortifications. Some worked as blacksmiths and masons.

I worked hard at the hospital, and was eager to do anything the Union Army needed me to do in order to enlist with them. I was paid $7.00 a week, and was elated to get it. My earnings were added to the money already saved. I heard that the white men who did menial labor were paid much more, but I was not concerned about that. There were more important things to think about, such as how to get Hannah to Fort Monroe, and how to find my family.

As time passed, some of the white soldiers came to find fugitive slaves useful and trustworthy. A few, like Andrew, even showed an interest in our welfare. Andrew seemed to be genuinely concerned about me finding my family. He said he could not imagine not knowing where his family was, or if they were well. I told him there were lots of things our people had endured that he would never understand.

I missed Hannah dearly and decided to write to her. I had no idea how to get the letter to her, but writing helped to ease the pain of not seeing and talking to her. Hannah managed to learn to read and write simple words by being around the tutor who taught John Mundy's children. Knowing Hannah, she was concerned about me, so I wrote a letter:

*Dear Hannah*

*I ges you know by now dat I ran from Charleston You an me always talk bout bein free an I had to tak a chanse an run I made it safe to Fort Monroe in Vaginia I got so much to tell you Dont wory bout me cause Is well Dey aint gonna sen me away cause Genral Butler got a camp heah for us slaves Evry day I wuk hard at de hospetol doin de wuk I lak to do I wont you heah wit me an I will fine a way to git you heah Plees wate for me I luv you.*

*Tom*

After I wrote the letter, I wanted to tear it up because it seemed so useless. Instead, I decided to ask Andrew if he would help me get the letter to Hannah. Although I had never met a white man as kind as Andrew, I still did not trust him. After years of being abused by white men, there was no way I could trust one of them because he was kind to me. Was it worth the risk to ask him? Yes, it was.

Most days Andrew talked on and on about his family. At first it was painful to listen to his stories about his parents and brothers, because I missed my family so much. But, after a while, it did not bother me to listen to him because he was a kind person. Like me, he was a young man who loved and cared about his family. Unlike me, he had been fortunate enough to grow up with them.

We had lots of walls to repair throughout the Fort. I was glad because the more I worked, the less time I had to think about Hannah and my family, and it was an opportunity to get away from the crowded camps.

Andrew got permission for me to continue to work under his supervision. He even told the commander about the quality of my work. Although several of the soldiers watched me work each day, Andrew was the only one who ever said anything positive about my work. He said more than once that he had never met anyone with masonry skills as good as mine. His words meant a lot to me.

After lunch one day, Andrew read a letter from his mother. She was a kind and caring person. I could tell by her words to her son. Andrew's face would light up every time he read a letter from her. He also got letters from Susan. After he read his mother's letter, I told him about the letter I had written to Hannah.

"I wrote a letter to Hannah las night, but don't have no idea how to git it to her." I expected Andrew to ask questions about who taught me to read and write, but he did not. Instead, he asked where Hannah lived.

"She live on a plantation in Savannah, Georgia. John Mundy is de master of dat plantation."

"If you can tell me the name of the county or the road, I will try to get your letter to her." I looked away because I did not want anyone to see the tears that welled in my eyes. Just the thought of that letter getting to Hannah was more than I could bear at that moment; and, a white soldier was willing to help me get it to her.

I sometimes wondered if God put Andrew in my life for a reason. Perhaps He wanted to show me that all white men are not cruel. I did not know the answer, and it really did not matter. All that mattered was that I met a kind, white man amongst Union soldiers, who could be brash and demeaning at times. Andrew's kindness was like a glimmer of sunshine on a rainy day.

I told Andrew as much as I knew about the location of John Mundy's plantation, which wasn't a lot. I remembered the name of a road near the plantation. He said he would do all he could to get that letter to Hannah. I thanked him and we went back to work. Even if she was unable to write back to me, I really wanted her to get that letter.

The Union soldiers talked amongst themselves as we worked around the Fort, and I could hear some of their conversations. For example, one of the soldiers said that General David Hunter, a Union commander in the South Carolina Sea Islands, had requested permission to arm Negra men for military service. The soldier went on to say that General Hunter had taken it upon himself, without permission, to begin recruiting on his own authority. Unfortunately, the War Department refused to pay or equip the regiment.

The soldiers supported the War Department's decision. One of them said that fugitive slaves were valuable to the Union for the duties they had been assigned, but that fugitive slaves did not have the ability to acquire the duties of a soldier. Their comments made me angry, but I worked on as if they did not exist. I had better masonry skills than any soldier in that group. Still, they did not think I was capable of being a soldier, and fighting for the Union.

There was a newspaper that circulated around Fort Monroe, and Andrew read it daily. He often talked about articles in the newspaper. Based on what he said about President Lincoln, it seemed as if the President wanted slaves to be free. I understood why many southern planters hated the President. One morning in July 1862, Andrew said the paper reported that President Lincoln had appealed to congress for the border states to support gradual, compensated emancipation, with colonization of freed slaves outside the United States.

He also read that the Second Confiscation Act forbade military personnel to decide on the validity of any fugitive slave's claim to freedom, or to surrender any fugitive to any claimant. Andrew said that was great news for my people. He seemed to be happy for us. I sure was happy to hear that news.

Some of those soldiers were content to have me around Fort Monroe; not because they cared about me, but because I was a hard worker, willing and able to do the work that was assigned to them. Samuel and I had skills that could have earned us a lot of money if we had had the opportunity to work for ourselves. We vowed that we would provide a good life for our families.

By July 1862, I had known Samuel for about a month and grown to respect and care about him because we shared some of the same values. He, too, believed in working hard, and cared about the quality of his work. He loved his wife dearly and they wanted the very best for their baby son. Samuel often said his son would not grow up as he did, toiling from sun up to sun down for the white man.

We talked about ways to improve living conditions in the contraband camps, and came up with an idea to teach the boys and young men in the camp how to become masons and carpenters. It was important to think about surviving and living without depending on slaveholders for food, clothing and other needs. Most of the refugees did not have skills because they had spent their lives working in fields, cleaning, cooking and doing other menial labor. There was certainly nothing wrong with working in fields, cleaning and cooking, but we had to teach our people so they could become skilled laborers. That would enable us to support each other, by paying *our* people to work for *us*.

Some soldiers were responsible for seeing that the refugees got up early, ate breakfast and were ready for work by 7:00 a.m. Some thought we had no right to be at Fort Monroe, and that General Butler was wrong to have declared Fort Monroe a haven for fugitive slaves. They thought we should have been returned to our owners. Unfortunately, the resentful Union soldiers vented their frustration with us by cursing or not speaking to us.

Not only were some soldiers offensive to us, but some officers were rude and berated us as well. On the other hand, a few understood that we were valuable to the Union, and assigned refugees burdensome jobs the soldiers hated to perform themselves, such as cooking, washing clothes and cleaning camp. To my knowledge, the refugees who did menial labor for the Union were usually paid approximately $2.00 a week.

Samuel and I finished our work at the Fort, and still had enough time to work with the older boys and men. Teaching them skills to become masons and carpenters would enable them to work outside the camp, constructing fortifications, erecting batteries and repairing structures.

It did not take long to get a group of boys and men together who wanted to learn and develop masonry and carpentry skills. We met with them each evening around the same time, in a small area within the camp, and began teaching them.

We talked about the layout, and about how carpenters needed to know how to measure and mark materials. We explained how we began carpentry work when we were young boys, by cutting and shaping wood. Samuel showed them some of the tools we used each day at the hospital, including planes and saws. We explained how wood and other materials are joined together with nails and screws.

Each day most of the boys and men showed up, but there were days when some could not attend because they were assigned to other duties around the camp. Most of them seemed really interested in what we taught. There were lots of questions, because we spoke words some of them had never heard, and showed them tools and materials they had never seen.

There was one young boy who came every day, promptly. He was usually the first to arrive for the lessons and the last to leave. His eyes had a sparkle that caught my attention. He did not ask questions, but listened attentively as Samuel and I spoke. He appeared to absorb every word. When everyone left to return to their shanties, that young boy lingered. He touched and studied each tool carefully. I sensed that he did not want to leave us.

"I kin do dis wuk," he said to me one evening. "I wont to build things jes lak you. See, I kin hamma dis nail wit out hurtin' my fingers." He hammered nails into the wood blocks that Samuel brought from the Fort for the men and boys to work with.

"What's your name?" That boy was different from any of the boys I had met at the camp. He seemed so eager to learn; so eager to get that nail into the wood just right. The other boys left to eat supper or play around with each other; but, not this one.

"My name's Caleb." He continued to drive nails into the wood blocks. When one of the nails did not go perfectly into the wood, Caleb threw his hands up and appeared to be quite frustrated.

"Kin you please show me how to git dis nail out? Dis one ain't right."

"Caleb, it's nice to meet you, an I's glad you's heah to learn. Let me show you how to take dis nail out. You gotta be careful when drivin' a nail into wood, 'cause if de nail ain't straight, it will not go in de right way." I proceeded to show Caleb how to use the hammer to remove the crooked nail. He watched without saying a word, then asked if he could try to do the same thing. I said "Yes," then put a nail into the wood the wrong way.

"I kin git it out, jes you watch." He began working to get the nail out of the wood. I watched him work hard for several minutes before he was able to get it out. When he finally succeeded, a big, bright smile covered his face.

"See, see, Mistah Tom, I told you I kin do it! I'm gonna be a good carpenta one day, I jes know it. Mistah Tom, kin I wuk wit you at de Fort tomorra?"

Caleb's enthusiasm brightened my day. As I watched him work with the hammer and nails, my mind drifted back to the days when I was about his age. I was very young when I first watched Edward Carnes hammer nails into wood, while he and other white men and slaves worked to build a house in Savannah. I was familiar with tools because Pappy had carpentry skills, and he taught me as much as he could before I was snatched away. Although Pappy did not have time to teach me everything he knew, I quickly learned by watching other carpenters.

Like young Caleb, I was eager to learn as much as possible. Learning new things helped me deal with the pain of losing my family. Caleb reminded me so much of myself. That sparkle in his eyes was captivating.

"You tired, Caleb?" He had been with us for over two hours, and it was time for him to get back to his shanty. I did not want his mother to worry about him, and he needed to eat. However, he did not show any signs of being tired or hungry. Instead, he continued to hammer nails into wood, trying to get every one in perfectly.

"Caleb, I asked you a question. Don't you have to get back to your mother?" He stopped hammering and looked down at the ground. His big, bright smile disappeared. I assumed he simply did not want to leave us, and wanted to continue hammering. I certainly did not mind if he stayed, as long as his mother knew where he was, and he was not hungry. I enjoyed teaching, and would have stayed as long as needed.

"I ain't hungry, an I ain't got no mammy." He stared at the ground. I knew what it was like not to have a mammy. Although I believed Mammy was still alive, I had grown up without her. Caleb stood there, looking sad and lost. There was no way I could leave him like that, so I picked him up and sat him on my knee. Samuel asked if I wanted him to hang around, and I told him to go on because I wanted to talk to Caleb. Samuel had a wife and baby to get back to.

"Caleb, whur is your mammy?" I wanted him to talk to me. There was something special about him. Perhaps it was just the fact that he reminded me so much of myself many years ago. I wanted to help him adjust to life in the camp. It was not easy living in the crowded camps because the refugees did not have the food and supplies they needed.

"Mammy died. She got sick on de way, an she gone to heaven." Tears welled in Caleb's eyes. I wanted him to continue to talk, but he did not. Instead, he said he wanted to finish working with the tools.

"Caleb, I's sorry 'bout your mammy. Who did you come heah wit?" I had no idea how long Caleb had been there. He looked so sad, so alone, sitting on my knee. It was almost dark and the two of us sat alone. I did not know anything about him, other than what he told me. Still, I felt a sense of responsibility for him.

"I come heah wit Miz Flora an all de othas. We come from Richmond. Miz Flora said if we kin git to Fort Monroe, we would be free."

"When did you git heah?"

"I don't know. It wuz many days ago." He wiped his eyes and asked if he could continue working with the hammer and nails. I told him it was late, and I had to take him back to Miz Flora so that he could eat and get some rest. He looked at me with the saddest eyes.

"Mistah Tom, I wont to be a carpenta, jes lak you. You kin build lots of things, an I wont to be jes lak you." There was silence because I did not know what to say. I certainly wanted to help Caleb, as well as the other men and boys, learn new skills.

"Caleb, Samuel an I will be teachin' heah evryday after we finish wukin at de Fort. You an all de othas will learn to lay bricks an do carpentry wuk. You kin come as early as you wont to. Thar is so much for you to learn. Now, it's time for you to git on back to Miz Flora. You ain't had no supper, boy. Don't know 'bout you, but I need to git some food." I picked him up from my knee and patted him on the shoulder. We walked back to his shanty.

Miz Flora, as expected, was worried about him. I apologized to her, and told her why Caleb was late getting back. Just as Caleb said, Miz Flora told me that she and several other slaves ran off from a farm near Richmond. Caleb's mother had been with them, but after running through some water, she got sick and did not recover. Caleb was her only child. Miz Flora did not know a lot about Caleb's father. She and Caleb's mother had known each other a long time, and she was responsible for him.

I patted Caleb on his shoulder and told him I would see him the next day, and that there was a lot for him to learn. He still looked sad, but said he would be there early. That night I did not rest well. I thought about young Caleb most of the night. He was so eager to learn, but clearly missed his mother. He was a sad, young boy, who wanted to learn and become a carpenter. I decided to teach him everything I knew, and help him develop the skills he needed to be the best carpenter and mason ever.

The next day I arrived at the hospital and heard some news that made me sad. Andrew was there when I arrived, which was unusual because I was usually the first one to get to the work site. It was my job to set up for the day. I wondered why Andrew had come in so early. He was getting some tools when suddenly he announced that he had great news.

I assumed it was news about his family, perhaps something his mother had written in her letter. I had to be patient, because once again, I was faced with listening to him talk about his family.

After talking to some of the soldiers, Andrew said again he had good news to share with us. No one seemed particularly excited about hearing his news. They probably assumed it was about his family. Some of the soldiers rarely said anything about their families. I put my tools down and listened as he began to speak.

"Well, guys, just in case you're wondering about my good news, here it comes. Sargent Crater called me in last evening and told me I'm about to be armed. Yes, I am going to battle, finally! I have nothing against carpentry and masonry work, but repairing walls is not why I enlisted in the army. I came to fight for the Union, and I have been anxiously awaiting the moment to be called to duty. I can't wait to get out there and defend the Union. This is a proud moment for me!"

Andrew had a big smile on his face. Although I should have been, I was not happy for him. That was selfish of me, but it was the truth. First, I did not want Andrew to leave because he had always treated me like a human being should be treated. I would miss talking to him and hearing about his family. Second, I was envious because I wanted to be armed and fight for the Union. I wanted to help them because I believed they were fighting against slavery.

With Andrew gone, I would have to deal with those cold, unpleasant soldiers at Fort Monroe. I did not care that they did not want to talk to me. Actually, I did not want to talk to them. Some of the soldiers congratulated Andrew, but I turned and went back to work. He was the first white man who had ever been kind to me, and he was leaving.

He eventually came over and asked what I thought about him going to battle. Although I was not happy about that, I did not let him know. I knew how to treat people, and had never been rude to anyone. My parents taught me how to treat people; something you never forget.

"Andrew, I know dis is whut you wont more dan anything, an I know you will be great on de field. You treated me well since de day I met you, an I will neva forgit dat. You will make de Union proud."

"I sure will. Tom, I hope to see you again someday, and I really hope you find your family. You deserve to have them in your life."

I sensed that Andrew wanted to say more that day, because he knew how much I wanted to go to battle. Here were two men, one white, and one a fugitive slave, who wanted the same thing – to fight for the Union. Unfortunately, the President and other leaders did not think fugitive slaves and people of African descent were suited for battle. It did not make any sense to me, but that was the law.

I watched Andrew cheerfully put his tools away and run off to meet with his commander. He could not wait to get away from those torn down walls that would require months of hard labor to repair. Like Andrew, I had not come to Fort Monroe to be a carpenter or mason, but to fight for the Union. However, unlike Andrew, I had no choice.

That day I had no idea if I would ever see Andrew again. If I did not see him again, at least I knew that all white men are not cruel. I had to think differently if I wanted to survive in this country, as a free man, to become all that God created me to become. I did not spend much time with Andrew, but he certainly had an impact on my life.

# CHAPTER 10

We stayed busy at *The Dress Shoppe* and needed more space to work, but I was quite comfortable with the location of the shoppe because it was close to my home. One morning as I walked to work, it appeared that the people who lived in a house across the street from the shoppe were moving out. One of my customers said the owner of the house was looking for new tenants. I decided to take a look.

The one-story house had four rooms; a kitchen, living room and two bedrooms. The rooms were bright because each had a large window. The house was quaint, with a fireplace in the living room. It was the perfect home for a small family, or, for my dress shoppe. I envisioned us working there with enough space to move around freely.

"I like this house, and would like to lease it," I said to the owner, Richard Fulton. "My home is closeby, and this is a nice area."

"If you have a home, why do you want to lease this house?"

"I own the shoppe across the street, and we need more space to work. I will decorate this house and take good care of it, just as if it was my very own home. How much is the rent?"

"Slow down, Mrs. Harper. There are others who are interested in this house as well. Check back with me later in the month and I will let you know what I intend to do."

I left that house and knew it was the perfect location for my business, and prayed about it. The following week Mr. Fulton came to tell me I could rent the house if I was still interested. After much discussion and negotiation, we reached a rental agreement.

The following week we moved our fabric, sewing machines and supplies across the street to our new, larger shoppe. That first day we danced around the shoppe like young girls because we were so happy to have more space to design, cut and sew dresses. We dressed the large windows with white, neatly pressed curtains with ruffles, and put plants in each room. That shoppe became a second home for all of us. We made it as comfortable and pleasant as possible, because we spent so much time there.

After the Christmas parties, women continued to come in and order dresses from us. Helena Austin, Eve Grant and Jane Merritt spread the word about how pleased they were with their dresses. Those three women were instrumental in helping to build my business as a dressmaker and designer. Wealthy white women and prominent Negro women supported us.

I read everything I could find on women's fashions in order to grow as a fashion designer. I went to department stores, Jordan Marsh in Boston and Macy's in Haverhill, Massachusetts, to see what was selling in women's fashions. I discovered that, for evening dresses, women preferred short, puffed or ruffled sleeves, although some were long and slim. Skirts were mostly bell-shaped, and were trimmed with embroidery, ruches, ribbons or lace. Skirts, often worn over a crinoline frame, were cut to spread out at the back. They flowed out from the waist to a wide hemline. Most of my customers preferred that decorative trim be confined to the edge of the skirt. Trim was most often applied in horizontal lines.

Some sleeves were made of a different fabric than the bodice, in the same color, where the sleeves matched either the overskirt or the underskirt. That design appealed to some of my younger customers. I enjoyed working with most fabrics, but preferred silks, satin, taffeta, moiré, velvet or faille when making formal dresses. Taffeta was quite suitable for bouffant styles. I did not trim skirts made of taffeta, a very valuable fabric, because it was beautiful without trim.

This country gradually changed from an agrarian society to one dependent upon mechanization during the course of the war. In the early 1860's, production in the woolen industry and cotton textiles rose substantially, as well as the production of shoes and leather, thanks to army contracts. Firearms, gunpowder and wagon manufacturing increased because of military contracts. There was no shortage of fabrics at that time. I used cotton, linen, wool and silk to make less formal dresses. Cotton was the least expensive of the fabrics, but easy to work with. Thank God, more women chose to be fashionably dressed, which was good for us.

As the business flourished, Callie, Cora and Naomi became more creative. Callie and I began to focus on accessories to be worn with the dresses we made. She had a good business sense, and believed we could sell more dresses if we were able to advise women on how to complete their look. Callie learned how to make gloves, and before long we began selling them. Gloves were short, to the wrist or longer, and added a final touch to evening dresses. We sold mostly white gloves, but occasionally there was a request for pink or yellow gloves.

Naomi had been fascinated with hats and bonnets as long as I had known her. She said as a free woman, she would not think about wearing kerchiefs ever again. Naomi loved wearing hats and bonnets because they made her feel special. She wore them everywhere.

Naomi had the ability to draw pretty much anything she could envision, which included dresses, hats and bonnets. Before going to bed each night, she would draw because it helped her relax after a long day of cutting and sewing fabric. One Saturday evening I visited them at their home, and Naomi showed me drawings of hats she had designed. I was absolutely amazed with her talent.

Her drawings included cloth bonnets with large ruffles around the edge to protect the face from the sun. Some bonnets were trimmed with flowers or strings of ribbon. The more decorative bonnets were trimmed with feathers and ruching. There were straw hats with wide brims, and some with ribbons wrapped around the top of the brim.

I preferred the silk hats, some trimmed with ribbons and some with flowers, and imagined Helena Austin, Jane Merritt and their wealthy friends raving over those hats. Naomi explained that she would use various colors of silk, ribbons and flowers, and that some of the ribbons would match the dress fabric. It was exciting listening to her talk about her hats and bonnets.

The style of hats, like other apparel, was a statement of class and rank in society, as well as various fabrics. This custom was a carry over from life in Europe.

Naomi dreamed of designing and making beautiful hats and bonnets, just as I dreamed about designing and making beautiful dresses. I asked her what she wanted to do with her drawings.

"I like drawin' an thinkin' about how purty women can look in dese hats an bonnets. It makes me happy to know dat I can draw something dis purty."

"Naomi, have you ever thought about actually making the hats you design, so that women can enjoy wearing them?"

"How on earth can I do dat, Sarah? I would have to get de materials, an den I would have to find de time to work on dese hats an bonnets. Dat's a lot to do, an I ain't got de time."

"You can do it, Naomi. I had the same ideas about designing and making dresses. Now, thank God, I have my own dress shoppe. You have a gift for making dresses and for designing hats and bonnets. I will help you find the materials you need, and then you can begin working on your hats and bonnets. Women will love them. Think about all the women we've seen wearing hats and bonnets."

"I ain't got de time, Sarah, to do all de work. I work for you all day in de dress shoppe. I like drawin' hats an bonnets because it makes me happy, but I ain't got de time to make dem."

"If necessary, I will cut the hours you spend working on dresses at the shoppe, and that will allow time for you to work on and develop your dream. You can do this, Naomi. You must believe in yourself."

"I don't know nuttin about runnin' no business. Where would I sell de hats after I make 'em. Sarah, dis is jes too much for me to think about."

"You can sell your hats here at the shoppe if you want to. That way women who come in to order dresses will see your hats, and they will be interested. The thought of making and selling hats and bonnets might frighten you now, but as time passes, you will learn to operate your own business. You are a free woman, Naomi; free to do what you choose to do."

"What about all de dresses we gotta make? It jes don't seem right for me not to help you, Sarah, because you been so good to me. What if we git behind in makin' all dose dresses?"

"That is not for you to worry about. I will manage, even if I have to hire another lady. There are lots of women here in Boston who can sew and are looking for work. Now is the time for us to think about helping each other start our own businesses. I will work with you, and teach you everything I know about operating a business. I am still learning, and things are getting better each day."

"What if my hats an bonnets don't sell, Sarah? Den what will I do?" Naomi was afraid, and I understood why. Still, she had a gift, and someone had to encourage and help her develop that gift. Most women enjoyed wearing hats and bonnets. Some liked the plain, basic styles, and some liked the more decorated styles. Each of my customers had different tastes, and I knew pretty much what they liked and did not like. If I did not know, I asked.

"Well, Sarah, if you will help me, I will try to start makin' hats an bonnets. You a smart woman, an I wont to be lak you. Please be patient wit me, because I gotta lot to learn. I will work hard to make purty hats an bonnets."

"I am so proud of you, Naomi. You will do well because you take pride in your work. Women will love your hats and bonnets. You, Callie and Cora are the best." I gave her a big hug, and she smiled as if she finally believed her dream could come true.

Prominent, fashionable ladies in Boston found it necessary to have different dresses for taking tea, dinner parties and various social occasions. Of course, there was always a request for a special gown for weddings and other formal events. Eve Grant continued to be one of my loyal customers after the Christmas festivities. She was white, wealthy and traveled to Europe quite often. One bright morning in April 1862, she came into the shoppe talking about her recent trip to Paris.

"Oh, dear, I had a most wonderful time in Paris. My husband worked, and I shopped," she said, with a giggle. Naomi, Callie and Cora, who had been busy cutting fabric, stopped to listen as Eve described the dresses she purchased.

"My favorite gown is very similar to a gown worn by Empress Eugenie last year. She is the wife of Napoleon III. The green silk is the finest I have ever touched. The sleeves, like the skirt, have several flounces. The sleeves are trimmed in notched, white lace, as is each flounce. The white, lace collar compliments my neckline. I wonder if Empress Eugenie looked as lovely as I look in this well-designed dress." Eve broke into laughter. She was quite charming.

"A second gown caught my eye and I had to have it," she continued. "The jacket-style bodice is a style I have not seen here in Boston. The emerald green silk moiré is embroidered with green flowers around the edge of the skirt and the jacket. The sleeves are long and slim. I don't know where I will wear it, but most certainly I will be invited to the perfect occasion to prance around in it.

"Then, in a whimsical moment, I purchased a yellow silk dress with a double skirt. The skirt has pleating, rosettes and silk ribbons. The long sleeves are puffed at the shoulders. The belt, made of the same material, accentuates my narrow waistline. Oh, I cannot wait to wear these dresses. Let me add that I bought two hats, one trimmed with feathers, and one with flowers and embroidered gauze. Sarah, they are simply lovely. My husband will be speechless when he sees me in these dresses; and, when he finds out what they cost." Eve laughed again, as if she did not have a care in the world.

"Tell me more about Paris," I said.

"Well, from a fashion sense, there is no place on earth like it. The women take pride in being fashionable, just as I do. It is a treat to watch them parade along the streets in well-designed garments. On the other hand, the architecture and art are simply breathtaking. One must spend time at Le Louvre, and study the paintings. It is a most wonderful experience."

As Eve described some of the paintings at Le Louvre, I realized that she appreciated the arts, and was just as enthusiastic about Parisian culture as she was about its fashion. She was a very pleasant, sophisticated, young white woman.

"Sarah, you must think about visiting Paris someday. I wore two of your dresses and received several compliments. You must expand your thinking beyond Boston, Massachusetts. I have some catalogues that illustrate fashion from Paris and London that I will give to you. You are a gifted dressmaker, capable of competing with European dress designers. Who knows, perhaps someday you may meet the French designer, Charles Frederick Worth. He designs dresses for famous people. Well, I must run, dear. My husband left a list of things for me to do today, and I have yet to begin. I'll get to them, maybe." Eve laughed and left the shoppe.

We returned to our work, but I could not get Eve's words out of my mind. She said I should expand my thinking beyond Boston. My goal was to be the best dress designer in Boston, but I had not thought about designing dresses for women outside of Boston, and certainly not in Paris. All things are possible, but I had not thought about selling dresses in other places.

Within a few weeks, Naomi made five hats and six bonnets. I will never forget the day her first hat sold. That morning, a well known Negro lady, Suzanna Cross, came into the shoppe. Her husband was a respected undertaker. Suzanna had bought about three or four dresses from us, and was quite delightful to work with. It was a pleasure to design dresses for her almost perfect figure. Suzanna was tall and thin. She wore her long hair neatly pulled back into a bun. She was very attractive, with large, brown eyes and keen features. She was wearing a pale green dress with a three-flounce skirt that day. The full sleeves were split in front, revealing the white sleeves of the soft blouse underneath. We had just finished taking her measurements for a dress she needed to wear to a dinner party. As she was leaving the shoppe, she turned to ask a question.

"Oh, by the way, where can I find the perfect hat to compliment my dress? I haven't had time to look around. Perhaps you all know of some place I don't know about."

Naomi looked at me as if she did not know how to respond to Suzanna's question. We had not reorganized the shoppe to set her hats on display.

"Suzanna, I apologize for not having them on display yet, but Naomi designs and makes beautiful hats and bonnets. She has about ten that I would like for you to see," I said. "Naomi, will you bring your hats and bonnets out." Naomi went to the back room to get her hats and bonnets. Suzanna gasped as she carefully studied each one.

"Why, Naomi, your hats and bonnets are beautiful. I had no idea you design and make hats and bonnets. These definitely need to be on display."

"Dis white silk hat, wit de yellow ribbons an white flowers, is my favorite," Naomi said. "Dis pink silk will look wonderful wit de dress you're wearin' today."

107

"They are simply lovely," Suzanna said. "I love the black silk hat trimmed with coral ribbon and flowers. This straw bonnet with the black ribbon is quite stylish. I want these two, and the pink silk hat."

The biggest, brightest smile covered Naomi's face. I believe it was that very moment that she gained confidence in her skills as a hat designer. Although Suzanna Cross was kind and polite, she was very particular about her dresses, and about fashion in general. She would never have said she liked something if she was not sincere about it.

The moment Suzanna Cross left the shoppe that day, the four of us jumped around with excitement. We then made space around the fireplace to display the hats and bonnets. Naomi talked about what it meant to her to have sold three hats the moment they were put on display.

"If Suzanna likes my hats an bonnets, den maybe otha women will to. I feel real happy today, because sewin' an makin' hats an bonnets is what I love to do. Sarah, thank you for lettin' me sell my hats here. I neva dreamed dat something dis good could happen to me. Lord knows I'm thankful."

"Naomi, I believe your hats and bonnets will sell just as well as the dresses we make. You have a gift, and you work very hard. More wonderful things are going to happen for you."

"Women will run in here evryday lookin' for purty hats," Cora said.

"Befo long, Naomi will be makin' lots of money, an will have her own hat shoppe, because dis shoppe won't be big enough to hold all de women," Callie added. We laughed and embraced each other. That day Naomi began selling her hats and bonnets was truly a wonderful day for all of us.

# CHAPTER 11

By spring of 1862, people were still talking about the war that began with the attack on Fort Sumter in April 1861. Everyone had an opinion about how and why the war started. Negroes gathered at Aunt Clara's home, and other homes, to discuss how we could best support the Union. William and I attended a meeting at Aunt Clara's home one evening.

"President Lincoln must understand that Negroes here in the North are eager and willing to fight for the Union," Calvin Jackson said. Calvin was a barber. His shoppe was in his home and William was one of his many customers. To my knowledge, Calvin had never been a slave. "We are not afraid to fight for what we believe is right and honorable. We believe that victory for the Union will lead to freedom for our brothers and sisters in the South. The President should allow us the opportunity to enlist, so that we can strengthen our claim to freedom, our claim to equality. This should not, and does not have to be a white man's war."

"Many of our brothers and sisters have fled slavery and seek refuge within Union lines," Larry Wilson said. Larry was the butcher at a local market. "I have heard that General Benjamin Butler, the commander at Fortress Monroe in Virginia, gives food and shelter to our people, and puts the able-bodied men to work. If General Butler can see the worth in our people, then why can't our President and leaders see it? We should petition the President to allow Negroes to enlist; those who are free, and those who have escaped slavery."

"Our people provide a wealth of benefits to southern planters and farmers. They toil in cotton, corn, sugar and rice fields throughout the year. Allowing us to fight with the Union Army will deprive the Confederacy of the benefits of slave labor. We want to use our energy and resources to aid and strengthen the

Union cause," Herman Palmer added. Herman was a member of our church, and worked on the railroads.

"President Lincoln must reconsider his decision on the prohibition of Negro enlistment. Our people can be valuable to the Union by building fortifications, cleaning camp, preparing meals and scouting the countryside. I have no doubt that we will be as valuable when armed. We are just as capable of fighting the enemy as are white men. There is no good reason for Union commanders to turn us away," Franklin White said. Franklin grew up with Mrs. Baker and Aunt Clara. He was from a well-known family in Boston, and worked in one of the banks in the area.

"Both the Union and Confederate Armies have labor requirements," William said. "It is my understanding that President Lincoln promised that the Union Army would respect the property rights of slaveholders, including their slave property. Apparently General Butler doesn't agree with the President. It is reported that he has determined that slave labor is very valuable to the Union Army.

"I have read that fugitive slaves have been received at Fort Monroe in Virginia, that General Butler has not hesitated to let them stay, and that he has put them to work. General Butler has declared runaway slaves 'contraband of war'. This expression refers to property subject to seizure because of their military value to the Confederate Army."

That meeting at Aunt Clara's home lasted until the early hours of the next day. Everyone was fired up when they left that meeting, because they believed that helping the Union Army win the war would lead to freedom for our people. We tried to attend as many meetings as possible. One evening in July 1862, William and I had a long discussion about the war. I was quite surprised when he said, "Sarah, I want to go to Fort Monroe, to *attempt* to talk to General Butler."

"What do you want to talk to General Butler about? There are people who report to *The Liberator* about what's going on with the war. Do you think the General will actually talk to you?"

"There is only one way to find out, and that is to try to speak to him, so that the newspaper can accurately report what's going on at Fort Monroe. I want you to come with me. It will be good for you to get away from the shoppe for a few days. Mammy and Pappy can take care of Will."

"I have never been away from Will for any length of time and hate to leave him. I can ask Mrs. Baker and Aunt Clara to come over to help my parents."

"Your parents don't need any help. They are strong, generous and loving people. You are so fortunate to have them as parents. I see so much of you when I talk to them. They taught you well, Sarah. I am thankful that you are my wife." Although I addressed his parents as "Mr. and Mrs. Harper", William affectionately addressed my parents as "Mammy and Pappy." That meant so much to us.

"Why, thank you, William Harper. That is very kind of you. I have enjoyed being your wife. Our marriage will last forever, and I will do everything possible to make you happy, including going with you to Fort Monroe. Although the thought of going there makes me anxious, I will go."

"Why does going to Fort Monroe make you anxious?"

"It's not going to Fort Monroe that makes me anxious; it's going back to the South that worries me. After I got my parents away from Mississippi, I vowed never to return to the South. I am a fugitive slave, and we are going back to where our people are enslaved."

"Would you rather stay here, Sarah? If you would, I certainly understand. I can go alone."

"No, I'm going with you. I'm going to support you as you have supported me."

"Thank you. Your coming along means a lot to me. I don't know if General Butler will talk to me, but I want to know for certain if he is accepting runaway slaves at Fort Monroe. If he is, I can write about this in the newspaper. Sarah, you were very brave to go back to the plantation to get your parents. People respect you for your courage and devotion to your family. I have made the decision to go, and will do it."

"When are we leaving?"

"We are leaving a week from Sunday and will take the train to Richmond, and from Richmond we will take a carriage to Fort

Monroe. After we speak with General Butler, we will leave. This should be a most interesting trip."

I could see the excitement in William's eyes as he talked about visiting Fort Monroe. He so wanted to meet and talk to the General. I didn't think anyone would talk to him, but William was determined to go. Just as no one had been able to stop me from going back to Holly Springs to get my parents, no one could stop William from going to Fort Monroe.

We boarded the train and left early one Sunday morning. William talked about his frustration and disappointment in President Lincoln and other politicians because of their rejection of Negro soldiers. He had read about the Revolutionary War and the War of 1812, and learned that Negro soldiers were committed and proficient soldiers in both wars. He talked about those wars as we traveled to Richmond, Virginia.

"During the Revolutionary War, countless numbers of free and enslaved Africans in the colonies chose to join the American war for liberty from Britain, and thousands of them died alongside white colonists in the fight for freedom. We are not afraid to fight for what we believe in. As you know, our people did not willingly come to this country, and violently fought the slave trade in West Africa."

"Why did our people fight in the Revolutionary War?" William's family was educated, and he knew about America's history, and about the history of our ancestors. He talked about the courage our people had shown in past wars.

"Some fought to help America win the war, some were offered emancipation in exchange for their service, and some joined the British forces."

"Why would they join the British?"

"I suspect some did not believe they would ever be released from their owners, even if America won the war. What's important to understand is that Africans were brave, courageous and not afraid to join the white men in the Revolutionary War."

"After enlisting, did they all fight?"

"No, they all did not fight. Some were foot soldiers, and others were spies, gravediggers, laborers and servants. Some did whatever they were asked to do."

William explained that the Continental Army had little choice but to enlist Africans because a significant number of the colonists supported the British. The Continental Congress and state legislatures were torn with the idea of enlisting Africans in the Revolutionary War, just as President Lincoln and legislators struggled with whether Africans should be allowed to fight in the war between the North and South.

"African soldiers fought, and died, alongside white soldiers in the Revolutionary War, but were not treated the same as the white soldiers. When they were not fighting, they were assigned to do some of the most menial work. Our soldiers were rarely promoted, and did not get the same treatment when they were sick as the white soldiers. Still, somehow, they kept going and continued to fight for what they believed in. The First Rhode Island regiment was the first all-Black unit in America. The 54th Massachusettes Volunteer Infantry Regiment was the first military unit composed of men of African descent to be raised in Massachusetts.

"Although African soldiers, free and enslaved, fought in the Lexington, Concord, and Bunker Hill battles, their contributions to Revolutionary War battles have been virtually ignored." William talked about African soldiers he heard his family refer to as brave, courageous, motivated men whose contributions should have been recognized and honored, such as Peter Salem, Barzillai Lew and Salem Poor.

"Anyone who has knowledge of those earlier wars should know that our people can be quite valuable to the Union Army. Our soldiers fought valiantly in those wars, and they will fight valiantly for the Union Army, given the opportunity. Immediately after the attack on Fort Sumter, free Negroes in Boston, New York, Philadelphia and other New England cities willingly offered their service to the Union Army. They have even offered to form and finance black regiments."

William went on to explain how several politicians interpreted the 1792 Militia Act to mean that Negro men could not enlist in the army. They apparently believed that wars could be won without any help from Negro soldiers. However, abolitionists argued that Negroes should be allowed to join the Union Army, because they would be fighting against slavery, and therefore fighting to gain their rights.

We finally arrived at the train station in Richmond. I was anxious to get to Fort Monroe so that William could learn more about the war and the Union Army, and we could get back to Boston as quickly as possible.

Shortly after we exited the train, we stepped onto a carriage headed to Fort Monroe. There were two Negro women, who appeared to be slaves, traveling with their mistresses, and two white men on the carriage as well. We sat behind the white men. They spoke in a loud tone and we learned that they were physicians who had recently finished medical school, and were on their way to Fort Monroe to care for soldiers. Their conversation was quite interesting.

"The U.S. Army medical department was clearly not prepared for this war," one of the physicians said. They both appeared to be around thirty years old. I specifically remember that one had red hair and one dark hair. The red-headed physician continued to speak. "Likewise, the death of our Surgeon General hasn't helped matters. Scurvy is quite common amongst the troops at Fort Monroe and elsewhere. It has been reported that berries may cure, or even prevent the disease, but I think we're going to need a whole lot more than berries when we get to Fort Monroe."

"The medical service budget was cut a few years ago, but surely our leaders must have foreseen that this war was coming," the dark-haired physician said. "It was inevitable in light of the growing hostility between the states. And, what does Dr. Lawson do? He slashes the medical services budget, and then dies, just after the war begins. Unfortunately, there is now a shortage of doctors and people trained in medicine to treat and care for the wounded.

"The good news is that many of us just out of medical school are eager to do what we can to help the Union. I cannot think of anything I'd rather do more than serve the Union. I see this as a duty, a responsibility that I am proud to accept. The wounded desperately need physicians. Robert informed me that he has been very busy working as an assistant surgeon at Fort Wagner, removing bullets, controlling hemorrhages, amputating limbs, administering pain medications and stitching lacerations."

"I agree with you, Bradley," the red-headed physician said. "It is my understanding that many of the makeshift hospitals located behind the front lines of battle lack adequate sanitation, including proper dressings for wounds. We both know that disease can be reduced with proper sanitation. Our new Surgeon General, Dr. Clement Finley, must immediately focus his attention on increasing the medical services budget. Our troops are certainly worthy of the best medical care."

The two young physicians seemed to be quite passionate about supporting the Union. William looked as if he wanted to join their conversation. Although my husband was not a physician, he had strong feelings about the war, the Surgeon General, President Lincoln and other politicians.

"It is my understanding that wounds are contaminated with flies as soon as the wounded are sent to the rear of the battle grounds," the dark-haired physician continued. "I've been told that maggots form in the wounds shortly after the wounds are dressed. Also, any clothing or bedding soiled with blood or pus can also be expected to get contaminated with maggots."

"Anesthetics are available, but for some reason many wounded soldiers don't have access to chloroform, morphine or opium. It is my understanding that lots of doctors and apprentices are treating wounds with alcohol because that's the only drug they can get their hands on.

"Just think of the number of wounded men who are left on the battlefields, whose bodies are covered with flies and maggots," the red-headed physician added. "The more I talk about the need for improved medical care and sanitation for our troops, the quicker I want to get to Fort Monroe to do everything in my power to help the Union Army. It is not enough for me to practice as a civilian physician, making lots of money and living comfortably, which is what my parents want for me. No, I have to do more. My heart is with the Union."

"I understand," the dark-haired physician said. "Fortunately, my family thinks I'm doing an honorable thing by serving our troops. They taught my two brothers, sister and me that we must do our part to support what we believe in. Well, I believe in God, and I believe in the Union."

"My mother worries that I could get sick or die from being exposed to some of the unsanitary living conditions in these forts," the red-headed physician said. "You know how mothers are, they worry about everything. She has learned that hundreds of soldiers in the Union Army have been exposed to, and died from, common diseases such as measles, chicken pox and mumps. Fortunately, I had all of that as a child.

"Still, it is important that something is done, immediately, about the unsanitary living conditions that promote the spread of diseases such as smallpox, typhoid, malaria, diarrhea and dysentery. I want to make a difference by pushing for more sanitary living conditions in the Union Army, as well as the Confederate Army. That, most of all, is what I hope to accomplish."

The two young physicians talked on about how to provide the best medical care for the soldiers, and about how to reduce sickness and disease. I was impressed with the depth of their concern for the soldiers and for the Union, and sensed that they were both from prominent families. They grew up in Pennsylvania, and could probably have been successful physicians there, or wherever they chose to live. Instead, they chose to sacrifice their comfort to help make the soldiers at Fort Monroe more comfortable.

After riding on the carriage for several hours, we entered the Hampton area. One of the physicians said, "Fort Monroe is just a short distance away." I sat up straight and took a deep breath. I was anxious. After the carriage finally stopped, William grabbed my hand and we got off. The two Negro women and their mistresses did not get off. Perhaps Fort Monroe was not their destination.

We walked behind the two physicians because we did not know where to go. I saw a white church, St. Mary's Church, as we approached the entrance to Fort Monroe. We walked a short distance and crossed a moat, which led to the entrance of the large, stone structure. The moated walls were bordered with brick buildings and large oak trees that appeared to be very old. A group of white men dressed alike in blue jackets and blue pants stood near a house inside the Fort. We later learned that the white, two-story wooden house, with columns and a balcony on the second level, was the commanding head-quarters for Major General Butler. I assumed the men were guarding the house.

The men warmly greeted the two physicians. It appeared that they were expecting their arrival. After talking for a few minutes, the two physicians were invited to come inside the white house. The men stared at us as if they thought we had come from another planet.

"What are you two looking for?" a tall, thin man asked. "I can direct you to the contraband camps. That's where the fugitive slaves stay."

"We are not fugitive slaves," William responded. "We are here to talk to General Butler." The group of men laughed aloud. William held my hand. He did not appear to be frightened.

"Now, tell me, why in the world would you two want to talk to General Butler?" the man asked. "Do you really think General Butler would take the time to talk to you?"

"I don't know, but I would certainly like the opportunity to ask him," William answered. "We have come a long way to speak with General Butler."

"Where did you come from – Georgia, South Carolina, North Carolina? You ran off from your owners, and now you expect refuge here at Fort Monroe. Well, let me tell you, your people are over yonder, in the contraband camps, and that's where you two need to go. We don't need your kind to help us win this war. General Butler should never have started giving y'all food and shelter. If you feed 'em, they'll come back, every time." The men laughed again. I wanted to get out of there, quickly, but William did not appear to be moved by anything they said.

"We came here to speak to General Butler. May we please speak with him?"

"General Butler isn't here, and if he was here, do you think the General would speak to two runaway slaves?" another man asked. "I think not. Now, be gone; get on over to the contraband camps, where you belong. There's plenty of menial work to be done around here. I hope you two are good workers."

We followed the tall man a somewhat lengthy distance to what the soldiers referred to as the *contraband camps*, where the Union Army housed fugitive slaves. It was heartbreaking to see our people crammed into small shanties and brush tents. Women were busy caring for their children, some of whom were hungry and sick. The *contraband camps* were a painful reminder of the small, overly crowded cabins that slaves lived in on Frank Wilmington's plantation. Clearly, many of the people were suffering and destitute. We walked around trying to decide how to help them.

A mother held her crying baby close, and said to me, "He's sick, I don't know how to hep him." I took the child and tried to comfort him. The baby stopped crying and looked at me, as if he felt better. I held him close and rubbed his head.

"Well, I guess I have the answer to my question," William said. "General Butler has definitely granted refuge to our people. Living conditions are not very good, but at least they are allowed to stay. I commend General Butler for that. I hope he understands that our people are valuable because we have skills, and our men can fight as well as the white men.

"Sarah, we have to help the refugees here. It is important for the Union to win the war, but more important than winning the war, we must help our people. These shanties are crowded and some of the people appear to be sick. They are probably not getting enough food or any medical care. We should stay here long enough to find ways to help."

Although I wanted to get away from Fort Monroe and get back to Boston, William was right. I had grown comfortable with my life in Boston, doing what I enjoyed. We had a healthy child, a home, food to eat, and were fortunate to be able to work and earn money. Our parents were in good health, and most of my prayers had been answered. As I looked around at the fugitive slaves, I simply could not leave without talking to them and finding ways to help them. Although William was focused on gathering information for the newspaper, we knew there was more important work to be done.

The baby fell asleep on my shoulder and his mother took him. I asked her if I could talk to her. She was a young woman, perhaps in her late twenties. She was very thin and was dressed in a worn, cotton dress. Her dark skin was clean and clear. Her eyes were sad, but kind. Her short, thick hair was neatly braided. She, William and I sat on the ground under a large tree. It was a very warm day in July 1862. Although I was hungry and thirsty from the long ride on the carriage, I wanted to talk to that woman.

"What is your name?" William asked. The young lady wiped her forehead with her dress sleeve. She held her sleeping baby close to her chest and fanned flies away from his head. I sensed that she was a very caring person. She kissed the baby's cheek and rocked him in her arms.

"My name's Lydia," she answered, in a soft tone. She appeared to be frightened. I understood, because William and I were strangers. I soon learned that she was not afraid of us, but afraid that her baby would die.

"Lydia, my name is Sarah, and this is my husband, William. We want to help you all. Tell me, are you hungry, and is your baby hungry?"

"Yes, we's hungry. We ain't got our rations for today. It's comin', but sometimes it come late."

"Do you get rations everyday?" Lydia looked away, and then down at her baby.

"We gits it mos days. Y'all mus be free." She stared at us as she spoke. "Y'all don't look lak no runaway slaves. We come a long way, but we got heah."

"Where did you come from?"

"Me, my husban an chile come from a farm in Ashland, Vaginia. All we eva wont wuz to be free. Den we heard dat if we could git to Fort Monroe, we would be free. It ain't all I 'pected, but bein' heah is sho betta dan whur we come from. Lord, we's thankful to be heah." Lydia wiped her eyes. She smiled and looked down at her baby. "My son will have a betta life. I jes pray dat dey wont send us back to dat farm."

"They are not going to send you back to Ashland," William said. "General Butler has made this area a refuge for fugitive slaves. There is no need for you to worry about that. Where is your husband?"

"Dey got him wukin ova at de hospital. He can do mos any kinda wuk. He's a mason and carpenta. I'm real proud of my husban, 'cause he got some skills."

"How do most of the women keep busy during the day?" I wanted to know how to help them.

"Mos of us clean an cook. Some wash clothes, an do whut chores dey tell us to do. We wuk hard heah, jes lak we did on mastah's farm, but I sho lak it heah betta. We's thankful to be heah. You heah to stay?"

"No, Lydia, we are not here to stay, but we are going to help you and the others," William said.

"You don't look lak no slaves." Lydia stared at my dress as she spoke. "Dat sho is a purty dress. Maybe one of dese days I will git to wear a dress lak dat. Slaves don't wear dresses lak dat. Y'all mus be free."

"We are free, and one day, Lydia, you and all of our people will be free," William said. "I believe the Union will win the war, and there will be no more slaves. We are going to help the Union win the war."

Lydia held her baby close and kissed his face. "Thar ain't gonna be no mo slaves!" she shouted. As we talked, Lydia seemed to get more relaxed and comfortable with us. "Whur you come from?"

"We live in Boston".

"I sho wish you could stay heah wit us. We sho need people lak you 'round dis camp. Some days it gits real hard for us, but we manege to keep goin'. Thar's so much I wish I could do."

"What do you wish you could do?" I asked.

"I wish I could read an write. I can cook, clean, wash clothes an care for de sick, but thar's so much more I wont to do. I wont my baby to have a betta life. Thar's lots of people heah at de camp, an we gotta learn to hep ourselves. We gonna be free one day, an we gotta learn to do mo so we can make it."

As I listened to Lydia, it was obvious that she was an intelligent woman who simply wanted a better life for her family. She was no different from me or any woman who wants the best for our families. She wanted to learn to read and write so she could teach her husband and child.

There was something about Lydia I really liked. She repeatedly talked about how thankful she was to be at Fort Monroe, and how God had blessed her and her family to get there without harm. She talked about their son, and how she wanted him to get an education. She also talked about how much she enjoyed singing, and how she sang every night in the camp to help lift everyone's spirit. William asked her to sing for us, and she did. Her voice was clear and pleasant. As she sang, her baby gazed at her and smiled.

*Showd along, childrun!*
*Showd along, childrun!*
*Heah de dyin' Lamb:*
*Oh! take your nets an follow me*
*For I died for you upon de tree!*
*Showd along, childrun!*
*Showd along, childrun!*
*Heah de dyin' Lamb.*

"Thank you, Lydia. You have a beautiful voice. We are leaving in a few days for Boston, but we will return to help all of you here at Fort Monroe," William said. "We came to talk to General Butler, but I've been told that he is not here. At least I know our people are not being turned away. Things will get better here, but it will take time."

"I know things will git betta. We sho need some hep 'round heah."

"How can we help you?" I wanted Lydia to tell me what she wanted us to do for them. She was intelligent enough to speak for her people, and to know what they needed most.

Although I did not want to come to Fort Monroe, I felt an obligation to help improve the lives of the people in those camps. Some were sick and appeared to be weak. Women and children were barefooted, dressed in worn, torn clothing. Many were very thin. It was definitely time to start teaching our people how to survive away from those plantations.

"You can hep us by teachin' us to read and write. Lord knows we gotta learn to hep ourselves if we gonna make it on our own."

"In time you will learn to read and write, and how to survive on your own," William said. "Our people are strong and eager to work. My wife has taught children and adults to read and write, but it's difficult to learn if you are sick and hungry."

"Y'all is good people," Lydia said, with tears in her eyes. "I'm so thankful that you heah wit us. Well, look, heah come my husban. He been wukin hard ova at de hospital. He's a good man." Lydia pointed to a man walking toward us. She ran to meet him and gave him a big hug.

"Samuel, I wont you to meet dese nice people from Boston. Dey's free, an dey wont to hep us".

Samuel was a tall, big man. He wiped his hands on his soiled clothing before reaching to shake our hands. His hands were rough and his handshake was firm. He appeared to be a kind person. He kissed his son's face. Lydia asked him about his work at the hospital. He wiped his face with the front of his shirt before answering.

"Thar's a lot of wuk to do to fix dose walls. We stopped wukin long nuff to eat, an den we started wuk agin. No tellin' when we will finish up at de hospetal. Thar's a man whose hepin me. He's probly de smartes man I eva met. Lord knows he know how to do evrythang. An, he don't mind hepin de rest of us." Samuel talked briefly about a fugitive slave who had recently come to Fort Monroe, and about his skills as a carpenter and a mason.

"Tis mighty nice to meet you good people. So, you come from Boston to hep us out heah in de camps. Well, dat's mighty kind of you. Whut I would give for me, Lydia an our son to see Boston, an all de otha places whur our people is free. Y'all look mighty nice." Samuel's smile was big and warm. He shook our hands again, and asked William to tell him about Boston.

William told them where Boston is located, and a few things about the people who live there. Samuel and Lydia appeared to be interested in every word he spoke. It was obvious that they were eager to learn more about other places. Samuel took his son from Lydia and embraced him.

"Dat's de life I wont for my son. He will live de way y'all an otha free people is livin'. We made it dis far, an I know thangs will git betta. We come heah to hep de Union, but dey won't let me fight longside de white men. But, we heah, an Lydia an me will do all we kin to hep de Union. We bleeve dat if de Union win de war, den our people will be free. Praise de Lord, we will be free!" Samuel embraced his family and they laughed as if they were the happiest people in the world.

"Tell me, Samuel, when did you get here?" William asked.

"Me an Lydia been heah at Fort Monroe a few weeks. We come from a farm in Ashland. Lydia wuz on dat farm mos of her life, but I been sold from mastah to mastah ova de years. Don't know much 'bout my famly, 'cause I ain't seen 'em in years. We wuz all seprated when I wuz jes a boy. I dun been through a lot of pain in my years, but still thankfal dat de Lord bless us to git dis far. We won't born free lak y'all wuz, but me an my famly will be free one day. I ain't got no idea whut it lak to be free, but I sho waitin' for dat day." They embraced each other and appeared to be very much in love.

"Y'all wuz born in Boston, an dat's a lot to be thankful for," Lydia said. "It ain't been easy bein' no slave, but Samuel an me neva stop talkin' 'bout runnin' from de farm, an livin' as free people. One day we will tell y'all whut it's lak to live as slaves. You jes don't know 'bout some of the things we been through." Lydia held her head down and wiped her eyes. Samuel put his arm around her and rubbed her shoulder. There was silence. I walked over to Lydia and gave her a hug.

"You don't have to tell me," I said, "because I was a slave. I ran away many years ago. I did not tell anyone about my plan because I could not talk about that on the plantation. I never stopped dreaming about being a free woman. Believe me, I know what you both have been through. I have lived that life." Samuel and Lydia looked at me as if they were in shock.

"*You* wuz a slave?" Lydia asked. "Why, you don't look lak me or de otha women 'round heah."

"Yes, I was a slave. My master took me along on a trip to New York with him and his daughters, and I took a chance and ran away. I was blessed to meet some very kind people who sheltered me, and taught me to read, write, to speak properly, and to do many wonderful things. They became my family.

"I want you and Samuel to know that anything is possible if you have faith, and never give up on what you believe. I have always believed that our people were born to be free, and I never stopped dreaming about having a better life. There were times I wanted to stop believing that good things would happen for me and my family, but I could not allow myself to give up. It just did not make sense to stop trying, to stop believing. Mammy and Pappy instilled that in me. That is the most valuable lesson I ever learned."

"Hard to bleeve you wuz a slave," Samuel said.

"Yes, I was. Mammy and I worked in the big house, and Pappy worked in the fields."

"What wuz yo mastah like?"

"He was like most slaveholders. I ran away from him, and he may still be looking for me. If I am caught, I will become his slave again, but I cannot worry about that. Now, I am focused on how to help our people, and how to help the Union win this war. The Union has to win this war."

"Wuz yo husban on dat plantation wit you?" Lydia asked. "Y'all sho don't look lak y'all wuz slaves."

"I have never been enslaved," William said. "I was born and raised in Boston and work for *The Liberator*, a newspaper. My family cares about helping our people. I came here to talk to General Butler, to confirm reports that runaway slaves are actually allowed to stay here."

"You's a fine man, Mistah William, an you's a fine lady, Miz Sarah," Samuel said. "It's mighty decent of y'all to come down heah an try to hep us out. I hope you kin come back soon. We sho need yo hep 'round heah."

"We're going to do everything we possibly can to help everyone here," William said. "It's clear that you need food and clothing. Tell me, what else can we send to help out".

"We need tools an seeds so we kin grow vegetables," Lydia said. "We know how to plant an grow vegetables, and we wanna feed ourselves. We can't be lookin' to de white man for evrythang."

"Evrythang will be jes fine," Samuel continued. "It's good to be heah at Fort Monroe, away from de mastah, an all de bad thangs he dun to us. Evryday I learn somethin' new. I wanna be jes lak dat new wuker who jes got heah. He's really smart. He can do carpentry wuk an lay bricks lak I ain't neva seen nobody do befo. An jes think, he been a slave all his life, jes lak me."

"Maybe he will teach you some of his skills, and you can learn to be an even better carpenter and mason than you already are," William added.

"Oh, he's already doin' dat. He told me to wotch him as he wuk, an dat's jes whut I been doin'. He's a mighty kind man. Even de white wukers been wotchin' him an tryin' to learn his skills. Dey ain't neva seen no slave dat smart."

Samuel continued to talk to William about his flight from Ashland to Fort Monroe. While they talked on, Lydia asked me to walk with her. During our short walk, she asked if I could send her and the other women some dresses when I returned to Boston. She explained that most of them had only one dress. They washed that dress at night, and it was usually dry by the next morning.

That's when I told her I was a dressmaker. Lydia's eyes lit up when I told her I made the dress I was wearing that day, and that I owned a dress shoppe and had sold many dresses. She and Samuel were eager to learn all they could, and we were determined to help them.

We left for Boston the next day and promised Samuel and Lydia we would return to help them. Although we did not get to meet and speak with General Butler, our trip to Fort Monroe was quite productive. It was clear that the reports were true; General Butler had established a shelter for runaway slaves, and it did not appear that any of them would be returned to their owners. Although living in those camps had its challenges, the refugees said it was certainly better than being enslaved on farms and plantations.

We left Fort Monroe with a sense of peace, knowing that fugitive slaves would not be forced to leave.

# CHAPTER 12

We had dinner with my parents and talked about our trip to Fort Monroe. "Do de people in de camp have nuff food?" Mammy asked. "They have to eat to stay strong." She was always concerned about others.

"Yes, they have food, but not enough. The soldiers ration the food, but with more refugees coming in, they will need more. In addition to food, they need clothing and supplies. They have begun to establish their very own communities. Some of the men have skills, such as carpentry and masonry. Most of the women cook and clean, but they need supplies. William will write articles in the paper to get people involved to support them."

"You an William done a good thing by goin' down thar to see 'bout our people," Pappy said. "God bless dat Genrel Butler."

"Now, tell me, how have you all been? Will has gotten heavier. My, he has grown in the short time we were gone. It was difficult being away from him." I held my son close.

"We been good," Pappy said. "Sarah, you got a good chile. He's jes like you when you was a baby." My parents proceeded to talk about their memories of me as a baby.

Callie, Naomi and Cora were busy working when I got to the shoppe the next morning. They managed the shoppe quite well.

"Tell us about Fort Monroe," Naomi said. "Is it true dat runaway slaves can stay thar?"

"Yes, that is true. General Butler has allowed them to stay." I told them about Lydia and Samuel.

"Our men should be allowed to fight for de Union," Callie said. "Dey wont to help de Union win. If de Union win, we all might be free, foreva!" We clapped our hands and screamed. The thought of being free was something to shout about.

I was glad to be back at the shoppe because those ladies were wonderful to work with. They showed me the dresses they were working on, and Callie told us about a man she met at church. It was a humorous story.

"I met Joe at church two Sundays ago. He said I am de woman for him, an dat he jes can't wait no longer. He said he been lookin' for a good woman to jump de broom with."

"Why can't he court you, like a man suppose to?" Naomi asked. "Why's he in such a hurry?"

"Maybe he heard about all dat money you makin' sellin' your pretty dresses," Cora said. "Joe ain't no fool." We laughed and Callie continued to talk.

"Joe said after we jump de broom, he's gonna take me to New Yok, whur I can sell more dresses an make more money. Joe said he will buy me as many sewin' machines as I need, 'cause women in New Yok like pretty dresses." Callie could tell a story and make you laugh, even if the story wasn't intended to be humorous. It was a pleasure to work with her.

"Where will you live in a big city like New Yok?" Cora asked. "Dose folks in New Yok are pretty fancy, you know."

"Joe said he's gonna get me a fancy house to live in. I guess he's countin' on all dat money I will make sellin' my dresses in de big city." We continued to laugh about Joe's empty promises to Callie. The shoppe was a second home to us. We had a great time working together and those three women were like sisters to me. I still love them.

We were still talking and laughing when someone knocked at the door. I was in the back room and came out to see who had stopped by.

"Sarah, I'm glad you're back. I have three parties to attend this month, and don't have a thing to wear." It was Helena Austin, one of my best customers.

Helena described the dresses she wanted for the parties, and I sketched them to her satisfaction. Although I was thankful to have good customers, I did not want to get too busy too soon, because I had to make dresses for the women and girls in the camps. My customers were very important, but I would not disappoint Lydia and the others.

William made plans to return to Fort Monroe that August to take supplies, and I planned to go back with him. I got busy making dresses so they would be ready when we left. Cora, Naomi and Callie graciously agreed to help with the dresses for Helena, which saved a lot of time.

We made dresses and William wrote articles for the newspaper about life in the contraband camps. He wanted the readers to know that, although fugitive slaves are not turned away, they need help. The response was overwhelming after people read this article:

> *"Each day more fugitive slaves fill the contraband camps at Fort Monroe and other forts. These camps are hastily erected almost anywhere the Union Army is stationed. The refugees, or "contrabands" as they are referred to, seek protection behind Union lines. Many come to the camps barefooted, sickly and weak from hunger, after long flights by boat, wagon and foot. Still, they are grateful to be there and most eager to work. Although the small shacks where the "contrabands" live are crowded, they don't spend their time complaining. Let us take pride in knowing that our enslaved brothers and sisters are not simply waiting for emancipation, and hoping for things to get better. Rather, they seize every opportunity to pursue their freedom, often risking their own lives and putting the lives of family members in jeopardy. Their presence in those camps is proof that they are taking matters into their own hands.*
>
> *The able-bodied men are eager to be armed to fight for the Union. However, because our men have not been allowed to serve as soldiers, many have been put to work and aid the Union cause on numerous fronts. They build roads, construct fortifications and dig trenches. Some serve as scouts, guides, blacksmiths and masons. Our women wash for the soldiers, cook, sew, and take care of the wounded. Let it be known that our people, the "contrabands" are making vital contributions to the Union cause. They are valuable, and have much to offer the Union. Unfortunately, our leaders doubt that men of African descent have the courage or the ability to make good soldiers. They are wrong.*

*The Second Confiscation Act (July 1862) authorizes President Lincoln to 'employ persons of African descent in any capacity as he may deem necessary and proper for the suppression of this rebellion.' The Militia Act, passed the same day, provides for the employment of our people in 'any military or naval service for which they may be found competent', and grants freedom to those so employed.*

*We are making progress, and must continue to support and help each other. Our brothers and sisters in those camps need clothing, tools, seed, utensils and other necessities. They are learning to care for themselves in their very own communities, away from the oppression of slaveowners. There will be a meeting at the African Methodist Episcopal Church on Hampshire Street at 7:00 p.m. on Thursday, July 25, 1862. Please come to learn more about how you can help the refugees; and how we, together, can help the Union defeat the Confederacy.*

*President Lincoln said at the beginning of this conflict between the Union and the Confederates that he had no intention of interfering with the 'peculiar institution'. Instead, the Union's goal has been to quash the Southern rebellion – those states which have chosen to secede from the Union, and restore the Union. Our people, in fleeing to Union lines, are making slavery a central issue of this war..."*

Stories of deprivation, over-crowded living conditions, and need in contraband camps touched the hearts of thousands of men and women throughout the North. Before long, "freedmen's aid societies" were organized in many towns and cities, especially in New England. These organizations were established to prepare former slaves for lives as free citizens by promoting education, and teaching them to live independently. We heard about similar organizations in Boston, New York, Philadelphia, Cincinnati, Baltimore, Hartford, Providence and other cities.

William and I were actively involved in some of those organizations. The members worked hard to help the refugees.

Clothing, tools, utensils, seed and other necessities were sent to the camps. Also, large sums of money were contributed for the relief and education of the freedmen.

That Thursday evening, over one hundred people, white people and people of African descent, came to the African Methodist Episcopal Church to learn how they could help. Teachers volunteered to send educational materials, and some were prepared to relocate to teach in the camps. William was one of the organizers of the Boston affiliation. It was great to see the enthusiasm of the people at the church that night. As expected, Aunt Clara, Mrs. Baker and their friends were present.

Teachers talked about the best methods of teaching children and adults to read and write. Others talked about teaching skills, such as carpentry, masonry, sewing and knitting. Some wealthy Bostonians offered to send money to buy supplies and food for the refugees. There were two white physicians present that evening, Dr. Gregory Abbott and Dr. David Chase. Dr. Chase discussed his concerns about disease.

"There are reports that many refugees in those makeshift villages of huts, or should I say, *shacks*, have fallen victim to smallpox, pneumonia and other diseases. That is to be expected where there is an absence of proper sanitation. I went to medical school to care for the sick, and that includes fugitive slaves seeking protection in contraband camps. It is not humane for people to live like that. I want to do my part to help these people. If they need supplies, I will send them. If there is a need for physicians, I will go."

Everyone applauded Dr. Chase. Some cried, and some promised to support the cause, no matter what it took to help improve living conditions in those camps. The white people seemed to be as touched and moved about the refugees as the Negroes. I had never seen more love and concern amongst Bostonians than I saw that evening.

William announced that we would return to Fort Monroe on August 10, 1862, and encouraged those who could go to join us. About twenty people signed up to go. Those who could not go pledged to give money and other supplies. It was a wonderful evening and we were excited, but there was a lot to do.

Although I had been reluctant to go with William to Fort Monroe earlier that year, I was anxious to return. Mammy knew I was busy, and she wanted to help with the sewing. We had a long conversation one day.

"Baby, it's mighty good of you an William to help our people in dose camps. We been blessed to get to Boston, but we can't forget our people. Pappy an me are real proud of you. I wont to help make dresses, so you will have lots of dresses to take to dose women an girls. You know how I love to sew." Mammy smiled an hugged me. She then looked away, and her smiled faded.

"Sarah, I been thinkin' about your brotha a lot lately. I can see his face so clear. I ain't said nuttin to your Pappy, but I feel like my boy is tryin' to speak to me. Lord, if I could jes hear what he's tryin' to say to me."

"Mammy, are you afraid?" I hugged her. I did not let her know that her words upset me.

"No, I ain't afraid, my chile. I been prayin' about my boy, an feel like de Lord is tryin' to tell me somethin'. I know evrythin' will be alright, Baby. I jes wont you to know dat Tom been on my mind more than eva. A day don't go by dat I don't pray for my childrun. I know de Lord will give me peace about my son. He took care of you, an He will take care of my son. I jes wont to see Tom again befo I leave dis world." She looked away and wiped her eyes.

"Mammy, tell me, are you sick? Why are you talking about leaving this world? I need to take care of you."

"Baby, I ain't sick, but you know we all gotta leave dis world one day." She smiled. "I jes wont to see my son before I go, dat's all. I ain't seen him since dat day in Atlanta, so long ago."

We talked on about fabric and designs for dresses for the refugees, but I could not stop thinking about what Mammy said about Tom. I prayed for my brother everyday, and believed that someday we would find each other. I had to believe that. I refused to believe that my brother was dead. For all I knew, he could have been somewhere in the North looking for us. I had to start searching for Tom, even if it meant going back to Atlanta, where we last saw him.

Mammy and I worked hard to finish the dresses, and we did. She helped pack the dresses in boxes, along with lots of supplies that people donated for us to take to the refugees. About fifteen people joined us, as we headed back to the camps at Fort Monroe in August 1862. We brought utensils, tools, seeds, clothing, books and anything we thought they might need. Dr. Chase honored his word and came along with us. He brought medical supplies and was prepared to teach the refugees about sanitation.

Two teachers, Laura Smith and Angela Gannett, came along and brought materials to begin teaching children and adults how to read and write. We were amazed at how crowded the camps had gotten since our last visit. More shanties had been built, and the refugees were working together to help each other.

Samuel and Lydia were as excited to see us as we were to see them. They were clearly making the most of living in the camp. Like any proud mother, Lydia talked about her baby and how much he had grown.

"Sarah, he's tryin' to talk to me. Samuel an I already decided dat our baby will be a teacha someday, an he will be a good teacha, too." They laughed and talked about their son. Samuel then told us about how he and a group of men and boys worked everyday to build more shanties, because refugees continued to pour into Fort Monroe. They had finished working by the time we arrived, and had already left for the day.

"It's good to know that everyone is working to help each other. We brought some people who want to help you. Let me introduce you to Dr. Chase. Dr. Chase is a physician, and he is here to care for the sick, and to teach how to help prevent sickness and disease as much as possible." Dr. Chase shook Samuel and Lydia's hands, and said he was there to help as many people as he could.

William introduced the others who came with us, and asked them to explain to Samuel and Lydia how they could help. The teachers talked about how they planned to teach the children and adults to read and write. The men talked about the tools they brought and what they would be used for.

It was late, and everyone was tired from traveling, so we decided to rest and show them the supplies we brought the next morning. William and I stayed in one of the shacks, while Dr. Chase and the others stayed with relatives in the Hampton area.

We brought quilts because many of them slept on the ground. Needless to say, living in those camps was difficult. William and I made the most of it, but we were not there to stay. Unfortunately, those small shacks were the only "homes" for the refugees.

The next morning Lydia came to see us after Samuel left to go to work. I showed her the dresses Mammy and I made for her and the other women. She was very happy and grateful to get the dresses. She had two dresses, but most of the women had only one.

"We's thankful, Sarah, so thankful to you an yo Mammy. I kin sew a little, but I ain't neva made nuttin lak dis. Maybe one day you kin teach me to sew dresses lak dis."

"Lydia, I would love to teach you to sew and make your own dresses. It is not difficult. Mammy taught me to sew when I was a young girl. I love to sew and to teach. One day you, Samuel and the others will be free, and you will be able to do the things you have always wanted to do."

"Do you really bleeve dat, Sarah?" She was so excited.

"Yes, Lydia, I really believe that. Things are getting better for us. We just have to keep our faith."

Lydia told me she was well, but that some days were difficult for her and the others. She smiled as she spoke, but I could hear the pain in her voice and see it in her eyes. She was trying to be strong, but I knew she was hurting. I held her baby so she could wipe the tears she had been trying to hold back.

"Talk to me, Lydia. I want to hear about what you are going through. I am here to help, and one way to help is for us to take the time to listen to each other."

"Sarah, I ain't one to complain, 'cause Lord knows we grateful to be heah at Fort Monroe, but sometimes it's hard. I don't mind wukin hard, 'cause I been wukin all my life, but some days it jes ain't nuff food for evrybody. Dis camp gits more crowded evryday, an de men wukin hard to build mo shacks, but it ain't easy livin' lak dis. People is sick an dyin' evryday. We need hep. Thank de Lord you, William an de others is heah to hep us." Lydia tried to smile through her tears.

"Lydia, William and I like you and Samuel a lot. You are good, decent, hard- working people. We have liked you from the moment we met you. Would you and Samuel like to come to

Boston with us? We have discussed this, and William asked me to mention it to you. Samuel has good skills, and we will help him find work. I can teach you to sew and you can work in my dress shoppe. Why, you would love Cora, Callie and Naomi. They escaped slavery and came to Boston. I met them at my church and we work together everyday."

Lydia looked at me as if she could not believe what she was hearing. William had already talked to some men about hiring Samuel, and Mammy would have been thrilled to care for their baby. Samuel and Lydia were special people, and there was so much we wanted to do for them.

"Leave dis camp, an come to Boston wit you. Why, we don't know nuttin 'bout Boston. Me an Samuel is slaves; we been wukin on plantations all our lives. We ain't no fancy people lak you an William." She was cryin' and smiling.

"I was just like you, Lydia, but once I got to New York, God blessed me to meet good people who taught me to read and write, and to speak grammatically correct English. There is no reason why you and Samuel cannot learn as well. We will be there to help you."

"Sarah, I gotta talk to Samuel. I gotta tell him evrythin' you jes said to me. When is y'all leavin' to go back to Boston?"

"William has to get back to the newspaper, and I have to get back to the shoppe, so we will be leaving tomorrow, but Dr. Chase and some of the others are going to stay here longer. Talk to Samuel and let us know if you can come back with us."

"Sarah, you an William is good people. Now, let me git you somethin' to eat. I know you mus be hungry."

Lydia went back to her shack, and I got busy organizing the dresses to distribute to the women and girls. There was also clothing for men and boys that Mrs. Baker, Aunt Clara and others sent. I saw William talking to Dr. Chase. They had supplies scattered on the ground and were preparing to work with the refugees.

Lydia and I helped organize the children into groups so the teachers could begin working with them. At first things were pretty chaotic in the camps. The sweltering August heat did not help matters, but by the end of the day everyone had been assigned to a group.

I guess we must have helped about a hundred refugees get organized that day. Lydia said there were many more working outside the camps. Several men with skills had been assigned to make repairs around the Fort. Women also worked outside the camps, cooking, cleaning, washing clothes or caring for wounded soldiers. We only got to meet about half of the refugees during our visits to Fort Monroe.

Dr. Chase spent the next day treating the sick. He said some suffered from tuberculosis, yellow fever and malaria. He used a tent as a makeshift hospital. I heard screams as he gave injections. Most of the refugees had never had any form of medical treatment. Unfortunately, many were beyond help, and their lives could not be saved. Still, Dr. Chase worked on, tirelessly. He was a real trooper.

Women and girls sat patiently as they were taught how to sew and cook. Some asked questions, but most of them listened without saying a word. The elderly women cared for the babies. It was good to see our people organized, and being educated on how to meet their own needs. There was no better lesson to learn than how to help yourself.

We brought seeds to the camps because most of the refugees knew how to maintain gardens. Our people came from agricultural cultures in Africa and knew how to grow crops. Some slaves were allowed to keep chickens and hogs. It would have been difficult to survive on the limited rations provided to us by the slaveholders.

Some of the volunteers planned to stay until the end of August. Lydia was quite concerned that the groups would not be as organized, and that the lessons would not continue to proceed as well when more refugees entered the camps. Then she came up with a wonderful idea. She and Samuel were respected in the camps, and they had a feeling about which refugees would follow through on their assignments. She and two other women and men chose leaders for each group. The leaders would be responsible for seeing that everyone attended the groups they were assigned to.

The next day William and I prepared to leave Fort Monroe, although there was still much work to be done. Lydia came to see us before we left to tell us that they would not be coming to Boston with us. Samuel had already left to go to work, and we did not spend much time with him because he was busy.

"It wuz mighty kind of y'all to ax me an Samuel to come back wit y'all to Boston," Lydia said. "We wont to git thar one day, but right now we gotta stay heah to hep our brothas an sistas. Dey need us heah in de camps. Samuel an me kin hep dem stay strong, an hep dem do whut dey need to do. Maybe when things git betta heah, we kin come to Boston wit y'all. Please tell me dat y'all will be back heah soon. Me an Samuel will miss y'all so much."

"Lydia, don't worry, we will be back soon," William said. "This is only the beginning. There are lots of people in Boston who want to help you all. Some could not come this time, but they will come. The people who want to come to help have skills to share with everyone. Things are getting better. It's difficult now because of the crowded, poor living conditions; but, it will get better."

It bothered me that most of the children were without adult supervision. Sadly, most slave children did not live with their natural parents because families were separated. Many on the plantations did not have mothers to teach and guide them. We would have to find a way to help the children.

"I almost forgot to mention that one of the volunteers is a minister, and he will stay for some time. He will come to the camps to help during the week, and on Sundays he will come to preach and for Bible study."

"I want to heah him, 'cause I got so much to be thankful for,"Lydia said. "De Lord sho been good to us. Samuel is real sorry dat he did not git to spen time wit y'all dis time, but he an de othas been real busy wukin at de hospital. Thar wuz somebody he wonted y'all to meet. Next time I will see to it dat y'all git to meet him. He is a lot lak you, William."

"If you and Samuel like him, I know I will." We gave Lydia a big hug and said goodbye to those who came down with us. We told them we would be back with more volunteers and supplies.

"Did de women an girls like dose dresses we made for dem?" Mammy asked, when we got home.

"Yes, Mammy, they really like the dresses, and they asked me to thank you. There are far more refugees now than there were when we first went, and they are making progress. Of course, it's going to take time for them to get organized and learn to meet their own needs. The good news is that the camps are slowly becoming self-sufficient communities."

"The volunteers who went with us are quite enthusiastic about teaching the refugees," William added. "Many of them plan to stay on with relatives in the area and continue to help. Things are definitely getting better."

"We met the most wonderful people who live in one of the larger camps. They are married and have a lovely son. Their names are Lydia and Samuel. I believe they will come to Boston soon, but for now they want to stay to help the children and adults get organized. Samuel is a carpenter and a mason, and Lydia helps with teaching the girls to cook and anything else that needs to be done."

"We hear dat a lot of men are gittin killed because of dat war," Pappy said. "It's a mighty sad thing, men killin' men."

"It is sad, but I believe if the Union wins, our people will be free." William went on to explain why the Union was fighting the Confederates, and how our men wanted to help the Union win the war, but were not allowed to enlist as soldiers. My parents said they understood, but made it very clear that they believed it was wrong for men to kill men.

William came home from work the following evening with some exciting news. "General Butler has left Fort Monroe and moved on to New Orleans. He has incorporated into Union forces units composed of free Negro soldiers. It is speculated that he will soon begin recruiting both free Negroes and fugitive slaves for additional regiments."

Although many Bostonians thought General Butler was an advocate for freedom for slaves, one of our abolitionist friends, Richard Ware, explained that General Butler was primarily interested in victory for the Union.

"I'm not sure General Butler is an abolitionist," he said, while eating dinner at our home one evening. "He is a very intelligent man who has been recognized as a fine leader at Fort Monroe.

However, General Butler realized that it made no sense to honor the Fugitive Slave Law, and return those three runaway slaves to their owner." Richard was referring to Shepard Mallory, Frank Baker and James Townsend, three enslaved field hands on a farm near Hampton, Virginia, who were taken by their master to Sewell's Point and put to work building an artillery battery for the Confederacy.

"Those brave men soon realized that their owner had plans to take them to North Carolina, which would separate them from their families, and put them to work for the Confederate Army. Instead of going with their master to support the Confederate war effort, those intelligent men took a risk and escaped to the Union camp at Fort Monroe, where they managed to persuade the Union soldiers to offer them refuge.

"General Butler is no fool," Richard continued. "He learned that those three men had helped to construct a Confederate battery that threatened Fort Monroe. It did not make sense to him to send them back to strengthen that effort. Instead, he came up with a politically clever idea. Virginia had seceded from the Union, and Butler argued that he no longer had a constitutional obligation to return the slaves. Rather, in compliance with military law governing war between nations, Butler seized the three slaves as "*contraband of war.*"

"Regardless of his intent," I said, "General Butler's decision has been a blessing to our people and I am grateful to him. Because of him, fugitive slaves have found, and continue to find, refuge at Fort Monroe and other contraband camps. Although they are not free, once they arrive at Fort Monroe, fugitive slaves will have the opportunity to be self-sufficient and learn to care for each other. That is so much better than being enslaved."

William and Richard talked on about Fort Monroe, General Butler and other political matters, but I was focused on finding my brother. Tom had been on my mind more than ever in the past few weeks. I sensed that he was somewhere close, and that I would find him if I searched hard enough. My brother was strong, and I believed with all my heart that he was alive and well.

We talked about ways to find my brother after Richard left our home that night. We decided to put a notice in the paper, and to offer a reward to anyone who had knowledge of Toms's whereabouts. The notice read:

*INFORMATION WANTED on a tall Negro man, about thirty years old, with a scar on his right cheek. He was last seen in Atlanta about fourteen years ago, working as a carpenter and bricklayer. Please contact The Liberator in Boston, Massachusettes. There is a $200.00 reward for any information about Tom Johnson.*

Within a few days, someone came to William's office with news that they knew of Tom's whereabouts! I remember screaming and crying when William rushed over to the shoppe to tell me the good news. I was cutting fabric, but was too excited to finish, so I left the shoppe that morning to calm down. The man came to *The Liberator* and told William where we could find Tom. He then asked for his reward. I was prepared to give him the money, but William told the man he had to take us to Tom before he could receive the reward. The man said Tom was building a store not too far from the *The Liberator*, and told us how to get there. The man said he had worked with Tom a few weeks ago, and left that job for another job, but that Tom decided to stay to finish the store.

"Can you describe Tom?" William asked.

"He look lak mos of us. I jes rememba him talkin' 'bout tryin' to find his famly."

"My brother is tall and has a deep dimple in his left cheek. He has a big, warm smile, and he looks like our Pappy. He is so handsome." The man looked at me, but said nothing.

My heart raced with excitement as William and I rode with the man in our carriage. We decided not to tell my parents until we met with Tom and had a chance to talk with him. There was so much I had to say to my brother before taking him to see our parents. I had not been that excited since I reunited with my parents two years earlier. After years of waiting and praying, my family would finally be together.

When we arrived at that construction site, there were several Negro men working. I jumped down from the carriage and ran toward them, screaming, "Tom, Tom, it's me, Sarah!" William ran after me, but the man who had directed us to that site simply stood in silence, scratching his head. I waited for my brother to come running, screaming my name. I saw a man drop his hammer and start walking toward me, with his arms wide open, as if he wanted to embrace me. As he got closer, I stepped away from him and grabbed William's hand.

"Sarah, is this your brother?"

Tears rolled down my face. "I have never seen this man in my life! Please, get him away from me!"

"My sista, my sista!" that stranger shouted. He continued to walk toward me. "At las, we's togetha as a famly."

"Don't you touch my wife. She is not your sister, and you know it!"

"She sho look lak my sista." The man who brought us to the site looked down, as if he did not know what was going on. William asked him why he brought us there.

"Well, dis man is tall, an he gotta purty nice smile. I think he even gotta a dimple or two, but sometimes you can't see it. People change ova de years. Dis might be her brotha, an she jes don't know it. She ain't seen her brotha in years. Kin I still git my money?"

"No, you don't get any money," William said. He grabbed my hand and we walked back to the carriage. I was quite upset. William said I needed to calm down and not get too anxious about finding Tom. He said lots of people would probably respond to the notice in the paper, because lots of fugitive slaves were searching for their families, and we would find Tom.

The following week several people responded to the notice, but none of them was my brother. I was hurt, disappointed and discouraged. Although many seemed to be sincere, it appeared that some who responded were only interested in the reward.

I started asking around about my brother at different construction sites because, if Tom was in Boston, he would probably be working hard as a carpenter or bricklayer. He told us in Atlanta that he loved his work and would always do that type of work. I asked our close friends to let me know if they knew of anyone who might have information about my brother. I believed

Tom was alive and well, and we would soon be reunited. I had to hold on to that thought.

# CHAPTER 13

With Andrew off to battle, I continued to work at the hospital, but did not talk a lot, except when one of the soldiers asked a question or told me what needed to be done. I did not see Samuel during the day because he was assigned to another building. We still got together after work to teach other refugees.

The time I spent teaching was the best part of my day. Caleb faithfully came each day to learn more about carpentry. He still had that sparkle in his eyes. He stayed each day after everyone left to ask questions and to handle different tools. I enjoyed working with him as much as he enjoyed learning. Caleb stayed around until I told him he had to get back to his shack. He told me how much he enjoyed learning about new things and he was doing quite well. He was pleased that he had not hit his fingers with the hammer in two days.

"Tom, I lak learnin', 'cause you an Samuel is good teachers. I wont to see whut you do at de hospital. Kin I come to wuk wit you? I wont be no trouble, promise."

"Caleb, you's a chile, an you could get hurt at de hospital. Samuel an I will keep teachin' you, an you will learn a lot more. You gotta be patient."

"Please let me come wit you, Tom. I ain't no trouble, an I will do whut you tell me to do, promise."

Caleb was a lonely, young boy, who clearly missed his mother very much. What happened to Caleb was very common amongst our people. Children were separated from their parents everyday because of slavery. Families were often split up because the parents, and, or the children were sold to other slaveholders. Although Caleb was very interested in learning to be a carpenter, I sensed that he stayed around after everyone left because he wanted, and needed, a father.

I took Caleb back to Miz Flora and she thanked us for working with him. She said there were few men in the camp who had skills, other than working as field hands, and that Samuel and I were good for the men and boys in the camp. She then talked about Caleb.

"Tom, I wont you to know how much you mean to dis boy. His mammy, Lily, wuz lak a daughter to me. I luv Caleb, but I can't do for him whut you kin do for him. I's sixty-five years old, an I ain't well. Caleb talk 'bout you evryday, Tom, an he wont to be jes lak you. Evryday he tell me 'bout all de good things you an Samuel done taught him. Now, he wont to know if he kin go to wuk wit you at de hospitel. I told him he can't go, cuz he would be in de way. I jes wont to let you know."

"Miz Flora, I understan whut you sayin'. I told Caleb he can't come to wuk wit me. He could get hurt, an childrun don't belong 'round thar. I will continue to teach an wuk wit him heah at de camp." I patted Caleb on his shoulder and headed back to my shack for the night.

I hurt for Caleb because his mother was dead and he knew nothing about his father. His wound was fresh, since his mother died trying to get to Fort Monroe. Miz Flora loved Caleb, but she did not know how to help him. Caleb was among many children in the camp who did not have a parent present. The women in the camp cared for the children as best they could, but there was nothing like having your very own parents in your life. I was a grown man, and thought about my parents and sister everyday. I would have given anything to have known that they were alive and well.

The next day Samuel mentioned that Lydia had been assigned to care for sick and wounded soldiers. He said Lydia did not want to leave the camp because of their son, but she had no choice. Miz Flora and some of the older women would have to care for their son during the day. Samuel also mentioned that he had seen Caleb crying that morning.

"Why wuz he cryin'? Do you think he's sick or somethin' is wrong?"

"Don't know," Samuel said. "He wuz alone. I had to git to wuk, an thar wuz no time to talk to him."

"I will talk to him afta wuk. Caleb wuz probly cryin' 'cause he wont to come to wuk wit us."

"We can't have no childrun 'round whur we wuk. Much too dangrous for little ones."

That evening after work, as usual, Caleb was the first to get to us for carpentry lessons. We planned to teach the men and boys how to repair broken furniture that day and brought two broken chairs to the camp. Caleb jumped up to assist us. He did a good job and we told . him.

"I told y'all I kin wuk at de hospital wit y'all," he said. "Let me hep y'all build new chairs." As usual, I walked Caleb back to Miz Flora's shack that evening. I asked him if he was sick, or if anything was wrong, but did not tell him that Samuel saw him crying that morning.

"I ain't sick. I miss Mammy. She fell in dat water, an got sick, an now she dead." Caleb walked away crying. I could not leave him that night without saying something to try to lift his spirit, so I had a long talk with him.

"Caleb, I know how you feel."

"No, you don't, 'cause yo mammy ain't dead. I so scared, Tom. I wont Mammy to come back an be heah wit me." I let him cry. After he wiped his eyes with his shirt and calmed down, I picked him up and sat him on my knee. There were some things Caleb had to understand, and that night was the night to teach him.

"Caleb, I wuz once your age, an lived wit my parents an sister. Den, one day, dey wuz all gone, an, lak you, I wuz alone an hurt. I cried a lot, but cryin' didn't bring dem back to me. I had to go on wit out de people I luv mos in dis world. It wuz hard, Caleb, but I made it. I's a man now, an still miss my famly, an still think 'bout dem, but I had to go on wit my life."

"Whur's yo mammy?" He looked directly at me with his big, innocent, teary eyes.

"I don't know whur my famly is. Dey could still be in Missippi on dat plantation, or dey mighta been sold to anotha slaveholder. But, I's gonna find all of dem, an we gonna be a famly agin."

"Dey ain't dead?" I did not answer Caleb immediately. I sometimes wondered if my parents and sister were still alive, but forced myself to believe that one day we would be the close, loving family we had once been.

"Caleb, I bleeve dey's alive an well."

"I know Mammy is dead, 'cause I seen her when dey took her out de water. Her eyes wuz closed, an she said nuttin to me." Caleb started to cry again. When he calmed down, I talked to him about one of the most valuable lessons I learned over the years – those difficult times in my life made me strong.

"Caleb, when things hurt us an make us sad, in time, dose same things kin make us strong. You young now, an I don't 'pect you to undastan evrythin' I's sayin' to you; but, one day you will undastan betta, trus me."

"I trus you, Tom. You an Miz Flora de only people I do trus." Caleb hugged me that night. I rubbed his head and told him it was time for him to get some sleep. As I walked away, he called my name.

"Tom, I don't wont you to eva leave me." I did not know how to respond, but had to say something.

"I will teach you evrythin' I know, Caleb. One day you will be a fine young man, an a good carpenter. Now, git some rest for tomorrow."

He hugged me, and had the biggest, brightest smile I had ever seen on his face. Somehow, I knew I said the right words to him that evening. I also realized I wanted him to be a part of my life.

Refugees poured into the camps. The crowded, unsanitary conditions were more than Samuel and I could take, so we decided to build more shanties. The only free time we had to build shanties was after we finished our assigned work at the Fort. We were tired after working long hours, but that was no excuse not to help the others.

Building more shanties was the perfect opportunity to demonstrate to the men and boys the carpentry skills we had been teaching them. We had talked about measuring, cutting and shaping wood, and finally they would have the opportunity to actually do those things. I was not surprised that Caleb jumped up to help. He was young and I did not want him cutting wood, but Caleb was certainly old enough, and intelligent enough, to measure wood and hammer nails. He could not hide his excitement.

"Tom, I told you I could wuk wit you, an dat I ain't no trouble. See, I kin do a good job for you an Samuel. How many shanties kin we build? I lak doin' dis wuk."

"We will build as many as we kin, 'til we ain't got no mo wood. Don't worry, Caleb, thar's plenty of wuk for you to do."

Lots of refugees helped and that was wonderful because this was an opportunity to help each other. We were slowly learning how to take care of ourselves. Samuel and I created an opportunity for our people to learn, and a means for them to keep busy and to be productive. We were proud of this.

I kept busy working at the hospital and in the camps, but could not stop thinking about Hannah. I wondered if she was still on John Mundy's plantation, and if she was well. I wondered if she still loved me as much as I loved her. I also wondered if she had received the letter I wrote to her. Andrew took the letter and said he would try to find a way to get it to her, but he left to go to battle and we never discussed it again.

As the days passed, Caleb and I grew close. He looked up to me, and I was proud to be a part of his life. He asked questions that suggested he had plans for his life, such as, "How much money do carpenters make?" He was an amazing young boy. I worked with and talked to him everyday. I had to be strong because he watched me closely. He told Miz Flora he wanted to be just like me. I tried to be a good example for him and the other young men in the camps.

"Whur do you think Mammy is?" he asked one evening. I did not know a lot about the Bible, but went to church when I was a slave on John Mundy's plantation. The preacher talked about a place called heaven, where good people went when they died. I told Caleb his mother was probably in heaven, with all the other good people.

147

"Do you think dey treatin' her good? Mammy wuz a good person, an she should be livin'. Do you think God wuz mad wit her, Tom? Is dat why she died?"

"Caleb, I'm sure your mammy wuz a good person, an God is a good God. I think de people in heaven is happy, an dey ain't sick no mo. Your mammy wuz sick, an I know you did not wont her to be sick."

"One day I wont to go to heaven; but, not today. I got too many shanties to build." I stopped cutting wood and stared at him. That young boy had *worked* his way into my heart. I felt something for Caleb I had never felt before. I loved my family and Hannah dearly, but that day I realized I also loved Caleb. He gave me another reason to be thankful; to believe there is good in this life, despite the pain and suffering I had endured.

"Tell me 'bout yo mammy, Tom. Kin you rememba her?"

"Yes, I rememba Mammy quite well. She is a very kind person, an she always had a smile on her face. She could read a few words, an she read de Bible to me an my sister. She taught us dat we wuz special, no matta whut anybody said 'bout us. She also taught us to luv, an not to hate people. Lak your mammy, Caleb, my mammy is a good person."

"Tell me 'bout your Pappy, Tom. I don't know my Pappy."

"Pappy wuked hard in dose cotton fields on de plantation. He taught me how to build a chair, an dat wuz my first lessin on how to be a good carpenter. He an Mammy knew how to create things wit thar hands, an dey taught us a lot. Mammy taught my sister how to sew, an Pappy taught me to be a carpenter. I got good parents, Caleb."

"Do you wont childrun?" He stopped hammering and looked directly at me. He waited patiently for my answer.

"Yes, Caleb, wheneva I kin jump de broom wit Hannah, I wont childrun. I will teach dem evrythin' I know."

"Will you teach *me* evrythin' you know, Tom?"

"Yes, Caleb, I will teach you evrythin' I know." He smiled and continued hammering. He clearly liked my answer.

As the the camps became more crowded, sickness and death increased. There was much suffering and neglect. The dead were carried out by wagon and thrown into a trench. Although some refugees had worn quilts to sleep on, many slept on the ground.

I heard soldiers say some Union generals would not interfere with slavery, and consequently, they did not offer refuge to fugitive slaves. They talked about how the Union Army, as it pushed further into the South, discovered large, once profitable, plantations abandoned by their Confederate owners because the slaves had run off to Union lines for protection. There was great concern within the Union about what to do with the increasing number of refugees. When the conflict began, the Union's aim had been to quash the Southern rebellion. Months later, it seemed as if everyone was focused on the issue of slavery, and what to do about it.

Despite all the challenges they faced, the refugees found ways to entertain themselves. They sang, danced and ate together. They also shared stories about the farms and plantations they had lived on and escaped from. Everyone seemed to enjoy listening to one man, known as "the storyteller". He had been at the camp only a few days. As we taught the men and boys, and built more shanties, others gathered around "the storyteller". He seemingly had their undivided attention as he told one story after another.

One evening Samuel and I stopped to listen to "the storyteller" after we finished for the day. He was a large man, well over six feet tall, who spoke in a deep tone. If nothing else, his size captured my attention. He moved his large hands and arms as he spoke, as if trying to demonstrate what he was saying. His dark eyes were intense, as he looked from person to person. He appeared to be around thirty-five years old. His name was Big Willie. Big Willie clearly had a gift – the ability to tell a story.

That evening Big Willie talked about the scars he received from beatings he got from an overseer in New Orleans. He showed off his scars as if he was proud of each one. He talked on about his life on the plantation, and how he was later sold to a slaveholder in Georgia. He said slaveholders paid lots of money for him because of his size.

He said he was strong enough to pull wagons. He then said something that caught my attention. In fact, his words disturbed me.

Big Willie said he once lived on a farm in Savannah, and his master hired him out to do work on nearby farms and plantations. He talked on, and mentioned the name John Mundy; the John Mundy who had once been my master. I knew it was the same John Mundy because Big Willie described the plantation, and his description matched that of the plantation where I spent years of my life. I could still visualize the big house John Mundy and his family lived in, surrounded by large fields of cotton and corn, with slave quarters in the back, and horses grazing in the grass.

Big Willie said he was a blacksmith by trade, and was hired out to work with John Mundy's horses. That was one of the last places he worked before he decided to run. He then mentioned that there was a young woman on John Mundy's plantation, and he wished he could have brought her along with him to Fort Monroe. Everyone was quite amused with his story, except me. I listened intently as Big Willie described the young woman as being the "purtiest woman I eva seen."

"She got de purtiest brown eyes," he continued. "She is a tiny woman, wit a bright smile an white teeth. Her voice wuz sof an kind. She wuked in de big house for John Mundy. I reckon her purty brown skin wuz as sof as de cotton in de fields. She de kind of woman I dream 'bout jumping de broom wit one day. I shoulda brought her wit me. I might even run back an git her one day."

Big Willie talked on about the young woman. Clearly, just the sight of her captured his attention. As he talked on about her, I had no doubt in my mind that he was speaking of Hannah; my Hannah. Everything he said about her was true. Hannah captured my heart the moment I saw her. Like Big Willie, I had never seen a more beautiful woman. Everything about Hannah was lovely, inside and out.

It was difficult to listen to another man speak about the woman I loved. I wanted to strike Big Willie for speaking so affectionately about the woman I planned to jump the broom with, but he did not know I was in love with Hannah. He did not even know me, or that I knew her. I walked away because I could not stand to listen to any more of Big Willie's talk about Hannah.

That night I thought about Hannah and what Big Willie said about her. I decided to ask him exactly when did he see her on John Mundy's plantation. Perhaps he could let me know if she was well. The next day, as usual, Big Willie had a crowd gathered around him listening to more of his stories. I waited until he finished talking, which was a long time, then approached him. I was reluctant to even speak to that man, but thought he could help me.

"You got a minute?" Big Willie was headed toward his shack. He turned around and walked toward me.

"Yeah, do you wont to heah anotha story? I got plenty to tell. Evryone of dese scars got a story behind it. See, I got dis one when a horse kick me, back on a farm in…"

"I wont to know more 'bout dat purty woman you wuz talkin' 'bout, on John Mundy plantation. Tell me, when did you see dis woman?"

"Why, I seen dat purty woman 'bout a month ago, I guess. It ain't been long, 'cause I jes got heah at Fort Monroe. She a purty little thing; de kind of woman I wanna jump de broom wit."

"Do you know her name?"

"Yeah, I bleeve her name is Hattie, or somethin' lak dat," Big Willie said. "I ain't good wit names, but I don't forgit no purty face."

I had no doubt that he was talking about *my* Hannah. Although he did not pronounce name her correctly, it was close enough to know who he was talking about. He proceeded to talk on about Hannah, but I cut him short. I had no interest in hearing any more of what he thought about her.

"Is she well?" I had to know that Hannah was well.

"She sho look lak she was well," he said. "I tried to talk to her, but she seem to be a quiet woman. People 'round de plantation say she is a good woman, an she don't botha nobody. Maybe one day I kin git back to dat plantation, an take her 'way from dat John Mundy. Hattie need to be heah, at Fort Monroe, wit de rest of us, 'cause…"

Big Willie talked on, but I walked away. I heard exactly what I needed to hear – Hannah was well. That night I felt a sense of peace I had not felt since I left Hannah. I fell asleep with one thought on my mind – how to get her away from that plantation.

# CHAPTER 14

By the summer of 1862, the tide of the war drastically changed as northern troops under General Grant moved further into the South, especially Tennessee. Contraband camps grew and more volunteers and aids were needed.

There were days I wanted to leave Fort Monroe, because the living conditions were almost too much to endure. Unfortunately, the fugitive slaves who came were not strong and healthy. I watched several suffer and die. The sight of it sickened me. Still, I stayed to do as much as possible to make things better.

Although many days were dark, there were rays of sunshine and hope. The volunteers were committed to teaching us. Most of them stayed with family and friends in the area, and came to the camps each day to work with the men, women and children.

Samuel and I continued to work hard, making repairs around the Fort. Fortunately, Samuel, Lydia and I were amongst the refugees who had strong, healthy minds and bodies. Samuel and Lydia were like family. Lydia, in some ways, became a sister to me and Samuel, a brother. I had only been that close to one other person, excluding Hannah and my family, and that was Joe. I often wondered if he was still on John Mundy's plantation, and suspected he was. Joe played it safe and did not take risks. I guessed that Joe would probably be enslaved until our people were set free.

As the days passed, Caleb followed me around like a young duckling. The only time we were not together was when I worked at the Fort during the day. He begged to come with me each morning to run errands, such as cleaning up the construction site and getting nails and tools for the workers. I asked if Caleb could work with me, but he was not allowed because of his age. Caleb was a child, but in many ways he acted much older than his years.

Although I did not discuss this with Samuel or Lydia, I grew to love Caleb, and began to think of him as my son. He was obedient, and so eager to learn. After some time passed, I realized that I did not love Caleb because I pitied him; I loved him because he was special. That young boy loved to work. He would have worked all day if someone did not tell him he needed to rest, or that it was time to eat. He said he wanted to be just like me one day. I never forgot his words. I felt responsible for him. I made a promise to do everything possible to see that Caleb grew into a strong, intelligent young man, with carpentry and bricklaying skills, and whatever else I could teach him.

I asked the volunteer who taught Caleb to read to keep me informed about his progress. I could read and write simple words, but wanted him to get the best education possible. Having Caleb in my life helped me understand what my parents must have gone through when I was taken from them. After having known him for only a few weeks, I could not imagine my life without that boy.

I will never forget that special day I returned to the camp and he was waiting for me. He ran to meet me with excitement. That particular day he was especially jubilant. I remember him jumping around with paper in his hands.

"Tom, Tom, I kin read words!" he said over and over. It was a very hot evening in August, and all I wanted to do was drink lots of water and sit. Instead, I forced myself to listen to Caleb read. When he read those words to me that he had written on that piece of paper, I picked him up and held him close. *My* boy was actually reading words that he had written. *My* boy could read and write!

I sat on the ground with Caleb, in the sweltering heat, and held the paper in my hands. I do not remember the words on that paper, but they were simple words I could read, written by *my* boy. I did not want Caleb to see the tears in my eyes, so I looked away. At that time, I thought crying was a sign of weakness in a man, and did not want Caleb to grow into a weak man. Much later in life, I learned that sometimes it was good to cry.

From that day forward, I insisted that Caleb read to me every evening. He learned quickly, and I encouraged him to read as much as possible. His teacher, Miz Everett, was a refined lady who had taught school in Boston. She was amazed at the progress Caleb made in the few weeks she worked with him. She gave him lessons to work on each day, and said it was very important for me to continue to help and encourage him. I told her I would help and encourage him throughout his life. Not only did I help Caleb with reading and writing, I helped him develop bricklaying and carpentry skills.

We kept busy building tents and shanties. That was definitely our greatest contribution to improve living conditions in the camps. We finally finished repairing the first floor of the hospital, and I was assigned to work on another floor. One day, as we cleaned up and prepared to move to the next floor, I heard some men talking about a soldier who had been severely wounded. They said one of his legs might have to be amputated, but they were not certain about that. As they talked on, I continued to clean up. Then, I stopped cleaning when someone said the wounded soldier's name was "Andrew". I wondered if he was the talkative Andrew who had been so kind to me.

There was no way to know because I did not ask questions. I came to work each morning, did what I was assigned to do, and returned to the camps each evening. After Andrew left, only a few of the soldiers made conversation with me. I certainly did not think of Andrew as a friend, but I liked him and missed him when he left to go to battle. The more the men talked about that soldier, the more I began to think he was the Andrew I knew. Lydia worked in the hospital, so when I returned to the camp that evening, I asked her about a wounded soldier named Andrew. She said the hospital was filled with wounded soldiers, and that she would find out if one of them was Andrew. Unfortunately, the next day I learned that the wounded soldier was Andrew; the young, friendly Quaker soldier who enlisted in the army because he loved his country, and wanted to help save the Union. According to Lydia, Andrew had been badly wounded and the doctors debated about whether his leg had to be amputated.

Before Andrew left for battle, he said he would see us again, and would tell us what it was like to fight for something you truly believe in. Andrew was like a child the day he left to go to battle. He was more talkative than ever, and quite playful with everyone, including me. It was obvious that he grew up in a family who loved him very much, and taught him to love and care about people; even fugitive slaves. It was Andrew who taught me that all white people are not cruel.

The next day, as we prepared to start work, I managed to slip away from the others. Lydia mentioned that Andrew was probably on the second floor. I grabbed a broom and pretended to be one of the refugees assigned to clean the hospital. There were several refugees working throughout the hospital, cleaning, cooking, caring for the wounded, and doing whatever the soldiers needed them to do; or, whatever the soldiers did not want to do themselves.

I discreetly managed to move around until I found Andrew's bed. I recognized his name above the bed, and continued to sweep and dust until there were no doctors or nurses nearby. Then, I cautiously moved over to the bed where he lay. I looked down. There was no doubt in my mind that the wounded soldier was the Andrew I had grown to like. I would have recognized his head full of red, curly hair, anywhere.

Andrew's forehead was wrapped with a white cloth. His left leg was also wrapped in a hard, white material. His eyes were closed, but he was definitely breathing. He took deep breaths, as if each one was his last. I did not see anyone around, so I came close to his bed and called his name softly, several times. Finally, his eyes opened. I spoke to him, hoping he could hear me.

"Andrew, Andrew, it's me, Tom, rememba me? We wuked heah at de hospital togetha."

To my surprise, Andrew looked up at me and smiled. I smiled too, thinking there was no way he could have forgotten my face. I clearly looked nothing like the white soldiers at Fort Monroe. I was so happy he was alive. There was so much I wanted to say to him.

Still smiling, Andrew tried to speak to me. He appeared to be in a lot of pain, but kept smiling. In a weak voice, he said, "Tom, I'm hurt real bad; I think I'm going to die. You are a brave man, Tom, and I hope you get to go to battle some day. The Union needs men like you."

"You ain't gonna die, Andrew. You always wonted to be a soldier, an dat's whut you is, Andrew. You can't die now, 'cause de Union need you." Suddenly I heard voices nearby, and whispered, "I gotta go, but I will be back tomorrow to see you."

I swept near his bed as a nurse came to his side. She removed the white cloth from his head, which was soaked with blood. Poor Andrew had been severely wounded, but I did not want to believe he was dying. He was too young, too decent, too kind, to die. I thought about his family, especially his mother, and wondered if she knew about her youngest son. They needed to get to see him as soon as possible.

I left the room and rejoined the other soldiers. They were busy getting the work tools and materials in place and did not notice when I entered the large room. One of the soldiers in charge told me to go to another building to get more materials. I needed to get away from them because I was hurt over what had happened to Andrew. I knew how much he meant to his family, and did not want him to die.

Andrew was young and had so much to live for. The loss of a family member was painful, and had nothing to do with the color of your skin. I had to find a way to get back to see him, and thank him for his kindness, which meant so much to me.

That evening Lydia told me that Andrew's condition had gotten worse and his family was with him. She talked about how his mother held him close, as she cried and told him how much she loved him. Lydia said it was a very sad time for the family.

That night I wondered how much more sickness, dying and death I could stand. Several refugees died each day in the camp, and, unlike Andrew, they did not have proper medical care, or family hovering over them, telling them how much they are loved. Andrew was so fortunate. Life in the contraband camps was quite difficult most days. I did everything possible to shelter Caleb and protect his young mind from all the pain and suffering. Each evening we talked about what he learned that day. I wanted him to think on things that were good for him, instead of dwelling on the pain of losing his mother. I was more concerned about his well-being than about my own. I knew I could make it in this cruel world, and Caleb needed to learn that as well.

Caleb was a ray of light in my life. Not only did he learn to read and write new words each day, but he began to teach *me* to spell new words. I remember him saying, "See, Tom, I kin teach you jes lak you teach me. Tom, we kin teach each otha." We both laughed hard. I sensed that God put that young boy in my life for a reason; not only for me to teach him, but for him to teach me everything he knew.

One day Caleb came home excited about the new word he learned that day. He said Miz Everett did not feel well, so she only taught him one word.

"You know whut dat word wuz, Tom? She taught us to spell grow, 'g-r-o-w.'"

"Kin you tell me whut dat word mean?" I asked.

"Yes, I kin; 'g-r-o-w' means dat all things git taller," Caleb answered. He stood next to me. "See, Tom, one day I will *grow* tall, jes lak you. I ain't got far to go."

"You right, Caleb, you ain't got far to go. But, did you know thar's otha ways we kin grow?"

"No, will you tell me?"

"Well, our minds kin grow jes lak our bodies," I explained.

"How kin your mind grow?"

"Well, Caleb, as you get olda, you gonna think diffrent. You ain't gonna think lak you think today. An, when you think diffrent, you will speak diffrent."

"Do you mean I will speak lak you?"

"Yeah, somethin' lak dat. Dat's why I wont you to learn as much as you kin, Caleb, 'cause de mo you learn, de mo your thinkin' will change."

"Tom, do you mean dat de more I learn, de bigger my brain will git?"

"Yeah, Caleb, dat's whut I mean."

"I'm gonna learn evrythin' I kin, Tom, 'cause I don't wont to be a tall man wit a small brain." We laughed a lot that night. His eyes sparkled like the stars in the sky when he talked about the new words he had learned to read and write. I was so thankful to have him in my life. He was exactly what I needed to help with the pressure of daily life in the camps.

Over the next few days, Andrew's condition miraculously improved; but, he lost his left leg. From time to time I was able to get away from my work assignment to have a quick visit with him. Andrew said he looked forward to my visits. Most importantly, I got to thank him for being so kind to me.

Shortly after his leg was amputated, Andrew said he was leaving Fort Monroe to return to Philadelphia with his family. That was sad news, but I knew it was coming. His family wanted him at home so they could take care of him. My family would have wanted the same for me. Before he left Fort Monroe in September 1862, Andrew and I had a long talk one morning.

"Tom, won't be long before you get your freedom," he said. "Things will be changing in the South real soon. I don't know how much news you get over at that camp, but I want you to hear this." Andrew read from a newspaper: *President Lincoln recently issued a Preliminary Emancipation Proclamation. It proclaims that 'All slaves in those states or portions of states still in rebellion as of January 1, 1863, will be declared free. It pledges monetary aid for slave states not in rebellion that adopt either immediate or gradual emancipation, and reiterates support for the colonization of freed slaves outside the United States.'*

"That's good news for your people. I'm so happy for you, Tom. I don't understand all that you've been through, but I know it hasn't been easy for you. I think it's only right for you to go to battle for the Union. You can do a lot of good for the Union."

"Thank you, Andrew. I don't know whut all dose words mean dat you read, but I hope it's good news for us. I don't wont you to leave Fort Monroe. I ain't neva met a white man that talk and think lak you."

"How are things going in the camps?"

"We's struggling to make de most of it, but it ain't easy livin' in dose conditions, Andrew. I thought 'bout leavin', but I can't leave jes yet."

"Why can't you leave? Things will be much better for you in the North. You got good skills, Tom, and you could work and make a good life for yourself."

"I got otha people to think 'bout. Can't jes think 'bout myself."

"I guess you're thinking about your lady you left back in Savannah."

"Yeah, I been thinkin' 'bout Hannah a lot. I don't know how she doin', an dat's been tough for me."

"Well, I mailed that letter you asked me to mail."

"You did?"

"I told you I would try to get that letter to Hannah. If I say I'm going to do something, I do it. My word means a lot to me."

"Thank you, Andrew. I 'preciate dat. I will miss you. You goin' home, an your mammy will take real good care of you."

"I gotta get used to living with one leg. You think my lady will want a man with one leg?"

"I think your lady will still wont *you*, Andrew, 'cause you a decent man. Take care of yoself, an God bless you." I shook Andrew's hand and left the room. I did not think I would ever see him again, and would never forget him because he was the first decent white man I ever met.

More than ever, I wanted to leave Fort Monroe to find Hannah and my family. I felt a strong urge to go back to Savannah to get Hannah, and then come back to Fort Monroe to continue to help the refugees, but was reluctant to leave Fort Monroe because of Caleb.

He depended on me and looked up to me. How could I leave him, after all he had been through? Also, I had grown to love Caleb, and wanted him in my life. He had done as much for me as I had for him.

That night I had a long talk with Samuel and Lydia. I told them about my strong desire to leave Fort Monroe, to go back to get Hannah. I had not seen her in a long time and missed her very much. She was the only woman I ever loved and did not want to lose her. I could not expect her to wait for me forever. Hannah wanted to be free, and to have a family as much as I did, but she was stuck on John Mundy's plantation.

I could not sit around and wait for the President and our leaders to act on slavery, before making an effort to find Hannah and my family. I made it to Fort Monroe, and believed I could make it back to Savannah to get Hannah.

"I undastan how you mus feel, Tom, but it ain't gonna be easy for you to git back to Savannah," Lydia said. "Whut if Hannah ain't on de plantation no mo? Whut if she left dat place?"

"It's a chance I gotta take. Nuttin in dis life been easy for me, but I gotta do it."

"Tom, you do whut you feel is bes for you," Samuel said. "If you luv Hannah, den go back for her. It's a chance you gotta take. We will carry on heah at de camp."

"Thar's jes one thing I need you to do for me befo I leave. Promise me dat you both will take care of an look afta Caleb. Dat boy mean de world to me. Lydia, I need you to see to it dat he gits food to eat, an dat he continue to learn new words. I don't want him to stop learnin'. Samuel, I need you to continue to teach Caleb about bricklaying an carpentry. If y'all kin promise me dat, den I kin leave heah wit some peace. I *will* be back for Caleb."

"Tom, you's family to me an Lydia, an we promise to take care of an look afta Caleb. Don't you worry 'bout him. You jes need to be safe, an git back to git yo lady."

The next morning I had a long talk with Caleb. As expected, he cried to come along with me to Savannah. I would have taken him, had I not known that Lydia and Samuel would take good care of him.

Caleb had grown close to Samuel and Lydia, and I knew he would be in good hands until I returned for him.

"I won't be no trouba to you, Tom," Caleb pleaded. "You said dat I's a good boy, an dat I learn quick. You said we would stay togetha. I kin run fas, an I don't eat a lotta food. We kin hep each otha git to Savannah, 'cause…"

Caleb's words were hard for me. I almost changed my mind about taking him along. Every word he said that morning was true, but he was young, and I knew the journey back to Savannah would be a long, difficult one. I could not put that young boy through that unless it was absolutely necessary. Samuel and Lydia assured me they would take good care of him until I returned. I had peace of mind.

Before I left Fort Monroe that morning, Lydia put food, water, potion and other items in a sack for me. She and Samuel said they would pray for me every day until I returned. My mind was made up, and no one and nothing could change it. Just as I ran from that plantation in Charleston, I left the contraband camps at Fort Monroe on a hot day in September 1862, determined to get back to Savannah, to get the only woman I ever loved.

# CHAPTER 15

Once again, I was back in the woods, on the run; running back to the plantation I had been so desperate to get away from. That did not make a lot of sense to the fugitive slaves I left behind at Fort Monroe, but it made a lot of sense to me. No one knew what I felt for Hannah. My love for her was more powerful than the risk of going back to John Mundy's plantation, and possibly getting caught. I made a promise that I would come back for her, and did not go back on my word.

It was difficult living in the camps in crowded, unsanitary conditions, and working long hours. Still, I was thankful to have made it to Fort Monroe, and that slaves were not turned away. I planned to return for one reason – to get Caleb.

Fortunately, I had decent shoes on my feet, thanks to the Union Army. On my flight to Fort Monroe, sore, swollen feet had been my biggest problem. Lydia learned a lot by caring for wounded soldiers, and she gave me items to take along, such as a potion for sore feet and soft, white cloth to wrap them in.

Lydia, like Hannah, cared about people and wanted to make everyone comfortable. Watching her and Samuel share their love and lives together each day caused me to miss Hannah more than ever. Lydia and Hannah were so much like my mother – angles here on earth.

Although I had plenty of bread and fat back that Lydia packed, I did not eat for two days in the woods because there was so much to think about. I had to get to Savannah, to that plantation, and then somehow get Hannah away from that place. I believed she was still there.

It was torture not knowing about the people you love and care about. I did not know where my parents and sister were, or if they were alive, but had to think positive. Many slaves did not know where their families were, or if they were alive. I often thought about how we would recover from all we had to endure as slaves.

I had been on the run to Savannah for a few days when I saw a man lying on the ground near a fallen tree. From a distance he appeared to be a runaway slave who had been hurt. I was uncertain if I should approach him, because there was no way to know who was with him, or who was watching. Instinctively, I wanted to keep walking and let him lie there, but as I got closer, I heard him moaning. He sounded as if he was asking for help.

"My leg, my leg," he mumbled. I looked around, but did not see anyone, and came closer. "Kin you help me? It's my leg."

"I will try to help you." I looked around again, then set my sack against a tree. I reached down to help that man get up, but he could not move his left leg. Finally, I was able to turn him over and he pulled himself up to rest his back against the tree.

"Whut's your name?" I asked.

"My name's Adam, an I's tryin' to git to Fort Monroe. I heah dat slaves is free thar, at leas dey free from thar mastah. I fell ova dis stump, an been layin' heah, tryin' to git up."

Adam's round face was thin and his eyes were sad. He appeared to be around twenty years old. His body frame was small. Although his face and arms were scratched, he only complained about his leg. I asked him if he was hungry and he said he needed a drink of water. I gave him my pouch and he gulped the water down. Adam thanked me for helping him and said he would move on as soon as he was able to walk. Lydia put some white cloth in my sack, so I took some and wrapped it around the wound on his leg. He thanked me and talked about his life.

"I spen mos of my life in Georgia, an I done some wuk at Fort Pulaski."

According to the soldiers at Fort Monroe, Fort Pulaski was built to protect the port of Savannah. It is located between Savannah and Tybee Island. Fort Pulaski was under the control of Confederate troops until December 1861, when Confederate forces abandoned Tybee Island. That allowed Union troops access to cross the

Savannah River from Fort Pulaski. Soon, Union forces began construction of batteries along Tybee Island. Then, in April 1862, Union forces asked Confederate troops to surrender Fort Pulaski, but the commander of the Confederate troops rejected the offer. Union troops then began a long, sustained attack on Fort Pulaski. Reluctantly, the commander surrendered the Fort over to Union control.

"I was wukin at Fort Pulaski when I heard dat slaves was comin' to Fort Monroe, an dat once dey got thar, dey wuz not turned away," Adam continued. "I did not run right den, 'cause mastah had hounds evry whur. But, he lef one day wit his hounds, an dat's when I run as fas as I could. I come a long way. I wuz doin' real good gittin through de woods, 'til I fell. Twuz so dark, I couldn't see. Thought my leg wuz broke, but now I know it ain't. Whur you from?"

"Well, I come from Georgia, but been at Fort Monroe for some time. Lak you, I heard dat slaves could stay thar if dey got thar, so I run off from de plantation one mornin'."

"Is dat so." Adam sat up straighter after he heard I came from Fort Monroe. "Tell me, uh, whut is yo name? Sorry, I ain't axed you yet."

"My name's Tom."

"Tell me, Tom, is it true whut dey say 'bout Fort Monroe? Is slaves really free once dey git thar?" He appeared to be anxious to hear the answer.

"It's true. Slaves been pourin' in thar almos evry day, an de masters can't come an claim us back. But, let me warn you, de camps is crowded, an thar is much hunger, sickness an death thar. But, de good news is dat we's wukin togetha to help each otha. Also, people from de North been sendin' supplies, an even comin' down to help us. Things will git betta."

"Long as we free, I kin make it!" Adam shouted. "Lawd, I jes wont to be free befo I leave dis world! I don't know nuttin 'bout whur my famly is, but I gotta bleeve dat one day I will find dem. Tom, tell me, how do I git to Fort Monroe?"

I told Adam as much as I knew about how to get to Fort Monroe. He asked lots of questions. I also told him that it would be wise for

165

him to stay where he was for a few days, so that his leg could get stronger because he had a long way to travel. I then asked Adam how to get to Savannah.

"You's already in Norf Carolina, an you's headed de right way to Savannah." He told me some things about that region.

"Why in de world would you leave Fort Monroe to go back to Savannah? Nigger, is you crazy?"

"I lef de woman I luv on a plantation thar, an told her I would be back for her someday. I didn't wont to leave Fort Monroe, to go back to dat place, but I can't have peace knowin' she's on dat plantation. She's a good woman, an we gonna jump de broom one day."

"She mus be a *mighty* good woman for you to go back to dat plantation," Adam said. "I don't luv nobody dat much. Don't you know dat patrollas an hounds is waitin' for you? An, if dey ketch you, dey gonna surely kill you."

"I know dat, but I gotta go back for her."

"How you know she still thar waitin' for you?" I had been asked that question before, but would not allow my mind to linger on it. Hannah knew how much I loved her. She also knew that we planned to jump the broom one day.

"You don't know her. I bleeve she's still on dat plantation, an I's willin' to risk my life to go back for her. Now, tell me, you sure I's goin' de right way?" I was done talking with Adam. I had only discussed Hannah and my family with Samuel and Lydia because they were like family to me. I did not know Adam and had nothing else to say to him about Hannah.

"Yeah, you goin' to Savannah. I jes hope you make it thar safe."

"I betta git goin'. I been in de woods a long time, an still got a ways to go. Hope yo leg gits better."

"Thank you for yo hep. Sho wish we could run togetha. You got anythin' in dat sack to eat?" Adam was weak and looked as if he had not eaten in a while. I had some bread and fat back, but had not eaten much of it because it had to last as long as possible. Still, I could not leave him with a wounded leg and no food.

"Yeah, I got some bread an fat back. Here, take some an eat it, 'cause you need yo strength." I gave him half of my food and water, then started to walk away. I hated to leave him with a wounded leg, but there was nothing else I could do for him. Staying with him would not heal his leg.

"You gonna come back to Fort Monroe, afta you git yo lady?"

"Yeah, I gotta come back to git my boy."

"You got a son?"

"Yeah, you kin say dat." I had never referred to Caleb as my son, but sure loved him like a son. That young boy meant so much to me.

"I ain't got no famly, but one day dat will change," Adam said, from a distance. I sensed that he did not want me to leave him because he continued to talk as I walked away. I wanted to do more, but there was nothing else to do for him. I gave him food and water and wrapped his wounded leg. I also gave him some potion for his wounds.

"You will have a famly one day, don't worry." Those were the last words I said to Adam. He watched as I walked away and said something else, but I could not hear him. It was not wise to be shouting in the woods because anyone could have heard us. There was no telling who was in those woods, looking and listening to catch niggers.

I walked along at a good pace, but did not run because, although it was around September, it was still hot. Thank God my shoes fit and my feet were wrapped in cloth and did not hurt.

I thought about Caleb. He loved Lydia and Samuel, and I knew they would take good care of him. Caleb, like me, had to grow up long before his time. There was so much he had to learn and understand at an early age. I was committed to help him grow to be a strong, prosperous young man.

I felt responsible for him, and that responsibility brought new meaning to my life. He always watched me at the camp, whether I was building tents and shanties, or talking to other refugees. I was cheated out of growing up with Pappy. Perhaps Caleb came into my life so I could be the father to him I did not have. He was truly a blessing.

That night I looked up at the sky and prayed for my family. I asked God to take care of them and to help us reunite soon. I also prayed that Adam's leg would heal and that he would make it safely to Fort Monroe. Although I did not know my family's whereabouts, I had a family. Unfortunately, Adam did not have a family, but he would have one as soon as he made it to Fort Monroe.

I could not remember how long it had been since I left Fort Monroe, but hoped that Savannah was not far away. I had no water and only a few pieces of bread left. It was hard, but filling. Some rain would have been wonderful during those hot days.

Early one morning, as I walked through that dry, thick wooded area, which I believed was somewhere in North Carolina, I thought I heard voices. The sun had not come up and my vision was not clear. I wanted to run, but the noise from the dry leaves and debris would've brought attention to me. I saw a large tree near a body of water with thick branches, and decided to climb it. I enjoyed climbing trees as a child. I climbed as high as possible so as not to be visible. I thought about a Bible verse Mammy often read to us: *And he shall be like a tree planted by the rivers of water, that bringeth forth his fruit in his season; his leaf also shall not wither; and whatsoever he doeth shall prosper.* She used to say I would grow to be like that tree. She said I would be strong, and would prosper in everything I did, and would be planted; grounded like those large trees.

Soon the voices were close enough for me to see who was speaking. I wanted to see men who looked like me to ask them how to get to Savannah. Instead, I saw two white men carrying large sticks. I suspected they were patrollers, but there were no hounds.

They got closer to the tree and stopped walking. My heart started to beat faster because I thought they had seen me in the top of the tree. Although it was the crack of dawn, it was not hard to spot a nigger sitting in a tree. I listened as the two men talked and did not move, out of fear they would look up and see me.

"Which way should we go?" the shorter man asked. He looked around as if he was lost. "Ain't no telling where Ed might be, 'cause these Georgia woods is thick."

"If we don't find him soon, it's gonna be too late. Too bad they let him get away like that. Come on, let's head on back, 'cause we gotta get back to Augusta before dark. We'll find him, don't worry."

Finally they moved on and I came down from the tree. I wondered if they were looking for runaway slaves, or if they were trying to find one of their own. Regardless, they helped me by pointing out that I was in Georgia, somewhere near Augusta.

It was around September 1862. I assumed there were still some patrollers looking for slaves, although I later learned that many white men and boys deserted their plantations and enlisted to fight with the Conferederate Army.

There was no more bread and fat back, so I survived on wild berries and nuts, not knowing if all of the berries were safe to eat. When I could not find berries, I ate leaves and tree parts to keep from starving. Although some slaves escaped and lived in the woods, not so far from their master's plantation, living in the woods was not easy.

I slowly pushed on that day until I came to an opening in the wooded area, and heard people talking. From behind a tree, I stared at a wagon filled with my people, men and a few women. Most of them were sitting in the wagon, but several stood around the wagon. I moved closer to hear what they were saying and to try to find out where I was. There was a white man, probably the overseer, standing near the door of what appeared to be a store. Some were inside the store.

Since there were so many niggers, I decided to take a chance and walk into the crowd, hoping they would not pay attention to me. The overseer was eating and looking in another direction. I quickly walked from the wooded area and joined the group of men, who appeared to be around my age. They looked at me, but kept talking as if they knew me. They talked on, and I soon learned that they were slaves from different plantations and farms who had been hired out to work throughout Georgia, planting and harvesting crops.

They said they had been working in Atlanta and Augusta, and were leaving Augusta headed to Savannah. My heart pumped faster when I heard the word *Savannah*. The white men they had been hired out to work for stopped at the store to eat and buy supplies. Some of the slaves were eating and some rested in the wagon.

As they talked on about the crops they had planted and harvested, my mind raced, trying to decide if I should run back into the woods, or if I should jump onto the wagon, and pray that I would not be discovered. I still had a long way to go to get to Savannah and that wagon was a lot faster than my two legs. Also, I was tired and hungry, and the heat slowed me down. Most importantly, I was anxious to get to Hannah.

If the overseer did not recognize me as one of the hired-out slaves, I did not know what course of action he would take against me. I could have been whipped and taken back to John Mundy, or perhaps thrown off the wagon. I made a decision, then took a deep breath; I jumped onto that wagon and sat down amongst the other slaves.

Shortly thereafter, four white men came out of the store and began talking to the overseer. They talked and ate, with sacks in their hands, probably filled with goods from the store. One of the white men said, "It's time to go. Let's count to see if they're all here." The five white men walked toward the wagon.

"One, two, three, four… twenty-three; let me count again," the overseer said. My heart beat was faster than ever. Common sense should have told me that those white men knew exactly how many slaves were on that wagon. I had definitely been caught, and all I could do at that moment was wait to see what they would do with me. I sat motionless as the overseer counted the slaves again. Then, all five white men started counting.

"Robert, there's an extra nigger on this wagon!" the overseer said. "We had twenty-two when we left Augusta, and now, for some strange reason, we got twenty-three."

"You sure 'bout that," the man named Robert answered. "Well, I'll be damn, you're right, Ellis; we got us an extra nigger. Now, who's the extra nigger?"

There was silence on the wagon, then all eyes were on me. Everyone suddenly realized I had just joined them. Although we had the same skin color, we clearly did not all look alike. I had no choice but to stand up and confess that I was the extra one. I jumped down from the wagon and walked over to the overseer. I felt weak in my knees and began to question why I jumped onto that wagon. I had come so far and survived. Suddenly, I had to deal with five white men.

"Where you come from, boy?" the overseer asked. "You a mighty strong looking nigger. I bet you can plant and pick a whole lotta cotton. Turn around, and let us get a good look at you." The five white men laughed. I had no choice but to turn around and let them stare at me from head to toe. It was most humiliating. With the exception of Andrew, I had been humiliated by white men all of my life.

"You gonna answer me, boy?" the overseer asked. The other four continued to laugh and stare at me. Every slave on the wagon looked as if they were frightened for me. Even if I wanted to run, it was too late for that. I stood there, at the mercy of five white men.

"I come from Vaginia," I said, and looked away.

"What the hell you doing down here in Augusta? Looks like we got us a runaway nigger." They all laughed again.

"You done run from your master, ain't ya?" one of the white men asked. "Well, guess what, you belong to us, now, 'cause we show ain't gonna give a strong, healthy nigger like you back to your owner. We done got lucky, boys! We done found us a young, strong nigger! Get your ass on that wagon, and come on down to Savannah with us." They all laughed and patted each other on the shoulders.

I jumped back onto the wagon, wanting to shout for joy! They did not realize that they had done exactly what I wanted them to do. They were not taking me back to my master, who by the way, was not in Virginia. John Mundy was in Savannah, and that wagon would take me exactly where I wanted to go – back to Savannah to get Hannah!

# CHAPTER 16

It felt good to sit on that wagon and ride to Savannah, as opposed to running through those thick Georgia woods in the heat. The wagon stopped twice before we got to Savannah, and we were told to get off to clean up corn fields and prepare them for planting in the spring. I was anxious to get to Savannah, but we had to do what we were told to do.

When the wagon stopped the second time, and we were told to get off to clean more fields, I thought about running. I wondered if I could get to John Mundy's plantation quicker by foot than on that wagon, but decided not to run because there were too many slaves and white men watching. I had come too far to risk getting whipped, or maybe killed.

As we traveled, the slaves sang spirituals and talked softly to each other. The white men were much too close to risk talking about anything other than work. Some of the slaves wanted to know more about me, but I said little because it was not wise to talk too much.

After traveling for several days, we finally made it to Savannah. Oh, the splendor of Savannah, with streets lined with moss draped, large oak trees, and its unforgettable squares. John Mundy often talked about Savannah and its downtown squares, both of which were founded by General James Oglethorpe. The public squares were created to be a locale for people to congregate and enjoy themselves. One of the squares was named to honor General Oglethorpe.

I worked on a house near the squares for one of John Mundy's friends for several months. During that time, I watched people gather in the squares daily to socialize, and to see children jump around playfully. For a short time, I lived vicariously through those people who were free to enjoy life, and the view of the Savannah River.

I still remember large ships leisurely sailing down the Savannah River, loaded with supplies to be delivered to Savannah and other coastal cities. People gathered along the river front to buy or sell vegetables, seafood and other goods. Savannah also stands out because of the homes, with Victorian, English and Gothic architecture. If you were free, and established, Savannah was a great place to live. Unbeknownst to any of us at that time, Savannah would be saved from Union attack two years later, in December 1864, because the city surrendered rather than be burned like Atlanta.

I had to figure out how to get away from the others on the wagon without being noticed. I heard one of the white men say he was hungry, so I assumed they would stop before long to get something to eat, and that is exactly what they did. They must have been real hungry because they stopped when it was almost dark, which was something they had not done before. Two of the white men went into a store to get something to eat, and three stayed with the slaves on the wagon. They told us to get off, three at a time, to take care of our needs. I was one of the last to get off the wagon, and noticed that the white men were talking to each other and eating. They were clearly hungry and tired, and so were most of the slaves. If I was going to get away, that was the time to do it.

After we took care of our needs, we started back toward the wagon. One of the younger men stumbled over something on the ground. It was almost dark, and I do not know what he walked over, but that was the break I needed! While the others were bent over trying to help him stand up, I started toward the woods not so far behind the store.

I ran as fast as possible, and was not afraid because no one could see well enough to find me in the dark. Also, I was not afraid because there were no hounds. They had whips and large sticks, but thank God, there were no hounds. I was confident I could run faster than any of those white men or slaves.

I assume those white men did not have any hounds with them because they were familiar with the slaves on that wagon. They had been working for those men for several years; hired out to plant and cultivate fields. What those white men forgot, because they were tired and hungry, was that I had just joined the other slaves on that wagon, and they knew nothing about me. They were thrilled to have me because I was young and strong. They had seen that I was a good worker, and were eager to get me back to their plantation. I was not able to discern if the white men were from the same plantation or not.

I stumbled over things, and ran into a tree, but kept moving. When it was too dark to see ahead, I slowed down and walked. I never heard any loud screams that I was gone, or anyone chasing after me.

They probably did not realize I was missing that night until they counted, and realized they did not have twenty-three slaves on the wagon. Their "extra nigger" got away and never looked back. Once again, I was in the woods, alone; but, this time, *I knew where I was.* I knew that John Mundy's plantation was not far away because I had worked in those woods for years, cutting down trees and gathering firewood for the master.

I ran for the next two or three days with very little sleep. I was afraid to sleep for more than a few hours each day because those white men could have gotten some hounds and turned them onto my scent. I could not take any chances, and did not take any changes.

I was elated because John Mundy's plantation was not so far away. I had to get back to that plantation, and believe with all my heart that Hannah was still there. Every detail of her beautiful face was as fresh as ever in my mind.

Although there was a lot to do, I had to get through the first step, which was to get Hannah. I tried not to think beyond that because it was overwhelming. I could not allow frustration to consume my energy, and had to keep the faith that my dream would come to pass.

After about two or three days in the woods, I woke up one morning and gasped, because John Mundy's plantation wasn't far away. That area was very familiar. I was hungry and tired, but managed to keep walking. Finally, I stopped walking and stared at a big house, with horses and carriages. I heard voices, but did not know if they were real or not. I fell to the ground, too weak to stand any longer. I lay there, praying for the strength to keep going. As I lay there, the voices became louder. I needed help, desperately, and mumbled, "Help me". My voice was weak, but apparently someone heard it.

I did not want to die in the woods, but at that moment did not care who heard the moaning. I thought it was probably the people from the wagon. Perhaps they had finally caught up with me, and would throw my weakened body back onto the wagon. I would be punished for running off and leaving them.

I sensed that someone was looking down on me, but did not look up to see who it was. I was not afraid; simply too weak to care about who had found me. I expected to hear cruel words, but heard nothing. I was helpless, and at the mercy of whomever had found me. They could have done whatever they wanted to do to me at that moment, but, they walked away.

Perhaps they knew I was too weak to do anything, and left me there to die. Maybe they left to get the others, to ridicule and humiliate me first, before the punishment. Finally, Tom, the nigger with carpentry and bricklaying skills, who had been clever enough to escape slavery, had finally been caught. I was too weak to cry, but mumbled, "Lord, help me".

I tried to crawl away from that spot, but was too weak to move. I did not want to die in those woods, alone. Would anyone tell my family what became of me? Probably not, because no one cared about a slave who ran whenever he had the opportunity. I had so much to live for; so much I wanted to accomplish in my life. That morning I believed my life had been cut short, as I lay there, mumbling irrationally to God.

I don't remember at what point I passed out, and don't know how long I was out, but will never forget the sensation of that cold cloth on my forehead. Someone put their arm under my neck and tried to raise my head. They tried to get me to drink water, but the water ran down my neck. I choked before swallowing it, then opened my eyes. I will never forget those piercing, brown eyes that stared at me. I thought I was out of my mind, or dreaming, because those deep, captivating eyes were very familiar. They were Hannah's eyes!

I dreamed of Hannah often, only to wake up to reality and realize that she was nowhere near. That morning I did not want to wake up, because I did not want Hannah to disappear, yet again. I did not want that dream to end, because I needed Hannah more than ever. I wanted to see her before I died in those woods. There was so much to be said before leaving this world. She had to know that I loved her more than ever, and that she was the woman I wanted to jump the broom with.

But, I did wake up, because of that cold cloth on my face. I had been confused before, but that time it was different. It all seemed so real. Slowly, I came to my senses and heard a soft voice speaking to me. It was a very familiar voice; a very loving, caring voice.

"Tom, Tom, don't be afraid, 'cause I'm here wit you." I reached out to touch her arm, thinking that an angel was speaking to me. I desperately needed that angel, or whatever she was, to stay with me.

"Please, don't leave me. I don't wont to die alone. Please, talk to me." Tears ran down my face. I had been through so much, for so long. At that moment, more than ever, I did not want to be left alone.

"You ain't dyin', Tom, 'cause I'm gonna take care of you. Wake up, Tom. It's me, Hannah, wake up!"

"Hannah, Hannah, is it really you? Hannah, please don't go away, agin, please. I need you, Hannah." Suddenly, I realized I was *not* dreaming! By the grace of God, Hannah was wiping my face with that cold cloth, trying to wake me up. I had somehow made it back to John Mundy's plantation!

"I ain't leavin' you, Tom, an you ain't leavin' me again. She helped me sit up, then hugged and kissed me. Although very weak, I found the strength to embrace her. We hugged and kissed each other, and cried. No, I was not dreaming that time. Hannah came into that wooded area where I fell, after someone who worked in the big house with her heard and recognized me.

177

"It's Tom, it's really *my* Tom!" she said over and over. "I been waitin' for you, Tom." Our faces were soaked with tears.

I realized that Hannah could be in danger for being away from the big house for too long. "I don't wont you to git in no trouble. You betta git on back to de big house."

"I ain't gonna leave you lak dis," she said. "Let me get you some food, an I will be back. You jes lay here, an don't make no noise. Mary is de only one who know you're out here, an she ain't gonna tell nobody. You know Mary been lak a mammy to me all dese years."

"Be safe." I rubbed my legs and arms to be sure it was not a dream, and watched Hannah walk back to the big house. She was more beautiful than ever. I had never wanted to be with a woman the way I wanted to be with her. I lay against that tree, waiting for her to return, and thanked God I'd gotten back safely to that plantation. Most importantly, I thanked Him that Hannah was alive and well.

That morning I realized that all things truly *are* possible, if you have faith, and if you are persistent enough to push on, even when it is painful to keep going. Hannah was worth everything I endured to get back to her, and I would have done it all again for her. I knew from her embrace, and kisses, that she loved and wanted me as much as I loved and wanted her. In some ways, I am grateful I was too weak to touch her that day. Hannah was pure, and she wanted to stay pure until we jumped the broom. Had I been stronger that day we reunited in the woods, I could not, and would not, have restrained myself.

Hannah came back with hot food and water. She had worked in the big house since John Mundy bought her several years before. She and Mary did all of the cooking and cleaning for his family. Mary was an older lady, perhaps somewhere close to my mother's age, and she taught Hannah how to cook. Mary always cooked the best food. Her cooking was second only to Mammy's.

I ate the food so fast I almost choked. Hannah tried to get me to eat slowly, to properly digest the food, but that was hard to do when I had not eaten in days.

"How you feelin', Tom?" She rubbed my head, as she spoke in her kind, soft, compassionate voice.

"I feel a lot betta, now dat I got you heah wit me. I had to get back to you, Hannah, even if it cost me my life."

"Well, you're alive, an you will be jes fine. Now, no more talk 'bout you dyin'. I'm gonna take real good care of you. When you finish eatin', I'll git you all cleaned up."

"Hannah, I don't wont no trouble for you. Don't you need to git on back to de big house, befo mastah John come lookin' for you?"

"Yes, I need to git back, but not 'til you eat all your food, so go on an finish. Mastah John ain't heah right now 'cause he joined the Confederate Army. I think he might be a captain."

Thank God, John Mundy was not at the plantation at that time, which was around October 1862. That was great news, because with him gone, it would be easier to get Hannah away. Yes, there were overseers and drivers around, but none of them was as difficult as the master. With him gone, I would have some time to get strong enough to run again.

"Hannah, I risk comin' back heah for you, an I's takin' you wit me, back to Fort Monroe. You gotta be real careful, 'cause you know dey will kill me if dey find me. You can't say nuttin to nobody, not even to Mary."

"Mary know dat you're heah, Tom. Mary ain't gonna say or do nuttin to hurt you".

"Hannah, you kin not tell Mary dat we gonna leave dis place. I know dat Mary luv you, but she ain't gonna wont you to leave. Listen to me, please, don't tell nobody dat we gonna leave. If Mary ax, jes tell her dat I came by to git some food, an dat I will be gone soon."

"I will, Tom, I will do whut you say. Now, let me get back to finish cookin'. You get some rest, an I will be back to get you all cleaned up." She kissed me and walked away.

I watched Hannah walk back to the big house. I was still too weak to stand, but finished eating and drinking. It did not take long for my body to get stronger and to feel better. I could see the big house where Hannah worked every day, and a few slaves at a distance, working in the fields. Things had really changed on that plantation. There weren't as many horses and not as many crops in the fields as before I left. I also did not see as many slaves working in the fields. It was obvious that the master was away because the plantation did not appear to be flourishing as it once had.

I did not come any closer to the big house, out of fear someone would see me, so I walked further back into the woods, trying to stretch my legs so they would get stronger. I was ready to run again, but had to be patient because there were things Hannah would have to do before she could leave. Running would not be easy for her because she had trouble breathing at times. I felt strongly that she could make it if I was with her. We would have to support each other on the long flight back to Fort Monroe. I believed Hanna could make it.

Saying goodbye to Mary would be hard for Hannah, but she would get over it. Mary had been like a mother to her. Hannah was around sixteen when her mother died suddenly. Shortly after her mother's death, John Mundy bought her and she came to his plantation. Before she arrived, Mary had been the only house slave, but that changed when Hannah came. Mary never had children, so she watched over Hannah and taught her how to cook. Before long, Hannah began helping Mary with the cooking and cleaning in the big house. She loved Mary very much.

Mary also loved Hannah, but it was still dangerous for her to tell anyone about her plans to run away with me. There were some things slaves simply could not tell, and making plans to escape was one of them. News that slaves were planning to run somehow always leaked, and the master usually found out. Of course, those slaves who made the plans were severely punished, and sometimes killed.

It was almost dark when Hannah came back because she was busy with chores for the mistress. It was only after the mistress dismissed her and Mary to go back to their cabins that she was able to slip away. She had to wait until she was absolutely sure no one was watching. There were usually one or two slaves who reported everything to the master. That plantation certainly had its share of slaves who told John Mundy everything. I never understood why we betrayed each other. It just did not make any sense to me. Perhaps they had their reasons for telling on their own.

"I had to wait, 'cause thar was things the mistress needed me to do. Lord have mercy on you, Tom. I been prayin' for you evryday since Joe told me dat you ran off from Charleston. I missed you, Tom, but was happy for you, 'cause I remema all de plans we made. We could not jump de broom 'til we wuz free. I also knew dat you would somehow come back for me."

"Did you eva git de letta I wrote to you?" Andrew said he would do his best to get that letter to the Mundy plantation.

"I neva got no letter from you," Hannah said. "I neva told nobody how much we luv each otha." We embraced as we lay on the two quilts she brought from the big house. Her warm, soft skin felt wonderful next to my sore, scratched, weak body. I did not want to let her go, but someone would certainly discover that she was not in her cabin. Each night the overseers counted to make sure all of the slaves were where they were supposed to be.

"When kin you leave?" I held her close to me.

"I kin leave in de mornin'. Lord, it's gonna be mighty hard leavin' Mary behind. Mary been lak a mammy to me." Hannah cried softly on my shoulder. I understood, and knew the pain of leaving loved ones behind.

"Hannah, I know it's hard, but you can't stay on dis plantation 'cause of Mary. If thar was any way I could bring Mary along, I would, but I don't think she would leave dis place. Mary been on dis plantation mos of her life, an I don't think she's ready to leave."

"You're right, Tom. Mary done told me many times dat she would neva leave mastah John, 'cause she been heah too long. She also neva thought I would leave her."

"She said anythin' 'bout me bein' out heah in de woods?" There was no way to know if Mary had said something to the other slaves.

"She think you came back for food, 'cause we know of slaves who run off, an some time later dey come back for food an water. Some of dem actually live out in de woods, not so far from de plantation, an neva git caught. I let Mary think dat you're already gone, 'cause I did not want her to get suspicious. If Mary thought I was 'bout to leave her, she jes might say somethin' to de othas, to stop me from goin' wit you."

"Very good. Some day we will come back for her, if she wanna leave dis place; but, rememba, if she don't wanna go, ain't no need in tryin' to talk her into leavin'. Runnin' off ain't for evry slave. Tell me, Hannah, you ready to go wit me?"

"Yes, Tom, I'm ready to go wit you. I brought you dese quilts to sleep on tonight, 'cause you gotta get some rest. I'm ready to leave wheneva you say so. I been waitin' an prayin' for dis day, an I ain't turnin' back." I kissed Hannah passionately.

"How is Joe?" I would have given anything to have seen Joe and talked to him, but could not take the risk that he might tell someone I was back.

"Joe is well, but he don't need to know dat you're heah," she said. "Joe is still very loyal to mastah John."

Hannah packed food, water and other things. It was hard for her to walk away from Mary, and from the plantation that had been her home for many years. I understood, and did not rush her. I wanted the decision to leave the plantation to be hers, not mine. She cried, then took a deep breath and said she was ready to go. I grabbed her hand, and we walked away, together.

That was our first step to live the life we had dreamed of and talked about for so long. I felt great that day because I successfully rescued the woman I still love to this day. After we left that plantation, Hannah and I started our flight back to Fort Monroe. I could not wait to see Caleb.

# CHAPTER 17

Weeks passed, and several men responded to the notice in the paper about my brother. Unfortunately, none of them was my brother. I began to think Tom was not in Boston, and maybe not in the North. William put that same notice in papers in New York and Philadelphia.

I wanted to put my name in the notice, so Tom would know his sister was looking for him, but decided that was not wise. Frank Wilmington, or his men, could have been anywhere.

I made dresses and clothing for the refugees, while Callie, Cora and Naomi worked to finish gowns and dresses for customers, including Eve Grant, Jane Merritt and Helena Austin. Although those three women were quite demanding about their dresses, they were very loyal customers.

There were days I had more than enough to do and sometimes did not know where to begin. In addition to sewing, I helped William and other volunteers prepare boxes of supplies to send to the camps. I had to please my customers in order to stay in business, but also felt obligated to help the refugees.

Several women came in during the summer months asking for simple, as well as more fashionable day dresses. With Mammy's help, we were able to keep up with the orders. Mammy only worked a few hours each day while Pappy cared for Will.

I often prayed for my shoppe to prosper, and my prayers were certainly answered. Not only did we make and sell lots of dresses, but Naomi made and sold lots of hats and bonnets. Some evenings after the shoppe closed, we sat and chatted about our journey from slavery to becoming prosperous women who managed our very own businesses. We could do anything we wanted to do if we worked hard, and were persistent to see it through.

One day in late September 1862, Eve Grant came to the shoppe to pick up her dresses. After trying them on, she praised us on the quality of our work. Eve was a perfectionist. If she praised your work, it had to be well above average. Praise from her was truly a compliment. She loved to talk, and after she finished chatting, she said she wanted to talk to me about something. I had no idea what was on her mind.

"Sarah, as I have said many times, the quality of your work is very good. Everyone knows if I am not pleased with something, I will certainly let you know. People think I'm difficult, but I simply want perfection, that's all." She giggled. Although she was a perfectionist and quite demanding, Eve Grant was also quite humorous. She insisted I call her "Eve" because she was around my age or younger. It was known throughout Boston that Eve's family was very wealthy, and she had been exposed to the best of everything. I was truly honored to have her as a customer. She bought Naomi's hats and bonnets as well.

"Sarah, I'm going to Paris in a few weeks, and would like very much for you to join me. I have several friends there, and they will love your designs. You have great skills, and you need to expand beyond Boston. Furthermore, you will simply love Paris. Paris gets more beautiful with each visit. Now, tell me, will you come with me? I have gotten so many compliments on your dresses."

It was obvious that Eve was serious. Callie, Cora and Naomi looked up from their sewing machines, as if they could not believe Eve had asked me to join her. That was not the first time she had talked to me about expanding my business beyond Boston. I had not given it much thought because there was always so much going on in my life. Unlike Eve, I was not a wealthy, white socialite who had nothing to worry about, except which dress to wear to different events.

"Me, go to Paris? Paris is a place I have dreamed about, but when I wake up, that dream is gone."

"My dear Sarah, there is absolutely no reason why you should not come to Paris to meet my friends, and to expand your business opportunities. You have got to think big, Sarah. Lots of people make dresses, but yours are better than most of them. Why, Paris is the fashion center of the world. Think of the new, fresh ideas you can acquire by coming to Paris and meeting and talking with people. I must run along, dear, but let me know if you can come." Eve grabbed her dresses and left.

I watched Eve stroll down the street, looking as glamourous as ever in a bright pink dress with ruffles around the edge of the skirt that fit her thin body perfectly. She probably purchased the dress in Paris during her last visit because I had not seen that style in Boston. Eve was right; I needed to broaden my thinking about fashion so my business would continue to grow.

"Well, what you gonna do?" Cora asked. "You goin' to Paris with Miz Eve?" I did not expect Cora to comment on what Eve said. She stopped the sewing machine, looked directly at me, and waited for an answer.

"Cora is right," Naomi added. "You're one of de best designers and dressmakers in Boston, an you gotta grow an keep up wit de times. Sarah, I think you need to go to Paris wit Miz Eve. Think of all de people dat society woman knows. She can help you, Sarah."

"I agree wit evry word Cora an Naomi have spoke," Callie added. "Thar ain't nothing wrong wit bein' de best at what you do. Why, you can come back here an design dresses dat otha dressmakers ain't neva seen."

"I am surprised at each of you. I never thought you would agree with Eve. She is white, very wealthy, and she travels every where. I am not Eve, and I am not trying to be like her."

"Dis ain't about bein' like Miz Eve," Naomi continued. "We jes wont de best for you, Sarah. You got a wonderful gift, an thar is so much more you can do wit dis gift. Tell me, what is wrong about you goin' to Paris?"

"Well, first of all, I have a family to care for. Second, I've got a dress shoppe to run. Third, I've got to help the refugees at Fort Monroe. They need so much, and there is so much I want to do for them. My life is not just about doing what I want to do. I have others to think about and to look after."

"We ain't sayin' you gotta stop lookin' afta othas," Callie said. "All we're sayin' is dat you're a gifted dressmaker, an we wont you to make de most of dis gift. I can jes see you walkin' de streets of Paris, in one of your finest dresses. Sarah, you're so pretty, dose Paris people will think you're one of dem." They laughed.

"Well, ladies, thank you for your confidence in me, and for encouraging me, but my place is right here in Boston, doing the things I love to do, and being with the people I love and care about. Remember, I am still searching for my brother."

"I think you need to go, an dat's all I'm gonna say about it," Cora said. We went back to work and nothing else was said about Paris that day. However, I could not get their words out of my mind. I was happy in Boston with my family, and with making dresses with three women I had grown to love and trust. Still, thoughts of going to Paris lingered.

That night I thought about everything Eve, Cora, Callie and Naomi said. I had grown comfortable with designing familiar styles of dresses. Although my customers were pleased with my designs, I wondered if there would come a day when they might want something different, something more modern, or perhaps move on to other dressmakers.

That was quite possible. Perhaps that was exactly what Eve was trying to get me to understand, without actually having to say it. Eve had purchased dresses from several dressmakers in Boston and throughout New England, as well as from dressmakers abroad. Perhaps she was trying to help me build a larger business by suggesting that I come to Paris with her; or maybe it was simply casual chatter. Regardless, Paris was on my mind.

The next morning at breakfast I talked to William and my parents about what Eve said, and about the comments Cora, Callie and Naomi made. I needed to get to the shoppe, but wanted to talk and listen to what my husband and parents thought about me going to Paris. I respected their opinions and often asked for their advice.

"This is not the first time Eve Grant has mentioned taking a trip to Paris, is it?" William asked.

"No, it is not. As you know, Eve travels quite a bit. She seems to think I can benefit from going to Paris to meet other designers and to see their work. I cannot imagine being that far from home. We're talking about crossing an ocean."

"People cross oceans everyday," William responded. "Sarah, you must broaden your thinking about your business. Eve Grant clearly knows and appreciates the best in fashion, and she can certainly help your business. I think you should go." William's answer did not surprise me. His parents traveled quite often and they were business-minded people, always looking for fresh ideas and ways to grow. William's grandfather owned a grocery store, and his children learned the business and opened stores throughtout New England.

"Go to Paris, and leave my family? The thought of it frightens me."

"I didn't think anything frightened you, Sarah. One of your best qualities is your courage to face obstacles. Take a moment to reflect on your amazing flight from Holly Springs to Boston. You are the owner of one of the finest dress shoppes in Boston, and you had your business long before you met me. I'm proud to be your husband."

William's words were special. My parents smiled, but said nothing. I guess they thought that conversation was between me and my husband. They never interfered in our marriage.

"As for your shoppe, Cora, Callie and Naomi are more than capable of managing it until you return. They are like family, and we trust them. Mammy and Pappy are strong and independent, and they love taking care of Will. As for the refugees, they will make it, Sarah. Volunteers are coming to the camps each week, and some will be there indefinitely. We are following through on what we promised by sending clothing, food and supplies to them. We will get back to Fort Monroe as soon as possible.

"As for leaving me to go to Paris, that's not going to happen, because I will be on that ship with you. You don't think I would let my wife go to Paris without me, do you? Now, when are we leaving?"

I almost dropped my fork when William said he would be on that ship with me! For some strange reason I did not think he would leave his work to travel abroad, but I was wrong. My parents hugged each other and smiled.

"You will actually leave the newspaper and your work to travel with me"?

"Of course I will leave my work and travel with you. I don't want you to travel that far without me. We need to get with Eve as soon as possible to get the details about the trip. It will be good for us to get away, Sarah. I'm excited about going to Paris."

We had saved some money and William's parents offered to help with the cost of the trip, since the purpose was to broaden my business. I would get new, fresh ideas for designing dresses, and get to visit one of the most beautiful cities in the world.

I got to the shoppe late the next morning, and Cora, Callie and Naomi were already sewing. I apparently looked happy because they gave me a most interesting look.

"You're goin' to Paris!" Callie screamed. "I jes knew you would think about it an make de right decision." For a few moments I said nothing, but proceeded to stitch the hem of the gown I had been working on. They continued to stare at me. Finally, I stood up and shared the good news with them.

"Yes, ladies, I am going to Paris with Eve. I thought about what you all said, and you made some good points. If I want to be the best designer and dressmaker in Boston, I have to broaden my thinking and expand my business. I want to learn more, and Paris is known for fashion." Before I finished speaking, the ladies jumped around and screamed like young, playful girls.

"I knew it, I knew it," Cora said. "Sarah, we will look afta your parents and Will, as well as dis shoppe. You will have a great time. Think of all de people you will get to meet. You will have de best dress shoppe in Boston when you get back."

"Yes, I believe William and I will have a wonderful time."

"William is goin' wit you?" Callie asked. "You know what dey say about Paris? Dey say thar's lots of fashion, an lots of *romance*, too. You an William will have a *real* good time." My friends were just as excited as I was. Listening to them made me feel like a young girl about to explore a new world.

That evening my parents gave their opinion. They thought it was wonderful. "Chile, you're gonna see dis beautiful world, an you should," Mammy said. "You an William are young, an you should do de things you wont to do. You always been brave, my chile, an you will learn so much by goin' to Paris. Y'all be careful, an stay close to Miz Eve."

"Don't stay gone too long, Baby," Pappy added. "I know William will look afta you, 'cause he's a good man. Your Mammy an me

188

will be jes fine, so don't worry 'bout us. You know we will take good care of Will."

We met with Eve the following day to get the details about the trip, and learned that we would leave for Paris in two weeks. Eve carefully explained how to prepare for the trip, and what we needed to pack. She was excited that I was coming with her to learn more about the fashion industry. She said most of the people she had taken with her over the years could not wait to return. She also mentioned that Paris is a very romantic city, and no woman should be there alone. She winked at us, then giggled. Eve was quite a character.

Those days passed quickly, and before long, William, Eve, her husband and I boarded the largest ship I had ever seen. Eve's husband decided to come with her because he was prominent in the textile industry and planned to do business in Paris. I held William's hand as we boarded the ship and prepared to cross the Atlantic Ocean. There was no way I would have boarded that ship without my husband.

Lots of people boarded that ship, laughing and talking as if they were about to get into a carriage to travel around Boston. I suspected they were all wealthy and had traveled abroad before. Although I was frightened, William seemed to be as excited about crossing the ocean as the other passengers.

The ship appeared to be even larger on the inside. It was filled with people, some from New England and some appeared to be European. Although most of the passengers were Caucasian, there were Negroes who traveled abroad as well.

William and I did not stay in one of the palatial cabins, but we were quite comfortable in our cabin. Some passengers traveled on the lower decks in steerage. The meals on the ship were excellent and the service was wonderful. We enjoyed delicious French cuisine. One day William joined Eve's husband and other men for a tour below the deck. He was quite fascinated to learn how a large, luxurious ship crossed an ocean with so many people comfortably aboard. Thankfully, I did not feel every wave in the ocean, as expected.

Eve was most personable and talkative on the ship, just as she was in Boston. Almost everyone seemed to know and like her.

People were drawn to her because she was as charming as she was attractive. She was a wealthy, pleasant, well-educated socialite, who wore her clothes well. She was graceful and eloquent, and stood out amongst the ladies aboard that ship.

I was in awe of the equity aboard the ship, despite having lived in Boston for several years. Boston had its race problems as well. I did not think Eve would be as pleasant and friendly to me on the ship, and in Paris, as she had been in Boston, because I was a Negro woman who made her clothes, but she was. She was quite gracious to us. She introduced us to several of her friends and acquaintances, and made a point to tell people she was wearing one of the dresses I designed and made. To have Eve Grant strut around the ship in one of my dresses was a business opportunity in itself.

The interior of the ship was elaborately decorated with fine art and furniture that appeared to be expensive. There was so much I could not wait to share with my parents and friends. I was primarily focused on how the women were dressed. Most of them were well-dressed during the day, but especially in the evenings when they came to dinner. I noticed everything, including their hairstyles and headgear. Several of the younger women wore decorative hairnets, made of very fine material that closely matched their hair color.

Some wore fancy bonnets trimmed with colorful ribbons. I took notes in order to share those ideas with Cora, Callie and Naomi. The ladies had interesting hairstyles. One style, parted in the middle, smoothed over the ears and pulled back into a bun, was quite attractive. We had to be creative in designing dresses and in anything associated with fashion, including hairstyles and accessories.

After days of traveling across the ocean, we finally reached our destination. I was so thankful to get off of that ship and to be on land again, in Paris. We were invited to stay with Eve's mother in a house her family owned. It was my understanding that Eve's grandmother grew up in Paris and came to America when she was a young woman. Apparently her family still owned property in Paris, which was probably why Eve was able to travel there so often.

That evening we had dinner with Eve and some of her relatives. The house we stayed in was simply lovely. It was located on farmland near Paris. The white house was constructed of wood, stone and brick. It had six bedrooms and two large dining rooms, with cathedral ceilings throughout the house. I can never forget the breathtaking view of the French countryside from the bedroom window.

Eve appeared to be tired that evening, and was not as loquacious as usual. She told us to get some rest because she wanted to take us to *Musee du Louvre* the next day. She spoke French fluently. I later learned that she spent some of her childhood years in France. It was no secret that she loved the arts and her home was filled with a fine art collection.

Before we left Boston, I read about *Le Louvre* and other historical sites we planned to visit in Paris. *Le Louvre* was a fortress built to defend the Seine below Paris against the Normans and the English. It was also the former residence of King Louis XVI and Queen Marie Antoinette. During the French Revolution, the first state museum was opened in Le Louvre, where royal collections of paintings and sculpture were housed.

I had never seen anything as grand as that historical structure. We were speechless. It was hard to believe that I escaped from a plantation in Mississippi, and was visiting a palace in Paris. All things certainly are possible.

William appeared to be mesmerized as he studied each painting. As a child, I remember wondering what the world was like, and what life was like outside of Holly Springs. For years all I knew about the world was that my family, and other slaves, lived on farms and plantations owned by white people, and that we had to do what we were told to do. I now know that the world is big and full of things to see and do. Everyone should be free to learn about and explore the world.

The next day Eve took us to *Notre Dame de Paris*, which she described as a fine example of French Gothic architecture. She explained that Napoleon I was coronated there in 1804. It is a holy, sacred place. I felt close to God as I kneeled to pray, and thanked Him for all He had done for us. I counted my blessings, prayed for my brother, and asked God to help me find him. I believed Tom was alive and we would soon be together. I prayed for our people, that we would soon be free, forever.

As I left the cathedral, there was a sense of peace that everything would work out for us. We went back to the house we were staying in and Eve asked us if we were enjoying our visit. She had rested and was as talkative as ever.

"Yes, it is absolutely wonderful to be here," William said. "Thank you, Eve, for inviting my wife to come along with you. I did not want Sarah to travel this far without me, and thank you for this opportunity. You have supported Sarah's business, and I want you to know we are grateful to you. We are well aware that there are many dressmakers in Boston and throughout New England. You have worn, and continue to wear my wife's designs. We appreciate your support."

"I support Sarah because her work is very good," Eve responded. "Tomorrow I want both of you to meet some Parisian designers from whom I have purchased several gowns and dresses. Sarah, they have complimented your dresses, and they look forward to meeting you. I think it is wonderful when artistic people come together to share ideas. I think your business should expand beyond Boston, and I want to help you. Everyone knows I love fashion. It doesn't matter to me who designs my clothes, as long as it's quality, creative work.

"Tell me, Sarah, what is your source of inspiration? Most artists are inspired by something."

"Yes, Eve, you are right, most artists are inspired by something. My inspiration comes from the miraculous power of a tiny seed, planted in the ground. Think of all the good and beauty that comes from a tiny seed. When something is planted, one day it will sprout, grow and prosper. My favorite colors are those that most closely resemble the colors of vegetables. If you have noticed, I prefer to work with different shades of green, yellow and orange. I have a small garden, and every morning before leaving for work, I am anxious to examine the vegetables, looking for new growth, new sprouts, and to see something I did not see the day before."

"So, you are a gardener as well as a dressmaker and designer?" Eve looked at me as if she was trying to understand how a vegetable garden could inspire someone to design and make dresses. Eve knew me as a dressmaker and designer; but, she did not know Sarah, the person. She did not have any understanding of the hardship of growing up on a plantation. She did not understand that what little spare time Pappy had after working in the fields, he taught me how to grow vegetables, explaining that they needed water and sunshine to grow. She did not understand that Mammy worked long hours in the big house, but still found a little time to teach me how to make quilts from scraps. My parents taught us to survive. Despite a life of slavery, those days with my family were some of the happiest days of my life.

"Yes, I am a gardener, dressmaker and designer, and thoroughly enjoy all of it."

"Sarah, your dresses flow so well. Why, sometimes I feel as if I am floating across the room when I'm wearing your evening gowns." Eve laughed, and twirled around with her arms stretched out, as if she was attempting to fly.

"Although my dresses are designed so that the bodice fits perfectly, I like a full skirt that flows as the lady walks. That gives her the appearance of being *free* and *unconstrained*. I believe life is to be enjoyed, and *everyone* should be *free*. That *principle* is my inspiration to create full, free-flowing skirts." There was silence for a few moments. Eve looked at William and me.

"I agree with you, Sarah," she said. "All people should be free." There was more silence. Although Eve socialized with abolitionists in Boston, she had never mentioned that she was an abolitionist. It was good she had not mentioned that, because actions are more powerful than words. Eve not only supported me, a Negro dressmaker and designer, but she had also sent several of her friends to my shoppe and they bought lots of dresses. She and her husband donated large amounts of money in response to William's articles in the paper that money, food and supplies were needed to help the refugees in the contraband camps. I did not know what Eve Grant believed in her heart about slavery, but she had definitely supported me and the refugees at Fort Monroe.

The next day was most interesting because Eve took us to a fashion show, where women modeled dresses and gowns of several designers. I had never seen or heard of anything like that, and it was a fascinating experience I never forgot. As the women walked down the corridor, the designer talked about the design, and why women should buy that dress. I watched in awe as lovely ladies clothed in fashionable dresses and gowns filled the room. Then, by the end of the day, Eve had a most pleasant surprise – she introduced me to Charles Frederick Worth.

Charles Frederick Worth, an English-born fashion designer, came to Paris and changed the fashion industry forever. His story, which Eve shared with us, was most interesting. After working in drapery shoppes in London, he moved to Paris and worked for a company that sold ready-made garments and textile goods. He excelled as a salesman, and eventually opened a small dressmaking department for that company. He was recognized for his designs, some of which were displayed in the Great Exhibition in London and the Exposition Universelle in Paris.

Empress Eugenie, wife of Napoleon III, other European royalty, as well as wealthy American ladies, wore dresses he designed. Their support helped him become a front-runner in the fashion industry. I only spoke briefly with Mr. Worth that evening because people gathered waiting for the opportunity to meet him. More important than speaking with him, Eve wore one of my gowns and mentioned that to Mr. Worth. I clearly remember hearing him say to her, "Your gown is lovely."

Eve's husband had to get back to Boston earlier than expected, so our visit to Paris was cut short. Over the next two days, we visited other historical sites and attended two more fashion shows. I was determined to work with Callie, Cora and Naomi to plan our first fashion show.

As we traveled back to Boston, I wrote about my experience in Paris, and how to expand my business. Mr. Worth was the first designer to put labels in his designs, and I would do the same.

Paris was wonderful, but we were ready to get back to Boston. I admired Mr. Worth for all he had accomplished in the fashion industry, but was quite comfortable with my gift as a designer and dressmaker. I had my very own style, would continue to develop it, and work hard to make *The Dress Shoppe* one of the most prosperous shoppes in New England.

# CHAPTER 18

In the fall of 1862, Hannah and I left John Mundy's plantation early one morning, two days after we reunited in the woods behind the plantation. I was stronger, and ready to run again, this time with my lady. Hannah was quiet as we walked away. She was sad about leaving Mary, who had been like a mother to her. I made it clear to her that she did not have to leave with me; and she made it clear that she wanted to come with me.

My sack was filled with food, water and other things she thought we might need for our flight back to Fort Monroe. That was one of the happiest days of my life. With Hannah by my side, I could do anything. Our love for each other was, and is to this day, powerful. Nothing compares to having a strong, wise, caring woman in your life.

I wanted to sprint through the woods, but couldn't because that would have been too exhausting for Hannah. I was very careful with her because she had a history of having breathing problems at times. Those problems were triggered by stress, illness, or exceptionally long days of work in the big house. I did everything possible to prevent her from getting sick.

The temperature dropped, but it was not terribly cold. We had warm clothing and comfortable shoes, and walked each day until Hannah was too tired to keep going. Whenever she needed to rest, we stopped, spread quilts on the ground and rested until the sun came up the next day.

We did not talk a lot because there was no telling who was around. We were quite pleased that John Mundy joined the Confederate Army. Still, I wondered if his overseers were aware that Hannah had left. Mary loved Hannah dearly, and she may have kept that secret out of her love for her. Thank God we did not hear or see any patrollers.

Although we moved at a slow pace, each step took us farther away from that plantation, and closer to our destination, Fort Monroe. As expected, the days began to get colder. One evening we sat under a large tree, wrapped tightly in each other's arms. Hannah wanted to talk, and I listened.

"Tom, somehow I knew dat you would make it back to de plantation to get me. When Joe came to tell me dat you had ran off, a part of me was sad, but a part of me was so happy for you. I prayed for you evryday, and bleeved dat you would make it to Fort Monroe safe. You's a good man, Tom. Mammy used to say dat good things happen to good people. Now, my prayers been answered, an we's togetha again. Tom, we gonna stay togetha dis time. From now on, I'm goin' wit you, where eva you go. You ain't leavin' me behind no more."

I pulled the quilts up around Hannah's neck to protect her from the cold wind and prayed that she would not get sick. I didn't think I could keep going without Hannah in my life. She was a source of strength.

"Tom, did you have a rough time gettin' to Fort Monroe?" Hannah's big, enchanting, brown eyes stared at me. We were so close I could feel her heart beating.

"Yes, I had a rough time. One day I will tell you all 'bout de people I met in de woods, and 'bout how I got caught, an 'bout how I had to stay with Jim for a long time befo I made it to Fort Monroe. Still, I neva stopped prayin' an bleevin dat I would make it. Dat's what you gotta do, Hannah – pray, bleeve, an keep movin'.

"What was Jim like?"

"He was just anotha white man who 'pected me to work for him for nuttin. The only reason he caught me was because my feet was swollen an cut an I could not run. I coulda beat Jim an got away from him, but I couldn't run."

"How did you get away from him?"

"He made de mistak of takin' me to a pretty place, Williamsburg, an he didn't bring his hounds wit him. Thank God, dat was de break I needed. Fort Monroe ain't far from Williamsburg, an I found my way. Afta runnin' for a few days, it won't long befo I saw dis large body of water. Fort Monroe is right on de Chesapeake Bay."

"Tell me about Fort Monroe. What is it like thar? Joe didn't think you would make it. He said dey put de hounds on your scent soon as dey heard dat you was gone."

"Well, thank God, Joe was wrong. I made it to Fort Monroe, me an lots of otha slaves who dared to run to be free. Joe could be free if he had come wit me, but I can't worry 'bout Joe. Fort Monroe is crowded wit men, women and childrun who want to be free. Genral Butler don't turn no slaves away. De people live in shanties, but it gets more crowded each day, an thar is much work to be done."

"What do de women do?" Hannah appeared to be captivated with learning about Fort Monroe. She wanted to be free as much as I did, and wasn't afraid of running any more.

"De women care for de childrun, wash, clean, cook, grow vegetables an care for wounded soldiers. I met some very nice people thar, like Samuel and Lydia. Dey's good, decent people who want a betta life. Also, I have someone special I want you to meet. His name is Caleb."

"Who is Caleb?"

"Caleb is a fine young man. He wuks hard an is eager to learn evrythin' he can. You will love him, Hannah." I told her about Caleb and that he was the reason I was headed back to Fort Monroe.

She asked more questions about Fort Monroe, then fell asleep on my chest that night. She was tired and cold. I was quite concerned about her because I had always escaped during warmer months. Unfortunately, we could not sit around on John Mundy's plantation and wait until spring to escape. It just didn't work like that. Slaves had to run whenever they got the opportunity to get away.

After a few days in the woods, Hannah began to cough a lot. I had to find a way to get her out of the cold, or she wouldn't make it. She packed some kind of potion for her cough, and I gave her some and put the quilts around her small body. We had finally escaped from the plantation together, and I did not intend to let her die in those woods.

Early that next morning I took a big risk and made a fire with some sticks and dried leaves. That probably was not the wisest thing to do, but it was a chance I had to take to keep Hannah warm. I was certain the smoke would attract attention to us, and it did. About an hour after I made that fire, I heard someone's footsteps. Hannah had gotten weaker and we could not run, so I had no choice but to wait to see who was approaching us.

It was a Negra man, walking alone. I didn't know if he was a slave on the run or if he was working for someone. He stopped for a few minutes to talk.

"Whut you doin' out heah in dis cold?" he asked.

"We gotta do some wuk for de mastah." That was all I intended to reveal to him. He was short and heavy, and dressed appropriately for the weather, with a hat and a worn coat.

"You betta do whut you gotta do 'cause it's gonna be colder tonight. I's headed back to de plantation. Whur is yo plantation?" I assumed he was a slave and he assumed I was one.

"My plantation ain't close, an dis lady is sick. I gotta get some help for her." I did not let him know Hannah and I knew each other. I wanted him to think I was in the woods trying to help a sick lady. I thought he would move on, but he did not. Instead, he came closer and looked down at Hannah.

"She could die in dis cold. I ain't got nuttin wit me dat can help her. I seen a house back yonda. Maybe somebody thar can help her."

"Where is dis house?" Hannah was coughing a lot and I had to do something. I even thought about taking her back to John Mundy's plantation so Mary could care for her. I could not let her stay out in the cold and die. I decided to look for the house the man had seen and try to get some help. It was a risk that could have cost us our lives, but to save Hannah's life was worth the risk.

Hannah was weak, so I picked her up and carried her through the woods that cold day in November 1862. After walking for several minutes, I saw a white house with smoke coming from the chimney. I knew that house had to be warm, so I walked up to the door and knocked. It was not long before the door opened. A white lady, who appeared to be around forty years old, looked directly at me without saying a word. I expected her to slam the door in my face, but surprisingly, she did not.

"Why are you here?" she asked. Her gaze shifted from me to Hannah. "Is she alive?"

"Yes'um, she's alive, but she real sick. She's cold an she cannot stop coughin'." I stood there, still expecting the door to slam in my face. The lady turned and called for someone I assumed was her husband. A man came to the door and the woman stepped behind him. The man appeared to be a little older than the woman.

"Come in out of the cold," he said. "You can die in this weather."

The man opened the door wide and stepped back so we could enter what appeared to be the living room. The first thing I noticed was a fire burning. I stood near the door staring at the fire. That room was so warm. I felt as if I had walked into the gates of heaven. Hannah continued to cough.

"Put her down near the fire," he said. "She sounds pretty sick. Rebecca, get her something warm to drink."

The lady soon came back into the room with a cup. "Here, see if you can get her to drink this," she said. "It's warm water with herbs that should help her cough."

I held Hannah in my arms and raised her head so she could drink from the cup. She slowly sipped the warm drink. I managed to get her to drink all of it, and then laid her back on the floor near the fire. Her eyes were closed and she looked weak, but it wasn't long before she stopped coughing. Finally, the man asked me why were we out on such a cold night. I paused for a few minutes to think before answering.

"I been tryin' to get some help for dis lady. I did not wont her to die in dis cold."

"Rebecca can help her," he said. "She's real good at caring for the sick. Where did you come from?"

I knew that question was coming. I could not confide in that man and woman because they were white. I could not tell them we were running away from John Mundy's plantation because they may have known him. I suspected they were willing to help Hannah get well so they could turn us in. At that moment, all I cared about was for Hannah to get better. Her life was more important than being forced to return to the plantation.

"We's from a place near Savannah." I did not say anything else, because the less said, the better.

"Where're you going in this cold weather?" The lady was busy trying to help Hannah get comfortable on the floor. I could not imagine those white people wanting to help us. I thought without a doubt they had plans for us, but not good plans. At that moment, all that mattered to me was that Hannah was warm.

"As soon as she stops coughing, we'll leave heah. We don't want to cause you no trouble."

"There's no way this woman can leave this house tonight and expect to live," the woman said to the man. "She needs to stay here for a day or two. I don't want her to die."

Her words shocked me. Those people knew nothing about us, yet they didn't want Hannah to die. They must have known, or at least suspected, we were slaves on the run. Then it all became very clear to me. They wanted to trap us in their home for a few days to allow time to get a message to slaveholders that they had captured two slaves. Reward money for catching run away slaves was good. I figured that man and woman needed money, and had found the perfect way to get it.

We stayed in that house two or three days. I was quite anxious because I expected a slaveholder to knock at the door to claim us at any moment. Surprisingly, that did not happen. I soon learned that the man, William, and his wife, Rebecca, really wanted Hannah to get well. She got better, and William asked a most interesting question.

"Are you two trying to get to the North?" I looked away and, for some reason, gave him an honest answer. I didn't trust the man, but didn't lie to him.

"Yes, we's tryin' to get to Fort Monroe." Those people saved Hannah's life, and I didn't lie to them. If they had turned us over to John Mundy that day, I would not have been angry with them because they saved Hannah's life.

"If you need me to help you out 'round dis place, I will stay to help you," I said. I felt indebted to them because of what they had done for us. I could see there was work that needed to be done in the fields, and was willing to help them out.

"No, I got some hired help. We can manage those fields," William said.

"I want to do somethin' for you to show my 'preciation for what you done for Hannah. She coulda froze to death. You saved her life, an I wont to pay you for what you done for us. We's real grateful to both of you."

"I'm glad you made it here," Rebecca said. "She was a real sick lady. William and I believe in helping people; all people."

"Thank you from de bottom of my heart," Hannah said. "Dem herbs got me feelin' better in no time. Miz Rebecca, I'll be more dan happy to stay heah to help you wit yo cleanin' an cookin'. I'm real good at cleanin' and cookin'."

"Thank you," she replied, "but I don't need no help around here. I just hope y'all make it safely. It's mighty cold in these parts for anybody to be walking through the woods. By the way, we know someone who might be able to help y'all." Rebecca looked at William and then back at us. There was a brief silence, and then William spoke.

"We know some people who go to Virginia from time to time, and they may be able to help you. They don't live far from here. Tell them that William and Rebecca sent you."

William proceeded to tell me how to get to the home of one of his friends he thought might be able to help us. I listened carefully to his directions. I had made it to Fort Monroe once and knew I could do it again, but didn't think Hannah could make that long flight without getting sick again. We couldn't go back to the plantation because we would be punished for running away. I had to think about Hannah's health, and took William's advice.

Hannah was much stronger when we left William and Rebecca's home, and she was wrapped up from head to toe. I didn't know if I could trust William's friend or not, but it was a chance I had to take. Although William and Rebecca had been very kind to us, I still did not feel good about going to the home of another stranger, to ask for help. Still, we walked on in the cold weather.

After walking for maybe an hour, I saw a house that looked like the one William described. I held Hannah close as we approached the door. It was cold and I was worried about her. She held my hands and said a prayer, then I knocked at the door. A short, round white man, with bulging eyes and little hair, opened the door to the white, two story wooden house.

"We's heah to ask for help gittin to Vaginia," I said. "William and Rebecca sent us to you." I felt very uncomfortable standing at that white man's door, asking for help. It wasn't in my nature to ask anyone for help. I guess that was because I had always struggled so hard to get what I needed. If Hannah had not been with me, I would never have gone to that house. We were there only because of her health.

"Did you say William and Rebecca sent you?" the man repeated.

"Yes'um, dey sent us heah. We don't want to trouble you. We can keep walkin'."

"Come on in out of the cold," he said. His home was as warm and comfortable as William and Rebecca's home. "Anne, we got company. Bring these people something hot to drink."

Before long, a thin, short woman brought two cups of hot coffee to us. I assumed she was the man's wife. She invited us to sit and get warm. I couldn't imagine white people being that kind to two strange niggers. They appeared to be as kind as William and Rebecca. I thought this was all too good to be true. My heart pounded as I sipped the hot coffee, waiting for someone to break in to claim us. I sensed that Hannah was equally as concerned about our safety.

After a few minutes, the man, whose name was Horace, asked where we were headed on such a cold night. I didn't know what to say to him. I didn't want to lie, but couldn't tell him we were runaway slaves, out of fear he would turn us in. After a short silence, I answered.

"We tryin' to git to Vaginia, 'cause we got a chile thar an we want to be wit him." Horace looked at the woman and then at us. The woman lowered her head and stared at the fire burning in the room. She then looked at Hannah and spoke.

"I know all too well what it's like to have a child, and not be with that child. We lost our only child a year ago. A day doesn't go by that I don't miss my baby and wonder if he is alright. But, I know he's got to be alright because he's with the Lord. Still, I would give anything to see him and talk to him again." The woman wiped her eyes with a cloth she was holding. There was a long silence.

"It doesn't matter who you are; if you've got a child, you should be with that child," she continued. "Parents should not be separated from their children."

The woman walked away and sat in a chair near the fire. She appeared to be very sad. I assumed she was still mourning the loss of her child. Hannah looked as if she wanted to comfort her, but I gave her a look to let her know that the woman probably wanted to be alone for a few minutes. Hannah has a big heart and loves to care for others.

"Y'all taking a big risk walking about in these parts," the man said. "A lot of your people have been caught in these parts. Slaveholders pay well for the capture and return of slaves."

Hannah looked at me. My heart beat faster and hers probably did as well. I sensed that we had been trapped! It appeared that we had been sent to that house to be captured and returned to the plantation. I wanted to grab Hannah and run, but figured Horace and Anne's home was probably surrounded by patrollers and hounds.

"Anne, this is what we need to do," Horace said. She got up from her chair and walked over to her husband. I grabbed Hannah and held her tight. I didn't know what their plans were for us, but whatever they planned to do to us, I had a strange sense of peace. That peace was in knowing that we were together. If we had been captured, or if we were about to die, we were together. I kissed Hannah and held her close.

# CHAPTER 19

It wasn't long after we returned from Paris that we were busy preparing for another trip to Fort Monroe. Lots of people donated supplies to take to the refugees. We were anxious to see the progress they had made.

We left for a third trip to Fort Monroe early one Friday morning in late October 1862 with ten volunteers. Most of the volunteers were retired teachers who wanted to teach the refugees to read and write. Some came to teach skills to the men so they could earn a living and support their families.

"Welcome back, my friends," Samuel said. "Lydia an me been waitin' for yo return. It's so good to see you agin."

"It's good to see you, my friend." William shook Samuel's hand. "I see that you are still working hard. We brought more volunteers who want to help. Have things improved around here?"

"Yes, things is gittin betta for us. We gotta always bleeve dat things is gittin betta. Now, a lot mo boys an men kin build shacks an do carpentry wuk 'round heah. Come, let me take you to see Lydia."

We followed Samuel, and Lydia ran to us with open arms. She still had that big, bright smile. I often wondered if anything could stop Samuel and Lydia from being pleasant, kind, hard-working people. They were such an inspiration to everyone. Although they were fugitive slaves, living in a contraband camp, they were rich in so many ways.

"My dear Lydia, how are you?" I embraced her. "It is so good to be back. We have more volunteers, supplies, food and clothing."

"I'm well, Sarah. Lord knows, it's good to see you an William agin. Things is gittin betta for us, but, as you kin see, it's even mo crowded heah since y'all left us."

"I can certainly see that. How is your son?" Lydia was holding him.

"My Timmy is well, an he's growin' so fas. He wont be a baby too much longa." Lydia kissed her son and wiped his face with her hand. Caleb, a young boy, stood next to her. I remembered that he came to Fort Monroe with several adults, but his mother died before they arrived. Caleb, like so many of the young children, had no parents. Samuel and Lydia were very fond of him.

"Caleb is doin' good, but sometimes he gits sad 'cause Tom ain't heah. Tom said he will be back for Caleb, an I bleeve he will. Tom is a man of his word. I know y'all must be hungry, so sit down an let me fix y'all somethin' to eat."

We sat in wooden chairs that Samuel made. He talked to the volunteers about the supplies they needed in the camps, and about how he and other men and boys worked everyday to build more shanties. He also talked about the vegetables the women and children had grown.

Lydia returned with pork, beans, bread and water. After we ate, the volunteers left to get settled with relatives and friends in the area. Samuel and Lydia showed us the shanty they prepared for us. Lydia talked about how much Caleb had learned and that he was a good child.

"Tom been lak a father to Caleb," she said. "Tom ax me to take care of Caleb 'til he kin git back heah to git him. Me an Samuel think of him as our own."

"Yeah, Caleb kin jes 'bout build a shack by hisself," Samuel said. He patted Caleb's shoulders. "He's a fine young boy. I think it's 'bout time for you to git some sleep." Caleb said good night and left.

"Dat chile miss Tom so much," Lydia said. "Show hate dat Tom had to leave him."

"Who is Tom, and where is he?" William asked.

"Tom come from a plantation back in Savannah," Samuel explained. "He ran off from a plantation he was hired out to wuk on down in Charleston. Well, he lef a woman he luv very much back on dat plantation. He made a promise he would come back for her one day, an dat's whur he gone. He luv dat woman a lot, an he wont her to be wit him. Tom is a good, decent man." There was a long silence.

"Sarah, by the way, is looking for her brother," William said. "His name is also 'Tom'. I believe we will find him. Her brother was sold when he was a child, and the last time Sarah saw him was in Atlanta, many years ago." There was more silence.

"Tell us 'bout yo brotha, Sarah," Lydia said. "I know he mus be a fine man."

"My brother is indeed a fine man. I remember him caring for me when I was very young. Sometimes he worked in the cotton fields with Pappy, and sometimes he helped Pappy build things. He is a skilled carpenter and mason. The last time I saw him, he was building a veranda at a house in Atlanta. He is real good with tools and bricks." I noticed that as I talked about my brother, Samuel and Lydia looked at each other instead of looking at me. I thought that was somewhat strange, and stopped talking because I did not know what was wrong. Finally, Lydia spoke.

"Sarah, de Tom dat was heah at de camp kin build jes 'bout anythin'," she said. "Why, even de white men know dat he got good skills, an he kin jes 'bout do anythin' ova at de Fort an heah in de camps. Sarah, de Tom dat wuz heah in de camp, de one dat Samuel an me have growed to luv an trust, could be yo brotha!" I listened, but did not get excited because I had been looking for my brother for so long, without any success. There was a long silence, then Samuel spoke.

"Tom came to de camp afta we did. He got great carpentry and bricklayin' skills, an he kin build anythin'. I heard him say many times dat he come from a plantation in Missippi, an he wuked in Atlanta some years back."

"Tell us everything you can about this man. Can you think of anything special he said about his family?" William appeared to be more interested in what Samuel and Lydia had to say about the man than I was. I was tired from the long trip, but listened as they talked on.

"I rememba Tom talkin' 'bout some chairs he an his Pappy built," Samuel said. "His Pappy wuz teachin' him how to nail de wood togetha, an Tom hit his finger real hard. Tom said he wanted to cry, 'cause it hurt so bad, but he did not cry 'cause he wonted his Pappy to think he wuz a big boy, an dat he could build things. Tom said dat night, afta his Pappy wuz asleep, he started to cry 'cause his finger still hurt real bad. His mammy heard him cryin', an had a long talk wit him.

"Tom said his mammy said it wuz alright for him to cry. She told Tom he wuz a big boy, an a smart boy. She said it wuz good to cry sometimes, an nuttin for him to eva be ashamed of. She told him dat, jes lak dat hammer an nail hurt his finger, otha things in life would hurt him, an if he wonted to cry, he should. She told Tom his tears an pain would help him grow to be a big, strong man one day, just like de large trees "planted by de rivers of water".

"I wish somebody had told me dat when I wuz a boy. Tom an me got to be real close 'cause I enjoy listenin' to de things his parents taught him befo he got sold. He got a real good famly, somewhur, an dey taught him a lot. Tom show luv his famly."

"He show do," Lydia interjected. "He still got a quilt his mammy made for him. He took it wit him when he wuz sold as a boy. Dey said Tom wuz hired out, an he would come back to his famly, but he neva did. He wuz sold, not hired out. His mammy gave him dat quilt to take wit him befo he left his famly. Tom said dat quilt been wit him evry whur he been, 'cause his mammy gave it to him."

"Tell us about the quilt," William said. "I guess Tom took it with him when he left for Savannah."

"No, he did not take it wit him," Lydia said.

"I thought he took it wit him evry whur. Dat quilt is a part of his famly."

"Yes, it is a part of his famly. He left dat quilt heah wit Caleb, 'cause Tom think of Caleb as his son. He so wonted to take Caleb wit him to Savannah, but Lord knows, dat is a long journey for a chile. Tom thought it would be too hard on young Caleb. Dat is de only reason he left Caleb heah wit us."

"I would like to see the quilt," William said.

"I kin git it for you. Caleb lak to sleep wit dat quilt. Let me run to git it." Lydia left to get the quilt. While she was gone, Samuel talked on about Tom and about the good work he had done at Fort Monroe as a carpenter and bricklayer. She returned with a quilt that was clearly very old and worn, rolled up in her arms. As Lydia unrolled that old, worn quilt, my heart started to beat faster. I gasped, because I recognized that old quilt immediately. That was one of the quilts Mammy made when I was a young girl!

I even recognized some of my flawed stitches. At that time, I had just begun to use a needle and thread, and remember begging Mammy to let me help her make the quilt. Mammy, being the kind and patient person she is, let me make a few stitches. Although the stitches were crooked, and looked nothing like Mammy's, she hugged me and told me I could sew, and that one day I would make beautiful things with my hands. Mammy believed in me long before I believed in myself.

Mammy made *that* quilt for Tom, because he had always been so curious about trees. Tom used to ask questions like, "Why do trees grow so tall?" and, "Why are trees so big?" There were three trees embroidered on that quilt, with long, thick, brown roots. Mammy used to explain to him that it took many years for trees to get big, strong and tall. She talked about trees in the Bible, planted near water. Then Tom would say, "I wanna be big, strong an tall, just like a tree." Of course, Mammy assured him that he would grow to be big, strong and tall. I had absolutely no doubt that that was the quilt Mammy made for Tom.

We continued to talk about the man Samuel and Lydia believed was my brother. My heart ached, not only because the man had left the camp headed for Savannah, but because I knew that was my brother's quilt. I wondered if that man was really my brother, or if he was another stranger. Even if he was not my brother, that was Tom's quilt. I wondered if that person could somehow have found the quilt, or perhaps taken it from my brother. So much ran through my mind. I cried. It was simply too much to process at that time. William tried to calm me and Lydia gave me some water. I was desperate to find my brother, but was afraid I was in for yet another disappointment.

"Sarah, this man that Samuel and Lydia think could be your brother, may very well *be* your brother. You have been through so much searching for your brother. I don't want you to get hurt again. We need to be patient."

William was right. We had to be patient because I did not know if that man was my brother. Also, he had left Fort Monroe on a journey to Savannah. There was no way to know if he would ever return. That day I felt so helpless, so hurt, so anxious. I was angry with myself for not having asked around about my brother in the camps. That was our third visit to Fort Monroe, and I should have thought to ask about Tom. If I had only asked, I would have known if he was my brother or not.

For some reason, I believed Tom was somewhere in the North, perhaps even in Boston. I guess I believed that because I wanted it to be true; I wanted Tom to be close to us. That was why I had not focused on searching for him in the camps. I felt so foolish, as if I had somehow betrayed my own brother. The only thing that lifted my spirit that day was the fact that, if the man they described was my brother, then my brother had met Samuel and Lydia, two genuine, kind, wonderful people.

William was excited, but cautious about this man, because he did not want me to be hurt and disappointed as I had been so many times before. He knew I was desperate to find Tom, and how sad I had been because our search had been unsuccessful.

"Why didn't you tell me this sooner?" I asked Samuel and Lydia. They looked at each other as if they had done something wrong. I guess my tone was somewhat critical, but I was not thinking clearly at that moment.

"We's mighty sorry, Sarah," Lydia said. "We jes ain't neva heard you mention dat you had a brotha. You said you wuz a fugitive slave, but nuttin 'bout havin' a brotha."

"We did not mean no harm," Samuel added. "Lord, if we known you wuz lookin' for yo brotha, we woulda surely talked to Tom an tried to help you."

"Sarah is not blaming you," William interjected. "It's just that she has been looking so long for her brother, with no success. She will find him one day."

"If only I had said something; if only I had said something sooner to Samuel and Lydia. The first thing I should have done when we came to Fort Monroe was to have looked around and inquired about my brother. It was so foolish of me not to have done that. What if Tom has been here all along, working at Fort Monroe, and we have been here three times and overlooked him. I will never forgive myself if my brother was here all along and I do not find him." My heart and my spirit were broken that day in October 1862.

"Sarah, you were focused on trying to help the refugees," William said. "It's simply your nature to reach out to others. Furthermore, you thought your brother was in the North, and that's where you have been looking. We are going to find Tom. You must believe that."

"We shoulda ax Tom mo 'bout his famly," Samuel said. He held his head down. "If only I had ax him to tell me 'bout his famly, but me an Tom spent mos of our time wukin an tryin' to make things betta heah in de camps. Now I rememba Tom sayin' he had a sista, but he said his famly wuz probly still on dat plantation in Missippi. I guess dat's why I did not think to say somethin' to you, Sarah."

"We gotta bleeve dat Tom will make it safe to dat plantation, an dat he will git Hannah, an dat dey will make it safe back heah to Fort Monroe," Lydia said. "Tom is a good, honest man. If he said he will come back heah for Caleb, den I bleeve he will. Don't you worry, Sarah. If dat is yo brotha, we will let you know."

"Lydia is right," Samuel added. "Tom is a smart man, who kin do jes 'bout anythin'. I know he will find a way to git to dat plantation in Savannah, an git Hannah away from dat place. I ain't neva met a man like Tom. Lord, I show do miss him."

"Lydia and Samuel, thank you for telling me about this man. I hope and pray that he is my brother. I know for sure that Mammy made this quilt for him. Lydia, do you mind if I take this quilt with me? I'm sorry, I guess I should ask Caleb if I can keep this quilt, since it was given to him. No, forget it, I cannot take a quilt from a child."

"I will talk to Caleb in the morning," Lydia said, "but, I know how much he luv Tom, an he might wont to keep dis quilt."

"Let Caleb keep the quilt. Tom gave it to him. I would like to speak with Caleb before we leave."

I slept very little that night, on old quilts Lydia gathered for us. My heart ached as I thought about the man who had lived in the camp, then left to go back to Savannah. I wanted to believe he was my brother, but there was a strong possibility that he was not, since so many refugees entered the camp each day. I had to be patient and keep praying that I would find Tom.

The next morning Lydia prepared eggs and bread for Samuel, William, Caleb and me. After spending only a few hours with him,

I wanted to bring Caleb back to Boston with us. He was a most interesting child. It was very clear that he loved the man they knew as "Tom" very much. He told us about how Tom taught him to build shanties and to repair things.

"Tom said he's gonna teach me evrything he know," Caleb said. His bright, curious eyes sparkled as he shared with us how much Tom had taught him. Most important to Caleb, Tom taught him to build chairs.

"I help Tom build de chair you sittin' in, Miz Sarah. When I grow up, I'm gonna be de best bricklayer an carpenter of all. I wanna be jes lak Tom. He told me I can learn to do anything I wanna do."

"You love Tom very much, don't you?" I asked. "Tom sounds like a wonderful person and I am very anxious to see him."

"Tom gave me dis quilt, an told me to keep it for him 'til he gits back. Tom is comin' back heah for me. I hope he will hurry an git back, so we can build more things."

After listening to all the wonderful things Caleb said about Tom, there was no way I could take that quilt from him, although I knew Mammy made it. Caleb even said he was going to wash the quilt before Tom returned, so it would be clean when he gave it back to Tom. That child clearly loved Tom very much. Even if that man was not my brother, that was Caleb's quilt to keep.

We distributed the supplies we brought for the refugees. Of course, Caleb asked if he could help and Lydia gave him permission to help us. There was still a lot of work to be done in the camps. Some of the refugees had learned to read and write, and many had learned skills that would enable them to support themselves. After three days of working with the refugees, we had to leave the camp to get back to Boston. Before we left, Lydia and Samuel promised to let us know if the man they believed might be my brother returned to the camp, or if they heard any more about his whereabouts. We thanked them and said we would be back as soon as possible, with more volunteers and supplies.

# CHAPTER 20

One evening in November 1862, Mrs. Baker came to our home with some disturbing news. She had heard that Frank Wilmington was in Boston, looking for Daniel Broughton. Daniel left Boston to return to Canada shortly after his mother died. He did not tell Frank Wilmington about his departure. Mrs. Baker had heard that Frank Wilmington was asking people about Daniel's whereabouts.

Daniel had always been a private person. His neighbors probably did not know he had gone back to Canada, with no plans to return to Boston. Most people in that area knew Mrs. Broughton had died, and they told Frank Wilmington. Mrs. Baker informed us that Frank Wilmington was very angry with Daniel. As expected, he wanted to know where my parents were, and if Daniel had taken them with him.

"You must get out of the city!" Mrs. Baker said. "This man is making all kinds of threats, and someone will surely tell him where you are living. I cannot stand by and watch him take you and your parents back to Mississippi!"

"We are not leaving Boston," William said. "My wife has lived in fear of this man for years, and the time has come to deal with him."

"Deal with him, how? Sarah and her parents have not been granted their freedom. This man still has legal rights to them. Frank Wilmington has money and power, and the courts will rule in his favor. You know the law, William."

"I understand what you are saying, Mrs. Baker. I'm just ready to meet this man. I am not afraid of Frank Wilmington."

"This has nothing to do with your being afraid of Frank Wilmington. We have to think about what's best for Sarah and her parents." There was a long silence. William was ready to confront Frank Wilmington, but unfortunately Mrs. Baker was right. No court in Boston would deny him the right to reclaim his three fugitive slaves, regardless of the number of years that had passed since we left his plantation.

"William, let Sarah and her parents stay with Clara and me," Mrs. Baker pleaded. "Frank Wilmington is determined to find Daniel, because he believes Bertha and Joshua are with him."

"I think that's a good idea." William could be very stubborn at times. I could not allow his dislike for Frank Wilmington put my parents and me at risk of being snatched away and taken back to Mississippi.

"It's time I stood up to that man and protect my family," William said. "I don't want them to leave their home because Frank Wilmington is roaming around Boston asking questions. I'm ready to confront that man."

"Mrs. Baker, thank you for telling us that Frank Wilmington is here, and thank you for inviting us to live with you and Aunt Clara," I said. "We need some time to think about this, and decide what course of action to take. We will get back with you tomorrow."

William walked with Mrs. Baker to her home that evening, and I sat in our living room staring at the walls, wondering what would become of us. I wondered if we would ever be free of that man, and if Frank Wilmington would ever give up on finding us. I wondered if I could still run the dress shoppe if I moved in with Mrs. Baker and Aunt Clara. Cora, Naomi and Callie could run the shoppe, but we had so much work to finish with Christmas a month away. My customers would want to know why I was not in the shoppe. To my knowledge, none of them knew I was a fugitive slave.

Most importantly, I was concerned about my parents. I would survive, one way or the other, but my parents had grown to love living in Boston with us. I would rather have died than have had them snatched away and returned to that plantation. William was angry and not thinking clearly. He believed I could win the case against Frank Wilmington in court because I escaped years ago. Unlike me, my parents had permission to come to Boston, for a short time, to care for Mrs. Broughton. They did not stand a chance of winning against Frank Wilmington.

William came home the following evening angry about the news. I believe he would have killed Frank Wilmington that night if he had met him. He felt strongly about his responsibility to protect his family from anyone or anything that would harm us, and Frank Wilmington was clearly out to harm us.

The next day my parents, Will and I moved in with Mrs. Baker and Aunt Clara. I left my home to protect Mammy and Pappy. I could not stand by and allow Frank Wilmington to snatch them away. My parents loved Mrs. Baker and Aunt Clara as much as I did, and they did not mind living with them. Still, I did not want to leave my home, or stop working in the shoppe. I had two dresses to finish and decided not to take any more orders. Naomi, Callie and Cora would have to decide if they wanted to stay in my absence.

One day while Mammy and I were working to finish a dress, someone knocked at the front door. Aunt Clara opened the door. I instantly recognized Callie, Cora and Naomi's voices. They sounded as if something had upset them very much. I ran down the stairs to find out what had happened, and discovered that my life was in eminent danger.

"Sarah, Sarah", Callie screamed, "dose men came lookin' for you dis morning!" They appeared to be in shock.

"What men are you talking about?" Aunt Clara asked. I knew exactly who they were talking about, but managed to stay calm to hear them out.

"Dey walked into de shoppe, an axed, 'Which one of you is Sarah? We know she's here!'"

"Aunt Clara, it was Frank Wilmington and his men. Apparently they have heard that I work at *The Dress Shoppe*, or that I am somewhere in Boston."

"De tall, big man pulled us close, stared at us, den pushed us away. Dey looked around de shoppe, an before dey left, the tall one said, 'Tell Sarah, we know she is here in Boston, and we will find her, an take her back to where she belongs. She knows where she belongs.' Den dey walked out de shoppe an slammed de door."

Aunt Clara, Callie, Naomi and Cora embraced each other, while I stood calmly, trying to decide what to do. After so many years had passed, Frank Wilmington was still searching for me, his young slave girl, who cleverly got away from him.

"What are we going to do, Sarah?" Aunt Clara asked. "We cannot let this man find you. Thank you all for warning us, but you cannot come here again, because surely they are watching the shoppe and all of you. By coming here, you will only lead those men to Sarah."

I hugged Callie, Naomi and Cora, and thanked them for coming to tell me the alarming news. I told them they could continue to work at the shoppe if they wanted to, but if they did not, they could leave and lock the door. The safety of my friends was far more important than making money.

William came by later that evening and I told him what happened. He listened without saying a word. He agreed that my friends could continue to work at the shoppe if they chose to, but he did not want them to feel uncomfortable being there, not knowing when those men might storm in again.

It did not take long for Callie, Cora and Naomi to decide they did not want to work at the shoppe any longer. They were afraid that somehow Frank Wilmington and his men would learn that they, too, were fugitive slaves, and would take them back to their owners. So, I closed *The Dress Shoppe* and put a sign in the window to notify customers that the shoppe would temporarily be closed. It appeared that the dream I had nurtured, and diligently worked so hard to develop and build, had suddenly come to an abrupt end. I was very sad.

We were comfortable living with Mrs. Baker and Aunt Clara, but I missed my husband and home, and did not feel well. I did not tell anyone that I struggled to get out of bed each morning. I assumed the stress of having to hide from those men, as well as the disappointment of having to close my shoppe, was too much.

I did not tell anyone because my family would worry. My parents had gone through enough in their lives, and I never wanted to give them any reason to worry about me again. William was busy at the newspaper and with sending supplies to the refugees. I did not want him to be concerned about my health, so my illness was my little secret for days.

By late November it was especially difficult to get up one morning, and I collapsed onto the floor. I remember waking up with a cold cloth to my face and seeing my parents, Mrs. Baker and

Aunt Clara standing over me. They lifted me onto the bed. I was weak, and reluctantly told them about my illness.

"I have been feeling ill and somewhat faint for days, but this will pass. I will be fine, so please do not worry."

"You don't know what caused you to be so sick, an you gonna see a doctor," Mammy said.

"Sarah, I will have Dr. Andrews come over to see you," Mrs. Baker said. "That way, you do not have to leave the house. I will run out and get him now."

Within a couple of hours, my physician, Dr. David Andrews, arrived and asked questions about my health. He was around thirty-five years old, average height, and soft spoken. He was a personable, intelligent, handsome, dark-skinned man. My family had grown to trust and value his opinion.

Dr. Andrews did all the things that physicians do to examine their patients and then left. He said he would be back in a few days. As expected, my parents would not let me get out of bed. Caring for others was something they never grew tired of over the course of their lives. That was what kept them going. They did not leave my bedside as we anxiously awaited Dr. Andrews' return. He came back within a few days.

"Sarah, you are going to feel ill and weak for some time, but don't be discouraged. This is to be expected."

"When will I feel better? There is so much I need to do."

"You will be just fine, and you will soon be the mother of a second child."

I suspect my parents were eavesdropping, because as soon as Dr. Andrews left, they ran into my room, shouting, "Our Sarah is havin' a baby! Dis is wonderful! We're gonna be grandparents, agin."

They were quite happy, but I was too sick to be excited. We had talked about having more children, but I did not think I had the time for another child because of the shoppe and our work with the refugees.

As usual, William came over to visit me after dark because we did not know a lot about Aunt Clara's neighbors. For all we knew, they could have been watching and reporting to Frank Wilmington. Aunt Clara and Mrs. Baker were close to some of their neighbors, but not to all of them. When he came by that night, he looked tired and worried. I asked him about his day, but he did not want to talk about it. Aunt Clara told him that Dr. Andrews had been to see me.

"Sarah, what did Dr. Andrews say? What does he know about your condition? Tell me, how do you feel? Your eyes look weak." William held my hands as he spoke. His compassionate brown eyes looked sad. He loved me very much and was not happy that Will and I were living with Aunt Clara and Mrs. Baker. Since our marriage, we had never been separated until that time.

"I feel the same, Sweetheart, and have some news."

"Tell me it's not pneumonia." We knew of several people who had died from pneumonia that year.

"No, it's not pneumonia. William, we will soon be parents to a second child."

William was ecstatic and spent the next few days with us celebrating. Although I was too sick to celebrate, it was wonderful to have my husband and family living together again. My shoppe was closed and I missed going there each morning. I was concerned about my sewing machines, fabric and other items at the shoppe. One day William and I went to the shoppe to gather my belongings so that some of his friends could come in and move everything to a safe place. His uncle gave us permission to store those things in his home.

We made progress gathering things and organizing the shoppe that day. I got tired and William insisted that I lie down in the back room. I was almost asleep when I heard voices. Someone had stormed into the shoppe. I was startled and sat up to listen to what they were saying, and began to get sick. It did not take long to recognize Frank Wilmington's voice. The man who had terrorized me all of my life was in my dress shoppe, and he was not alone. Of course, they were looking for me.

"I lost a slave girl several years ago, and it is my understanding that she might be working here," Frank Wilmington said. There was no way I could ever forget the sound of his deep, cruel, penetrating voice that still frightens me. I felt like that helpless young girl who ran away from him, and tried to hide behind the dresses in that room. I asked God to save me from the man who still, according to the law, owned me.

"Who the hell are you, and what do you want?" William asked. "This is my shoppe, and you damn well better get out before I throw you out!"

"Sarah Johnson is a slave, *my* slave, and I know she is here in Boston. In case you don't know the law, it's a crime to hide a fugitive slave. I still *own* her, and don't intend to leave Boston without her. Now, does she work here or not?"

"I am telling you, again, to get the hell out of my shoppe! Who works in my shoppe is my damn business, not yours. I am not your slave, and you do not control me!"

"Do you know the woman I'm looking for?" William did not answer. Although he did not acknowledge it, William knew that man was Frank Wilmington. I was afraid those men would hurt him, but he did not back down. He hated Frank Wilmington for what he had done to me and my family. Although I no longer hated the Wilmington family, or any white person for that matter, my husband had not gotten to that point. He had not learned that it is more powerful to forgive than to hate.

"I will tell you one more time to get out of my shoppe! I am a *free* man, and you are on my property. In case you don't know the law, it is against the law to trespass on another man's property."

"Let me make it very clear that we will be back, and when we find Sarah, I will take her back to Mississippi where she belongs. Tell her that she is *still my property*." They left and slammed the door.

William came to the back room and found me hiding behind some dresses, shaking and crying. He held me close and said everything would be alright. We did not leave the shoppe until late that night because we suspected Frank Wilmington and his men might be watching. Even if they were watching, it was too dark to recognize me. I was exhausted when we got to Aunt Clara's house. William told everyone what happened, and my parents were quite upset, but not Mrs. Baker and Aunt Clara. They said if Frank Wilmington, or any of his men, touched their property, they would have some of their wealthy, powerful, white abolitionist friends destroy them.

They made it very clear that I was not to leave the house again for any reason. William and his friends closed the shoppe and stored the machines, fabric and supplies. After that horrible incident, I was very sad. I should have been happy about being pregnant, but instead felt a deep sadness about my past, and more importantly, about what my children would have to confront in their lifetime. I stayed in bed most days and cried a lot. I wasn't just sad about Frank Wilmington looking for me; I was sad about life in general, and did not want to get out of bed.

Someone must have told Frank Wilmington that he might find me at the shoppe. I had not discussed my past with any of my customers. To my knowledge, only William's family, Mrs. Baker, Aunt Clara, Naomi, Callie and Cora knew that I was a fugitive slave. Based on what I heard that night at the shoppe, Frank Wilmington was not certain that I was *his* "Sarah". It sounded as if he only suspected that I might be the "Sarah" he was looking for.

Then, one quiet, cold evening in December 1862, we heard a loud banging at the door. As soon as Aunt Clara opened the door, I heard Frank Wilmington's voice. He was very angry and spoke cruel words to Aunt Clara.

"It is my understanding that you are hiding a fugitive slave woman in this house, and I demand that you send her out to her lawful owner. There is a law against hiding fugitive slaves. If you don't send her out, I will come in and drag her out. Sarah is coming back to the plantation, where she belongs!"

"If you set your foot in my house, I will have someone drag you out!" Aunt Clara snapped. "Get away from my door, or I will fight you myself!"

"Do you know who I am? I am Frank Wilmington. You don't speak to me in that tone."

"I am Clara Washington, and *you* don't speak to *me* in that tone! I know the law, and I will damn well use it against you!"

"Look, woman, you're standing in the way of me getting a slave back who ran away fifteen years ago. She ran off from me, and I have been determined to find her. I'm taking her back to Mississippi, along with her parents, as soon as I find them. I'll see you in court, you smart talking nigger."

"You can go to hell, you cruel, ruthless beast!" Aunt Clara shouted back. "Don't you ever come back to my house. I hope you burn all the way to hell!"

Frank Wilmington said something else to Aunt Clara, but I could not hear his words. He and his men left and Aunt Clara slammed the door. My parents and I hugged each other and prayed together.

# CHAPTER 21

The Fugitive Slave Act was the most controversial of all the bills that made up the Compromise of 1850. It required citizens to assist in the recovery of fugitive slaves and it denied a fugitive's right to a jury trial. Under the Fugitive Slave Law, an accused runaway stood trial in front of a special commissioner instead of a judge or jury.

The Fugitive Law was intended to curtail the runaway problem, but it had the opposite effect. By the 1860's, more slaves escaped as the law became fuel to the abolitionist movement. This ineffective law was extremely vulnerable to criticism. It assumed that Negroes were guilty and forbade them to testify in their own defense. It reached back to cover runaway slaves living in the North for years. Many of them fled to Canada.

Abolitionists called the law the "Bloodhound Bill" or "Man-Stealing Law". When federal marshalls tried to enforce it in Boston, abolitionists incited whites and free blacks to rescue and hide fugitive slaves.

As expected, Frank Wilmington kept his word. Shortly after he left Aunt Clara's house that cold, dreadful evening in late December 1862, he filed a petition in the New York District Court, claiming to be my lawful owner. A few days later, a Federal marshal appeared at Aunt Clara's door looking for me.

"I have an affidavit signed by Frank Wilmington," he said to Aunt Clara and Mrs. Baker. "It is my understanding that a runaway slave, Sarah Johnson, has been living here. Take this and read it. This slave is expected to be in court on January 2, 1863. If she does not appear in court, both of you will have to answer to the Commissioner. I don't think either of you wants any trouble with the law."

Frank Wilmington somehow discovered that Aunt Clara had been hiding me in her home. After his confrontation with William at the shoppe, I suspect they watched the shoppe closely. Although I did not leave Aunt Clara's house again after he stormed into the shoppe, he knew where I was staying. He obviously did not know that Aunt Clara was also hiding my parents in her home. They had not left that house in weeks. Perhaps he thought they were somewhere in Canada, living with Daniel Broughton.

I was quite ill the morning I appeared in court with William, Aunt Clara, Mrs. Baker and Robert Douglas, the lawyer William's family hired to represent me. Attorney Douglas was a tall, thin, white man, with blue eyes. He had thick, black hair and eye brows. William's family, Aunt Clara and Mrs. Baker had known him for several years. He had the reputation of being one of the best lawyers in Boston. Attorney Douglas was very active in the move to abolish slavery. That was probably the main reason he was hired. I was pregnant with my second child and there were complications, but I had to be in court. I certainly did not want to go to jail.

The special commissioner assigned to hear my case was Fredrick Parren, a rather short white man with broad shoulders, dark hair with streaks of grey and dark eyes. He didn't appear to be a friendly person. Perhaps that was his demeanor in court. I didn't know much about him, but prayed that he would rule in my favor. When court was called to order, my entire body tightened. I had never been more afraid in my life. I would rather have died than have gone back to that plantation with Frank Wilmington.

Unfortunately, my case was the first one called. I wanted to sit and watch Commissioner Parren in action before I had to stand before him, but that did not happen. Frank Wilmington was present with some other men, who I assumed were his patrollers. I looked into his cold eyes for the first time since I was around thirteen years old. He had not changed a lot, except his hair had turned grey. He was the same tall, domineering man I remember from my childhood on the plantation. His look and demeanor were as cold as ever.

"In the Matter of the Petition of Frank Wilmington," Commissioner Parren stated, "regarding the case of Sarah Johnson. Mr. Wilmington, tell me why you're here today."

"Your honor, I am here today to reclaim a slave who ran away from me fifteen years ago," Frank Wilmington began. After he made his opening statement, he turned to look at me. "There she is, Sarah, my slave."

Although I was quite frightened, I found the courage to look directly at him. I sat with William, our family, Mrs. Baker, Aunt Clara and their friends, who were abolitionists. They were there to support me. I did not have the right to defend myself, but it was certainly wonderful to have my love ones and friends present. They spent quite a bit of time with Attorney Douglas to help him prepare my case.

"Your honor, many years ago, this woman, my slave, ran away from me in New York City. I vowed that I would find her and bring her back to the plantation where she belongs. I suspected for years that she was here in Boston, and then I got a tip that she was working as a seamstress in a dress shoppe. My beloved wife, Charlotte, God rest her soul, taught this woman how to sew."

I wanted to stand and scream, "You liar, Mammy taught me to sew, not your wife!" Unfortunately, I could not speak a word in court, no matter what Frank Wilmington said. I prayed that Robert Douglas would do a great job, and that I would win a battle I was tired of fighting.

"If your plantation is in Mississippi, how did she run away from you in New York City?" the Commissioner asked.

"I was in New York City visiting with my sister, and I only brought my slave along as a personal assistant for my daughters. Then, as soon as she got the opportunity, she left my sister's house in the middle of the night and ran off. I have been looking for her ever since. Finally, one day I got a tip that she might be in Boston. It took some time, but thank God, we found her.

"Slaves are not cheap, especially good slaves. I cannot begin to tell you what her running off cost me and my family. Not long after she left, my wife became ill, and I could not buy more slaves at that time. We really needed her to help in the house and to help with caring for my wife. I've found her, and I want my slave back!"

"Mr. Douglas, I would like to hear from you at this time," the Commissioner said. "Tell me why I should not release your client to Mr. Wilmington."

Robert Douglas stood and walked toward the Commissioner. He and Frank Wilmington stood before the Commissioner. Frank Wilmington stared at my lawyer as he began to speak, with that same cold look in his eyes.

"Commissioner Parren, I'm sure you are aware that the voluntary transportation of slaves into free states, with the intent of residing there, automatically makes them free," Attorney Douglas began. He was poised and spoke with confidence. His voice was deep and strong. He did not appear to be intimidated by the Commissioner or Frank Wilmington. William squeezed my hand.

"You've heard Mr. Wilmington say that he brought, *willingly* brought, my client to New York City with him. It is my understanding that Mr. Wilmington has a home in New York City, and that he has spent quite a bit of time there. My client, a young slave girl, ran from this man in self-defense. Commissioner, I'm sure you are aware of the barbarity of slavery. However, you and I cannot begin to imagine what this young woman has endured at the hands of this man.

"Frank Wilmington warned my client that she would be severely punished when she returned to the plantation, whenever they left New York City. Commissioner, if you had a chance to save your life, and avoid being severely punished, or maybe even killed, wouldn't you run for your life? I certainly would. This young lady was just a child then, a frightened child in a strange city where no one cared anything about her. She didn't even have her loving parents to turn to because they were in Mississippi on the plantation.

"She ran for her life. Let me tell you, Commissioner, what this young lady has done with her life since the day she ran away from Frank Wilmington. My client, a brave, intelligent young girl at that time, found her way to a church in New York City, where she was fortunate to meet some kind people. These people wanted to help her, and they took her into their home. My client worked in a shoppe as a seamstress to earn money so that she could take care of herself. She didn't want these kind people to support her. She supported herself and saved her money.

"Before long, she had to leave New York City because Frank Wilmington and his "hounds" were on her trail. She was only a young teenager when she came to Boston. Shortly after she arrived in Boston, my client opened a dress shoppe with the money she had saved. It was a small shoppe, but believe me, the quality of her work was not small. Women throughout Boston came, and still come to this shoppe to have dresses made because the quality of their work is so good. My client managed to hire three women to help her because her business continues to grow.

"Commissioner, my client is an outstanding citizen here in Boston. She is a wonderful wife and mother, she is active in her church, and she is active in the community trying to help others here in Boston and elsewhere. Frank Wilmington *chose* to bring my client to New York City, and my client made the wise decision to run for her life. No one *owns* my client. She has been living as a free woman for years, and she should continue to live as a free woman."

Mrs. Baker and Aunt Clara wiped their eyes. There were others in that courtroom, but I didn't look around to see their expressions or reactions to what Mr. Douglas said in my defense. I was pleased with his argument, however the longer I sat, the sicker I became. The stress and anticipation were too much to bear.

"Commissioner," Frank Wilmington interjected, "this woman is my lawful slave. I have papers showing that she was properly registered as my slave many years ago. How can planters survive if our slaves run off? We have lots of time and money invested in our slaves. It's taken me over fifteen years to find this slave, and I have spent a fortune trying to find her. Now that I have found her, I want her back. She is *my property!*"

"My client is nobody's *property*," Mr. Douglas interrupted. "Commissioner, my client has a family who needs her. She has a husband and a child, and she's expecting another child. She is a good, decent, honest citizen, who has never harmed or hurt anyone. She is a *free* woman. Ask around Boston; no one has anything negative to say about Sarah Harper. I've talked to lots of people about my client, and people respect her. Ask your wife, Commissioner, about my client. She has probably bought dresses from my client's dress shoppe!"

"Commissioner, we are not hear to discuss what people think about this slave woman," Frank Wilmington snapped. "Her character is not at issue. She is my slave, and I want her back on my plantation where she belongs! You know the law, Commissioner. The Fugitive Slave Act was passed by the United States Congress in September 1850. Under this Act, all runaway slaves are to be brought back to their masters. There are people in this courtroom today who need to be punished because they have knowingly detained a runaway slave."

Frank Wilmington looked directly at William, Aunt Clara and Mrs. Baker as he talked about the Fugitive Slave Act. He talked on and on about how runaway slaves had caused planters to lose their plantations, farms and more. I got sicker as he talked on. Finally, the Commissioner said he wanted to see Frank Wilmington and Mr. Douglas in his office, and called for a recess. I assumed he would return with a decision about my future. I would either stay in Boston with my family, or be ordered to return to Mississippi with Frank Wilmington.

The anticipation of hearing the Commissioner's decision was extremely difficult. I was sick, sad and disheartened. It seemed as if everything I had worked for and believed in had suddenly slipped away. I felt empty, hollow, and did not have the strength to count my blessings.

Finally, Commissioner Parren returned to the room, followed by Mr. Douglas and Frank Wilmington. I was too weak to sit up, but heard his decision. I will never forget his words as long as I live:

"We are back on the record. After a lengthy discussion with Mr. Douglas and Mr. Wilmington, I have reached a decision in this matter. The relation of master and slave does not exist upon the principles of natural right. Such relation is a matter of law, which is of no force and is not binding beyond the limits and jurisdiction of that State in which it is enacted.

"By the Constitution of the State of Massachusettes, it is declared, 'There shall be no slavery in this State, nor involuntary servitude, unless for the punishment of crime. Therefore, because slavery does not exist in this State, the master has no power or authority to control Sarah Harper within, or remove her beyond the jurisdiction of the State.

'All persons within the limits of this State, even for the shortest period, become subject to all the municipal laws, civil and criminal, and entitled to all the priviledges and protection which those laws afford. This is the law, whether the person is Negro or Caucasian.'

"Mr. Wilmington voluntarily brought Sarah Harper into New York, a State where there is no slavery. Construing said 3d clause of the 2d section of the 4th article of the Constitution of the United States strictly, Sarah Harper cannot be said to be a fugitive slave. She has lived as a free woman for over fifteen years, and is considered by many to be a productive citizen here in Boston.

"I am inclined to believe that this young woman ran from Frank Wilmington in self-defense, after he took her from his plantation and brought her to a State where there is no slavery. In such case, Mrs. Harper had no will in the matter, but was controlled by Mr. Wilmington in furtherance of his agenda. The common law gives way to statute; both common law and statute give way to and are superseded by the Constitution of the United States.

"…Whereupon, I pronounce Sarah Harper to be free from the control and power of Frank Wilmington."

I heard the Commissioner's decision, but his words did not register in my brain until days later. I couldn't even cry because I was in a state of shock! The last thing I remember was Frank Wilmington screaming, "I will appeal your decision and I will win! I will get my slave back! When I finish with you, Commissioner, you will be destroyed in this city!"

# CHAPTER 22

I woke up the next morning in a hospital room. William, Aunt Clara and Mrs. Baker were there, with strange facial expressions. William's was a combination of sadness and joy.

"Sarah, the Commissioner set you free!" he said. "You don't have to go back to that plantation." He held me close, and was crying. I thought they were tears of joy, but soon learned some were tears of pain, because there was no longer a baby moving around inside of me. Unfortunately, our child was no longer alive. Although the doctor explained that I lost our baby because of problems related to my blood pressure, I knew the stress of having to face Frank Wilmington in court was the real reason our child did not survive.

I left the hospital a few days later and returned to live with Aunt Clara, Mrs. Baker and my parents. They wanted me to stay until I was strong enough to go home. I was sad, but there was much to be thankful for. Frank Wilmington was furious, and vowed that he would appeal the Commissioner's decision to set me free. Although my attorney did not think he would win on appeal, his anger worried me. He always got what he wanted. There was no telling what he would do next to get me back to that plantation.

About two weeks later I left Aunt Clara's house and went home. I don't know who was more excited that day, William or me. It was late January 1863. I spent my time talking to and teaching my young son. He was a happy child, and thank God he had no idea what his mother had been through, or what was ahead. If Frank Wilmington won his appeal, I wondered if he would also claim my son as his property. I didn't think he would get away with that because William would probably have killed to protect his son.

I taught my son something new each day and wanted him to learn as much as his young brain could absorb. Just as my parents taught us all they knew to help us survive, I wanted my son to be

231

prepared for whatever he might have to confront in life. I read to him until he fell asleep in my arms.

I missed teaching my students at the church, and had not seen or heard from them because I had been hiding out at Aunt Clara's house for so long. I had to give up teaching and working at the shoppe after Frank Wilmington showed up. That man caused so much pain for me and my family. Still, I did not hate him. I just wanted him to go away – forever.

I thought about my friends in the contraband camps and wondered if Lydia and Samuel were still there, or if they had moved on. Since I was no longer carrying a child, there was no reason we could not go back to Fort Monroe to continue our work. There was so much more to do in those camps. We promised we would help them, and I intended to honor my word.

Mammy and I had a long talk one day. She was worried because I was unhappy. She was very perceptive and wise, and I always felt better after talking with her.

"Sarah, do you miss your work at de dress shoppe? I know how much dat shoppe means to you. Me an your Pappy see no reason why you shouldn't go on back to work. It will be good for you."

"Mammy, I've been through so much. I lost my baby, and Frank Wilmington isn't finished with me. I expect him to come banging on the door at my shoppe again. Yes, I would love to work again, but just don't know what to do."

"Baby, you cannot live your life in fear. Mr. Wilmington knows where you are. He can't do nuttin to you 'less he wins de appeal. I think you need to get on back to doin' de things dat bring you joy. 'Course, I must admit, Pappy an I sho do miss keepin' our grandson." She smiled and squeezed my hands.

"Let me think about it. You're right, I sure miss working in my shoppe, as well as working with Naomi, Callie and Cora. I miss my friends so much and feel strong enough to go out and pay them a visit. I'll talk to William about reopening the shoppe." That evening I discussed going back to work with William.

"Sarah, I think that's a great idea. I've been thinking about that, but didn't say anything because you have to be ready to take that step. It sounds as if you are ready. I will get some help with getting your machines and supplies back to the shoppe. I'm sure your customers will be thrilled to see the 'Open' sign on the door again."

"I hope my customers will come back. This is the second time I've had to close the shoppe. There are lots of skilled dress makers around this city, and my customers may have moved on. I certainly cannot blame them if they have. My customers are stylish, and they enjoy looking glamorous. I cannot expect them to wait around for me forever."

"I believe your customers will understand that you had to temporarily close your shoppe. I also believe they will be thrilled to have you back. Why don't you visit with Cora, Callie and Naomi. That would mean so much to all of you."

"I will do that tomorrow. Mammy feels the same about me going back to work. The last two months have been very difficult, but I have to keep going. Things will get better for all of us. Perhaps we can even go back to Fort Monroe soon. I would love to see Samuel and Lydia. We promised them we would come back."

"We will go back soon," William said. "I want to see Samuel and Lydia as well. People continue to send supplies to the refugees, so they know we have not forgotten them. It's time to put what happened over the past two months behind us. I feel confident Frank Wilmington will lose on appeal."

Unfortunately, I wasn't confident Frank Wilmington would lose, but was anxious to see my friends and talk about reopening *The Dress Shoppe*. The next day I went to visit Naomi, Cora and Callie, and it would be a bitter-sweet reunion. They knew the Commissioner ruled in my favor, but did not know about my baby.

Naomi opened the door to their home and screamed when she saw my face. Cora and Callie ran to the door, and they screamed as well. We had not seen each other in two months. William saw them at church and told them the Commissioner ruled in my favor.

"Sarah, Sarah, you are back, and you are free!" they shouted. "Please come in and let's talk!" Naomi said. "We wanted to come to see you, but didn't know if it was safe to visit you. Sit down and tell us all about what you been doing."

Before I could get comfortable in my chair, Callie gave me a large slice of chocolate cake and a glass of milk. She had not forgotten how much I love chocolate cake. I asked them to tell me what they had been doing since we last saw each other.

"I been makin' hats an bonnets an sellin' dem to women at church an whereva I can," Naomi said. "People been axin when de shoppe is gonna reopen. Dey miss comin' to de shoppe."

"Cora an me been makin' dresses an gloves," Callie said. "Now dat you're free, Sarah, I hope we can go back to de shoppe. We been waitin' for you to tell us it's time to get back to work!" We laughed and talked about the dresses and accessories they'd made, and about their personal lives.

"Thank de Lord, we met some good men," Callie said. "I met David at church, an I sho do like him. I think he likes me a whole lot." Callie winked and clapped her hands. "He's a bricklayer, an he's got some money saved up. He said he wonts to provide a good life for his wife an childrun."

"I met a nice man, too," Cora interjected. "Ed is a barber, an he been savin' to open his own shoppe one day. He said I'm de kind of woman he been prayin' for. He's a kind person. I'd jump de broom wit him tomorrow if he axed me." Cora looked so happy.

"Well, I got a good man, too," Naomi added. "Sam works at de grocery store down de street. He been watchin' me real hard, an den one day he axed if he could come to visit me. At first I said 'no', but he kept axin 'til I finally said 'yes'. Sarah, we gonna be happy, just like you an William." They talked on about the special men in their lives, then asked me to tell them about the Commissioner's decision to set me free. I told them what happened that day in the courtroom. Then, I reluctantly told them about losing my baby the day after the Commissioner ruled in my favor.

"It's been difficult for me and my family, but I am ready to get back to doing the things I enjoy. That is one of the reasons I came to see you all today. I am going to reopen *The Dress Shoppe* next week, and would love for each of you to come back to work. You may not want to at this time, but I would sure love to have you back with me."

Before I finished speaking, Naomi, Callie and Cora jumped around the room with excitement. "Sarah, you gonna reopen de shoppe?" Callie asked. "We been prayin' for dis to happen."

"You don't know how much we miss workin' wit you, Sarah," Naomi added. "I'm so happy to hear dis good news."

"We work togetha so well," Cora said. "I bleeve it was meant for us to work togetha."

The following week all of our machines and supplies were moved back into *The Dress Shoppe*, and once again it was open for business. William put an announcement in the paper that the shoppe had reopened. When we closed it in December, he announced in the paper that the shoppe would be closed temporarily. Aunt Clara and Mrs. Baker assured me that they would get the word around that I was healthy and strong and ready to start making beautiful dresses again.

My attorney informed me that Frank Wilmington hired an attorney to represent him on appeal, and that we would be back in court sometime in February 1863. I decided to focus on rebuilding my business, as opposed to worrying about what Frank Wilmington was up to, and was determined not close the shoppe again, regardless of what happened.

About a week later Eve Grant strolled into the shoppe, looking as glamorous as ever. To my surprise, she was wearing a yellow dress I designed and made for her.

"Sarah, I didn't know about your past, but I have heard about your case, and about the Commissioner's decision." Eve looked sad and then hugged me. I didn't want her pity, or anyone's pity. I never mentioned my past to any of my customers because it didn't concern them. However, I was concerned that people in Boston knew about my case, and that the owner of *The Dress Shoppe* was a fugitive slave.

"Sarah, you are a strong woman, and you will make it," Eve continued. "That horrible man will not win on appeal, believe me. You are free, and you will remain free. I will speak up for you, and will ask others to do the same. You are a hard worker, and you have built a prosperous business. You have every right to stay here in Boston and operate your business."

"Thank you, Eve. I appreciate your support." I changed the conversation to designing and making dresses, because I did not intend to discuss my past with Eve or any of my customers. I was their dressmaker, not their personal friend.

"It is so good to see you. We are back and ready to make dresses and lots of accessories. How can we help you today?"

"Well, I will be attending the annual Spring Gala next month, and need something different, youthful and refreshing to wear. I want all eyes on me when I walk through those doors! Now, this is what I have in mind. I want a bright color, maybe pink, with the top of the dress cut low. Of course, I don't want to show too much." Eve broke into laughter. It was wonderful to hear her laugh again because her joyful nature was contagious. She had the ability to lift your spirit if you were anywhere close to her. I was so glad she returned to the shoppe. Eve had been a very loyal customer, and apparently the news about my past had not changed her opinion of me.

I spent almost two hours that day talking with and designing the perfect dress for Eve to wear to the Spring Gala. Before she left, she assured me that she would spread the word that I was back, and *The Dress Shoppe* had reopened. She kept her word, because a few days later several of her friends came into the shoppe, including Jane Merritt and Helena Austin. We were as busy as we had ever been and it was wonderful.

Then, one day in February 1863, my priest, Father Paul, came to the shoppe to see me. I immediately felt a sense of panic and unrest. I thought something bad had happened to one of my family members, because Father Paul was known to comfort people at the death of a loved one. I prayed. We all had to die, but I wasn't ready to say goodbye to anyone in my family.

I couldn't understand why William wasn't with Father Paul. He had always been right at my side whenever I needed him. Then I thought something bad had happened to William. Perhaps Father Paul had come to break the horrible news to me. Everything was a big blur at that moment. Naomi, Cora and Callie held my hands.

"Sarah, I need you to come with me," Father Paul said in his calm voice. "Someone is here to see you."

"If it is anyone from that plantation, please send them away, and get William and my attorney. They can't take me back until we go to court." I was so afraid of what I had to face when I stepped out of the shoppe. Although it was February, the sun was bright and the weather somewhat mild. I will never forget that day as long as I live.

I walked out of the shoppe, and looked directly into the eyes of someone I had not seen in years! There was no way I could ever forget those eyes. I screamed and fell to my knees! Father Paul said, "Sarah, this man came to the church asking about you early this morning. He says he is your brother."

# CHAPTER 23

On February 28, 1863, my sister and I reunited after being separated for twenty-five years! When I looked into Sarah's eyes, I gasped, not sure if my perception was real. I caught Sarah before she fell to the ground. The thought of that moment still gives me chills.

Cora put a cold cloth to Sarah's head, and she finally came around. She stared at me as if she could not believe her eyes. I held her close for several minutes, and her priest prayed over us. Sarah cried on my shoulder like a lost child who had finally found her parents. I cried as well. It felt as if I had died and gone to heaven.

"Sarah, it's me, Tom. I been lookin' for you, an now I've found you! Samuel and Lydia told me dat you might be my sister, an dat is why I came to Boston. Dis is real!" The priest and I helped Sarah stand up, then we went into her shoppe. She sat and rested her head on my shoulder, and did not speak for several minutes. The shock of seeing me was simply too much for her.

"Tom, is it really you, is it really you? Tell me it's really you."

"It's really me, Sarah. Do you remember dis scar?" I showed her the scar on my right hand I got when I fell out of a tree. She and I were very young and I was teaching her how to climb a tree. It was a hard fall out of that tree, and I got a really bad cut on my hand. Someone told Mammy I would always have that scar and they were right. The cut healed, but the scar never left.

Sarah looked at my hand, kissed the scar and cried again. I assume she remembered that incident. Words cannot express what I felt at that moment. All the wonderful things I enjoyed with my sister when we were children flashed before me. I love my family dearly, and thought about them everyday. I kept the faith that someday we would reunite.

Sarah finally came around and started talking. She was choked up, but managed to get the words out. "Tom, it's really you; I know it's really you. Naomi, please get William and tell him my brother is here. He has come back to us."

"Sarah, I have someone I want you to meet." Hannah was waiting outside of the shoppe with Caleb. She wanted me to have some time alone with my sister. I asked Callie to ask Hannah and Caleb to come into the shoppe.

"Sarah, this is Hannah; Hannah, this is my sister, Sarah. Sarah, this is Caleb, my son." Sarah stood and embraced Hannah and Caleb.

"God has blessed me to reunite with my brother, and to meet his wife and child." Sarah cried again.

"Sarah, Hannah is not my wife, but she will be soon. Caleb is my son, but it's a long story that will take some time to explain."

"Tom has talked so much about you and his parents," Hannah said. "He's been determined to find y'all."

"Tom came back for me, just like he said he would," Caleb interjected. "Tom is de best Pappy a boy could have. He's taught me so much. I ain't neva had a Pappy before Tom an me met at Fort Monroe. I'm gonna grow up wit Tom an Hannah."

"Caleb, I remember you!" Sarah screamed. "You are the little boy who kept Tom's quilt! This is all too much!"

"It's a very long story. I will tell you about it real soon. Thank God I made it to Fort Monroe." I was about to say more about what happened at Fort Monroe when Naomi walked into the shoppe with Sarah's husband.

"I've talked to several men named *Tom*, but there's no doubt you are *the* Tom – Sarah's brother! You two look so much alike." William and I shook hands and then embraced. He was my brother because he was married to my dear sister.

"Now dat I have found my sister, I must soon leave to go back to de plantation to get Mammy and Pappy. I want dem to be heah in Boston wit Sarah an me." When I said that, I noticed that William and Sarah looked at each other and smiled, but said nothing. I didn't think any more about it.

"Tom, Hannah and Caleb, our family, please come to our home to rest and get a hot meal," William said. "This has to be one of the happiest moments of my wife's life, and it is time for us to celebrate."

I was too excited to be tired, or to think about anything other than having found my sister. That evening we all walked to Sarah's house, which wasn't very far from her shoppe. I was so very proud of my sister. She was married to a fine man, she was a mother, she had a lovely home and her own business. I knew she and Hannah would love each other because they had some of the same wonderful qualities. As we walked to Sarah's house, Caleb held Sarah's hand as if he had known her all of his life. I didn't think my life could get any better; but, it did.

When we got to Sarah's house, she grabbed my arm before we walked into her home. She looked at me with tears in her eyes and said, "Tom, I have another big surprise for you." I thought she was talking about her son, but I was in for the surprise of my life! Sitting in front of the fireplace were Mammy and Pappy! Mammy's face turned white as she looked into my eyes. She must have thought she was looking at a ghost. She screamed, "Thomas, my boy, my boy! Oh Lord, it's my boy!"

I helped Mammy out of the chair she was sitting in and hugged her tightly. "Mammy, it's me, Tom. Mammy, I've found my family! Thank God, I've found my family!"

Pappy got up from his chair and hugged me. "My son, my son is alive and well," he said over and over. "De Lord has brought our childrun back to us!" Sarah, Mammy, Pappy and I embraced a long time that day. It was as if no one else existed but the four of us. It was a miracle, and I knew it. My prayers had finally been answered.

It took some time for Mammy, Pappy, Sarah and me to calm down that unforgettable day. I would have given my life for them. Mammy embraced Hannah and Caleb, and told them she loved them. Caleb grinned from ear to ear. That may have been the happiest day of his life as well.

Mammy had prepared a wonderful meal, but no one was hungry. She wouldn't let go of my hand, and wanted to hear about how I managed to find Sarah. She just wanted to hear me talk. I think she wanted to be sure she wasn't dreaming; that I wasn't an apparition; that it was really me, her son, Thomas, who was snatched away from them many years earlier.

"Mammy, afta I saw you an Sarah in Atlanta years ago, I continued to be Edward Carnes' slave for a few more years. Den he sold me to John Mundy, and I was wit him for several years. I escaped while wukin for one of John Mundy's friends in Charleston, and made it safely to Fort Monroe, where I met two wonderful people, Samuel an Lydia. Dey met Sarah an William at Fort Monroe as well. Samuel an Lydia firmly believed dat Sarah was my sister. Afta I got Hannah from dat plantation in Savannah, she an I returned to Fort Monroe to get Caleb. I den came to Boston to look for my sister. I went to several churches to ax 'bout her. Finally, I was led to de *right* church.

"The priest said Sarah had talked to him about me, an he felt strongly dat I was her brother. Dat's when he took me to her dress shoppe. I don't need to say anymore."

Mammy and Sarah broke into tears. Pappy sat quietly and stared at me. He shook his head as if he couldn't believe his son had actually come back to the family. I stopped talking because the more I talked, the more Mammy and Sarah cried. I hugged Hannah and Caleb. Before long, we were all crying. That was the happiest day of my life!

After Hannah and I left John Mundy's plantation, I honestly believed that those white people who gave us shelter from the cold back in November 1862, had taken us in as captives, only to return us to John Mundy, or perhaps to enslave us at their farms. But, thank God, I was totally wrong about William and Rebecca, and about Horace and Anne. They, like Andrew, were kind white people who simply wanted to help us.

It was Horace and Anne who helped Hannah and me get back to Fort Monroe. They took us to the home of some of their friends, who hid us, and eventually arranged for us to get back to Fort Monroe. Hannah and I traveled back to Fort Monroe through what is known as the "underground railroad."

A week after I reunited with my family in Boston, Hannah and I finally jumped the broom. My son, parents, sister and her family shared that special event with us. I couldn't imagine being any happier; but, things got even better for us. William and Sarah told me about their ongoing problems with Frank Wilmington. Two weeks after my arrival, Frank Wilmington lost his appeal of the Commissioner's decision to set Sarah free. The Commissioner who heard the appeal determined that Sarah would be free if she was a slave in Mississippi in 1863, because of the Emancipation Proclamation President Lincoln issued in January 1863. Needless to say, we celebrated my sister's freedom for days!

Later that spring, I went back to Fort Monroe with Sarah and William to help the refugees in the contraband camps. Samuel and Lydia were still there, but not for long, because we brought them to Boston with us. Samuel and Lydia played a major role in my reunion with my family, and we became lifetime friends.

Later that year, I had the honor of fighting against the Confederacy, finally. I had long dreamed of doing my part to help the Union win the war, and joined the colored Massachusettes 54th regiment, where I met some courageous, dedicated men. Our regiment was one of the first colored regiments to enter Charleston when it fell. I fought with that regiment until the Confederate Army surrendered in April 1865.

After the war ended, I stayed in Charleston because there were more opportunities to build homes and work as a carpenter and mason. The city had to be rebuilt. I had planned to use the money I saved over the years to buy my freedom and my family's freedom, but, thank God, the Union won the war and all slaves were freed. Therefore, I used my money to purchase a home for my family. In June 1865, I went back to Boston to get Hannah and Caleb. I didn't ever want to be separated from them again, and knew I could make enough money to provide a good life for my family in Charleston.

The following year, Sarah, her family and my parents moved to Charleston to be closer to us. My sister opened another dress shoppe, and kept the shoppe in Boston as well, and her close friends, Cora,

Naomi and Callie, ran that shoppe for her. Sarah loves those women dearly and trusts them. She traveled back and forth to Boston to oversee her shoppe and to visit friends. She also traveled back to Paris to show and sell her dresses abroad. As expected, Sarah did very well as a designer and dressmaker in Charleston.

It has been an honor to bring our parents and children to visit Hampton Normal and Agricultural Institute, to see the Emancipation Oak, which grows at the entrance of this historical place of learning. It is important for our children to know that contrabands and free Negroes gathered beneath this tree to hear a reading of President Abraham Lincoln's Emancipation Proclamation, issued on January 1, 1863, which abolished slavery in the states that had seceded from the Union. They likewise need to know that pioneering teachers, Mrs. Mary S. Peake and others, defied a Virginia law and taught contrabands to read and write under the Emancipation Oak.

Our history is vivid, and I am very proud of it. We were, and are, an amazing family. Our strength is in our love for each other, our faith in God, and our determination to keep striving, no matter what we are confronted with. We are more than conquerors. *And we shall be like a tree planted by the rivers of water, that bringeth forth our fruit in our season; our leaf also shall not wither; and whatsoever we doeth shall prosper.*

## ABOUT THE AUTHOR

J. Carter-Ball currently serves as a central panel administrative judge in Nashville, Tennessee, where she lives with her husband, James H. Ball, Jr. They have two daughters, Ashley Ball, Esq. and Jamie Ball, MA-LPC.

She is a graduate of Hampton University and the University of Mississippi School of Law. She enjoys researching and growing a variety of plants, traveling, and writing. Her first novel, *As Soft As Cotton*, was published in 2008.